I0744774

Book 15: Dark Alpha's Command

SKYE DRUIDS SERIES

Book 1: Iron Ember

DARK KINGS SERIES

Book 0.1: Dark Craving

Book 0.2: Night's Awakening

Book 0.3: Dawn's Desire

Books 0.1-0.4 Bundle: Dark Heat

Book 1: Darkest Flame

Book 2: Fire Rising

Book 3: Burning Desire

Book 4: Hot Blooded

Book 5: Night's Blaze

Book 6: Soul Scorched

Book 6.5: Dragon King (novella)

Book 7: Passion Ignites

Book 8: Smoldering Hunger

Book 9: Smoke and Fire

Book 9.5: Dragon Fever (novella)

Book 10: Firestorm

Book 11: Blaze

Book 11.5: Dragon Burn (novella)

Book 11.6: Constantine: A History, Part 1

Book 12: Heat (short story)

Book 12.5: Constantine: A History, Part 2 (short story)

Book 13: Torched

Book 13.1: Constantine: A History, Part 3 (short story)

Book 13.5: Dragon Night (novella)

Book 14: Dragonfire

Book 14.5: Dragon Claimed (novella)

Book 15: Ignite

Book 16: Fever

Book 16.5: Dragon Lost (novella)

Book 17: Flame

Book 18: Inferno

Book 19: Whisky and Wishes, A Dark Kings Special Holiday Novella

Book 20: Heart of Gold, A Dark Kings Special Valentine's Novella

Book 21: Of Fire and Flame

Book 22: A Dragon's Tale (Bundle of Books 19, 20, & 21)

The Dragon King Coloring Book

Dragon King Special Edition Character Coloring Book: Rhi

Book 23: My Fiery Valentine

DARK WARRIORS SERIES

Book 1: Midnight's Master

Book 2: Midnight's Lover

Book 3: Midnight's Seduction

Book 4: Midnight's Warrior

Book 5: Midnight's Kiss

Book 6: Midnight's Captive

Book 7: Midnight's Temptation

Book 8: Midnight's Promise

Book 8.5: Midnight's Surrender (novella)

CHIASSON SERIES

Book 1: Wild Fever

Book 2: Wild Dream

Book 3: Wild Need

Book 4: Wild Flame

Book 5: Wild Rapture

LARUE SERIES

Book 1: Moon Kissed

Book 2: Moon Thrall

Book 3: Moon Struck

Book 4: Moon Bound

WICKED TREASURES

Book 1: Seized by Passion

Book 2: Enticed by Ecstasy

Book 3: Captured by Desire

Books 1-3: Wicked Treasures Box Set

HISTORICAL PARANORMAL

THE KINDRED SERIES

Book 0.5: Everkin (short story)

Book 1: Eversong

Book 2: Everwylde

Book 3: Everbound

Book 4: Evernight

Book 5: Everspell

KINDRED: THE FATED SERIES

(Spin-off series from THE KINDRED)

Book 1: Rage

DARK SWORD SERIES

Book 1: Dangerous Highlander

Book 2: Forbidden Highlander

Book 3: Wicked Highlander

Book 4: Untamed Highlander

Book 5: Shadow Highlander

Book 6: Darkest Highlander

ROGUES OF SCOTLAND SERIES

Book 1: The Craving

Book 2: The Hunger

Book 3: The Tempted

Book 4: The Seduced

Books 1-4: Rogues of Scotland Box Set

THE SHIELDS SERIES

Book 1: A Dark Guardian

Book 2: A Kind of Magic

Book 3: A Dark Seduction

Book 4: A Forbidden Temptation

Book 5: A Warrior's Heart

Mystic Trinity (a series connecting novel)

DRUIDS GLEN SERIES

Book 1: Highland Mist

Book 2: Highland Nights

Book 3: Highland Dawn

Book 4: Highland Fires

Book 5: Highland Magic

Mystic Trinity (a series connecting novel)

SISTERS OF MAGIC TRILOGY

Book 1: Shadow Magic

Book 2: Echoes of Magic

Book 3: Dangerous Magic

Books 1-3: Sisters of Magic Box Set

THE ROYAL CHRONICLES NOVELLA SERIES

Book 1: Prince of Desire

Book 2: Prince of Seduction

Book 3: Prince of Love

Book 4: Prince of Passion

Books 1-4: The Royal Chronicles Box Set

Mystic Trinity (a series connecting novel)

DARK BEGINNINGS: A FIRST IN SERIES BOXSET

Chiasson Series, Book 1: Wild Fever

LaRue Series, Book 1: Moon Kissed

The Royal Chronicles Series, Book 1: Prince of Desire

MILITARY ROMANCE / ROMANTIC SUSPENSE

SONS OF TEXAS SERIES

Book 1: The Hero

Book 2: The Protector

Book 3: The Legend

Book 4: The Defender

Book 5: The Guardian

COWBOY / CONTEMPORARY

HEART OF TEXAS SERIES

Book 1: The Christmas Cowboy Hero

Book 2: Cowboy, Cross My Heart

Book 3: My Favorite Cowboy

Book 4: A Cowboy Like You

Book 5: Looking for a Cowboy

Book 6: A Cowboy Kind of Love

STAND ALONE BOOKS

That Cowboy of Mine

Home for a Cowboy Christmas

Mutual Desire

Forever Mine

Savage Moon

Check out Donna Grant's Online Store at

www.DonnaGrant.com/shop

for autographed books, character themed goodies, and more!

EVERNIGHT

THE KINDRED, BOOK 4

DONNA GRANT®

www.DonnaGrant.com
www.MotherofDragonsBooks.com

1

Scotland

Breath billowed from Synne's mouth as the snow continued falling relentlessly, blanketing the world in white. The mare shook her head, dislodging the flakes from her black mane as they stood on the hilltop, looking out over the landscape.

Synne patted the horse's neck. "I'm cold, too, girl. But we've got a long way to go yet."

At least that's what Synne suspected. She had no idea where the Varroki lived exactly. All she knew was the direction: north. So, that's where she was headed.

She knew snow well, but the kind of cold she felt now was much worse than she was used to. It penetrated her layers of clothing to sink into her bones, making her movements slow, dulled. Her fingers were numb, and she couldn't feel her feet. She needed to move quickly if she ran into the Coven, and as it was now, she wasn't sure she could.

Just thinking about the Coven brought rage and grief so intense that her throat clogged with it. She would never forget the sight of those she had called family slain by the witch Sybbyl and her band of Gira.

Synne was a Hunter. She had been trained by one of the greatest knights, Radnar, and Edra, a powerful witch, to hunt those of the Coven and keep others safe. Now, Edra and Radnar were gone, as were so, *so* many others in their sanctuary.

For years, Synne had known love and safety. She was an expert with her bow, and for reasons she couldn't explain, she had a connection with nature. Trees, in particular. But everything she had known and loved was now gone. Because Sybbyl sought the bones of the First Witch. That's what all this was about.

Luckily, another Hunter, Leoma, and a nobleman, Braith, had stumbled across the Blood Skull. Braith was the Warden of the Blood Skull. It only responded to him. That meant no one else—especially those of the Coven—could use it. Since the Coven couldn't get to the Blood Skull, they had gone after the Staff of the Eternal. The piece of wood contained the thigh bone of the First Witch, granting the possessor immense power. And, unfortunately, Sybbyl had gotten her hands on it.

The scales had tipped in their favor when the Hunters learned that a witch named Helena was a descendant of the First Witch—the actual Living Heart. Helena's magic was greater than Sybbyl's. Regrettably, however, Sybbyl had been smart enough to get away during their battle.

Synne now believed that the Staff of the Eternal would allow Sybbyl to find the Varroki, who had been hidden for years. Everyone knew Sybbyl's next stop on her list of enemies was Blackglade, where the Varroki lived. And if the Hunters and innocents were really unlucky, Sybbyl would find yet another bone of the First Witch and make herself even stronger.

A long sigh escaped Synne. She had gone over this countless times since she'd burned those she loved at the abbey, but she hadn't come up with anything that might help her or anyone else. At least they still had Braith and the Blood Skull, not to mention Helena as the Heart. But there were other bones of the First Witch out there yet to be found.

Synne nudged her mare into a walk. The sky was thick with clouds, and it looked like the snow had no intention of stopping anytime soon. She needed to find some shelter. While the horse picked her way down the slope, Synne considered the Varroki. The Hunters hadn't known about them until recently, even though the Varroki had been waging their own war against the Coven since the days following the First Witch's death.

The Varroki were secretive, and for good reason. Their numbers included warlocks, something no one thought existed. For her entire life, Synne had believed that only women could have magic. Meeting the Lady of the Varroki, Malene, and her Commander, Armir, had opened Synne's eyes to a whole new world.

She'd never thought to leave the forest and the sanctuary Edra and Radnar had created. Yet her path now led her toward Blackglade and the Varroki. She had no idea what awaited her there besides war. There was no getting past what was coming, not that she wanted to. And she honestly didn't expect to survive the battle. After all, she had no magic.

It was the one thing she had wished for above all things. But wishing didn't change anything. As she had learned the hard way.

Synne glanced around. She liked that she was out in the open. She had purposefully traveled that way since crossing into Scotland. It allowed her to see all around her when she crested the ever-rising hills. However, the wide-open spaces were quickly coming to an end. Ahead of her was a vast forest. Her heart leaped at the thought of being in the confines of the woods again. But that quickly dissipated as she thought of the Gira.

For as long as she could remember, Synne had been terrified of the nymphs. Their skin and hair resembled the bark of a tree, allowing them to camouflage themselves so that no one could see them until the Gira chose to reveal themselves.

The tree nymphs mainly kept to the Witch's Groves, but they were known to venture out at times. Their whispers drew people. Once near the Gira, they pulled the unsuspecting person close, so the tree could surround them, holding them hostage for the Gira to torture and play with at their leisure. But it was the way the Gira killed that caused knots to form in Synne's stomach.

The nymphs devoured people.

Synne couldn't remember when she had first learned of the Gira, but she had known of their existence long before Edra had told her about them. Synne had never delved too far into her memories to learn *when* she had discovered the Gira—mostly because she didn't care. The nymphs were evil, and she wanted to stay away from them.

She hated that the Gira used trees to hide. Synne had always been drawn to trees. Just touching them calmed her, but her fear of the nymphs kept her away from them after the Gira had killed everyone at the abbey. And Synne felt the loss keenly.

Despite her need to be near trees, Synne wasn't looking forward to the approaching forest because of the dangers within. Her hatred of the Gira grew for taking that from her. Most of the anger inside her was directed at the Coven and the Gira. They had ripped her world apart. She didn't remember her family or the time before Edra had found her, but she felt nothing about that now. Maybe it was because she had no memories of that time that she wasn't consumed by the need for vengeance.

Unlike the sight of all her friends lying dead that she couldn't stop seeing each time she closed her eyes.

Though she hadn't spoken, the mare sensed Synne's turmoil and nickered softly while swiveling her ears toward her.

"I'm sorry," Synne told the mare. "I'm trying to control it."

And control was something she needed to do. She couldn't face her enemies while feeling such fury. It would cause her to make poor decisions. She needed to have a clear head and heart in order to succeed.

She did her best to let go of the anger. It took far longer than she liked, but eventually, Synne accomplished her goal. By that time, the forest lay directly in front of her. She pulled back on the reins to stop the horse.

The mare instantly obeyed. For the next few moments, both horse and rider stared at the woods before them. Synne looked to either side, but no matter how hard she searched, she didn't see a way around the forest. No doubt there was one, but she didn't want to waste time finding it. The shortest route was through the trees.

"Be vigilant," Synne told herself and the mare.

The horse blew out a breath in response.

She clicked, and the mare proceeded forward. Synne's heart raced with each step they took, and while her mind screamed for her to turn and run away, Synne didn't stop the animal. Soon, the woodland swallowed them up.

The moment they were within the confines of the forest, it was like entering a different world. Birds chirped, and a squirrel hollered nearby. The trees helped to protect her from the snow, catching the flakes on their thick, leafless limbs as well as the many evergreens. Wind whistled softly through the branches, almost like a lullaby.

Synne directed the mare, following a path as far from the trees as she could get, but it was still closer than she was comfortable with. The need to touch the bark warred with her fear that the Gira were nearby and hiding.

If she were Sybbyl, she would leave the Gira in the forest to slow anyone approaching. Then again, no one really knew where Sybbyl was. That in itself was terrifying. Everyone assumed that since the leader of the Coven had taken out the abbey, that Sybbyl would then head to Blackglade to attack the Varroki.

It made the most sense, but Sybbyl hadn't done things that made sense in the past, so Synne wasn't sure what to think. She could be allowing her fear to control her for nothing. Which was most likely the case. But when it came to witches, no one could ever really be sure.

Synne stopped the mare once more. This time, her anger was directed at herself. She was a trained Hunter. She didn't fear facing a witch, and she shouldn't be afraid of the Gira either. Witches could do all sorts of magic. Who was to say that one couldn't hide themselves like a nymph?

The last thing Synne should do was let fear sway her. She'd been in constant turmoil since she'd left the abbey. But the one thing that could help her was the very thing that surrounded her now—trees.

She eyed the foliage nearest her. None of the trunks looked as if a Gira were hiding there, nor did Synne hear any whispers. In fact, the forest appeared normal. Synne took a deep breath, inhaling the scent of pine and snow. Everything smelled…clean. Nothing seemed amiss.

Synne lowered her gaze to the mare. The horse was calm, seemingly not picking up on anything she'd missed. She nudged the mare forward once more and continued through the forest. Her gaze moved from side to side, searching for Gira, witches, or anything else that could be a threat.

When she could take no more, she reached out and touched a tree as she passed. Her gloved hand lingered for just a moment, but even that small contact bolstered her. Yet it wasn't enough. She removed her glove before she reached out to the next tree. When the rough, cold bark slid against her palm, she closed her eyes and sighed contentedly.

No one, not even Edra, knew why Synne needed to lay hands on the trees. Edra had found Synne in a forest, at least that's what the witch had told Synne. She had no memory of that time—or before that. Which was probably for the best.

The woods around her grew denser, the tall pines stretching high to the sky, their limbs extending out like fingers. She looked up, but the hood of her cloak prevented her from seeing directly above her.

With the mare weaving through the trees, Synne grew more and more relaxed. Never again would she allow fear to govern her. The fact that she had mastered her emotions proved that she needed the woods. She didn't want to think what would've happened had she continued to let her fear rule her.

Synne traveled for a while before she stopped the mare near a huge oak. She slid from the horse and dropped the reins. Synne wasn't worried about the mare bolting. The horse was too well trained for that. Synne lowered the hood of her cloak and took off her other glove as she approached the tree. Once she stood before it, she placed both hands on its bark and closed her eyes.

"I've missed you," she whispered.

While she didn't hear words from the trees, she did feel things. Right now, the oak was telling her hello. She smiled and pressed her cheek to the trunk as she spread her arms, giving the giant tree a hug.

"You will let me know if something is amiss, right?" she asked softly.

In response, the tree creaked as its limbs moved when a breeze slid around her. Synne's eyes snapped open. Thanks to the oak, she knew in an instant that she wasn't alone. The tree didn't tell her it was something dangerous, but Synne was on guard, nonetheless.

She straightened and dropped her arms as her head snapped to the left. Her gaze met that of a man sitting astride a white horse. The male's long, black hair hung loosely about his shoulders, and his eyes bored into hers. Even with the beard, she could see the sharp line of his jaw. He sat on his mount like one who had been born to ride.

The hilt of a sword could be seen over his shoulder. He likely had other weapons, as well, because he was, without a doubt, a warrior.

Whether Synne killed him or not depended on what side he was on.

2

He'd never seen a woman like her before. Lachlan wasn't sure what to think. She touched the trees as she passed them, and the action confused him. But it wasn't until she embraced the oak that he saw her lips move, almost as if she were talking to it.

His grandmother had once mentioned those who had a deep connection to nature, but he had believed it was the ramblings of her confused mind. Now, he wondered if she had been telling him the truth.

Lachlan had spotted the woman riding toward the woods. It was obvious that she was hesitant to enter the forest, but she hadn't let that stop her. At first, he'd thought it was because she might have suspected that he was within. While her cloak hid her face, her narrow shoulders and slight frame instantly marked her as female. He'd been so intent on watching her that he hadn't immediately noticed the bow she carried until she dismounted, but his attention had quickly shifted to the weapon.

And now, it was focused on the way she stared at him. There was no fear in her amber eyes. Instead, he gazed into the face of one who had faced death. Someone who had *delivered* death.

He was intrigued by this woman. She was unlike any he'd seen before, and while a part of him rebelled against it, another part was unable to look away. It was that interest that urged him to go to her, to discover her name and learn who she was.

Lachlan had wielded a sword before he could even lift it properly. His father and two uncles had trained him to fight for the clan, and he did it not just because it was expected, but because he knew it was what he was meant to do.

Because of his training, he recognized the difference between someone who carried a weapon for show, and those who knew how to use them. This woman was the latter. His sister had begged him to show her how to use a bow, but his father had refused. Lachlan didn't dare go against his sire. Yet someone in this female's life had taken the time to train her.

Lachlan tightened his fingers on the reins of his mount. He gave a slight tap with his heel, and the gelding moved forward. Lachlan didn't take his eyes from the woman, nor she from him. She didn't move, but he had the sense that she was prepared for an attack from any angle.

Damn intriguing.

The closer he got to her, the more he was able to take her in. At first, he'd believed her blond hair was cut short, but he now saw that it was held back from her face by several rows of braids hidden by the hood of her cloak. He wondered how long it was and had the desire to push the hood back to get a better look at it.

Amber eyes observed him carefully, warily. While her gaze was that of a warrior, her face resembled an angel's. Beauty, unlike any he'd ever gazed upon before, stood before him now. Her skin was flawless, her cheekbones high, and her lips delightfully full. If her face was this beautiful, he could well imagine what her body looked like. It was too bad the cloak hid it from view.

He stopped his horse a few yards away and managed to find his voice. "Are you lost?"

A blond brow quirked at his question. "Do I look lost?"

"You are no' from our clan, nor do you have the look of any neighboring clans." He shrugged. "So, aye, you appear lost."

"I'm not."

She said nothing more, but her accent gave her away. He didn't know what an English woman was doing in Scotland, but it couldn't be good. Despite his earlier assumption that she knew how to use the bow, he couldn't help but be concerned for her.

"You can be on your way," she told him.

Lachlan bit back a grin. Damn if she hadn't just issued him an order. "I'm no' going anywhere, lass."

She sighed and lifted her chin. "I am not some wilting female in need of a male."

"I didna say that you were. And I'm no' offering aid."

Several moments passed where she simply stared at him. Finally, she looked away, issuing another sigh, this one louder. "You aren't going to leave, are you?"

He shook his head.

She whirled around, the cloak billowing out around her as she did. That's when he saw that she wore breeches. He only got a glimpse of her legs before the cloak once more settled to hide her from view. But that brief second was enough to get his blood racing.

With interest and desire.

Lachlan wanted to see her legs again. And now, more than ever, he wished to see the rest of her. Was she really dressed like a man? If that weren't odd enough, no woman he knew would talk to him as this one did.

"You're staring," the female said.

Her back was to him now as she fiddled with her horse. He wasn't sure how she knew where his gaze was centered. It was most likely a lucky guess.

"So?" he replied.

Her head turned so she looked at him over her shoulder. "I'll leave the forest. I just want a few minutes."

"The fact that you say that tells me you have no idea where you are."

"Scotland," she retorted.

He rolled his eyes. "Aye, that you are. But you're also on MacCullum land."

"I've ridden over a lot of territory, and I'll continue riding onto others," she said and turned her attention back to the horse.

"Lass," he said with a sigh. "There is a war brewing between my clan and a neighboring one."

"There's always war of some kind."

"You're missing the point. You traveling alone as you are could make others believe you to be a spy. Or worse, someone to be kidnapped."

Her hands stilled. Then she turned and faced him with her arms by her sides. "I'm not a spy. And if anyone dares to try and force me to do anything, they'll regret it."

"MacCullum land is vast. If you want to get through the forest without anyone else bothering you, let me escort you."

"How do I know you're a MacCullum? For all I know, everything you've told me is a lie."

If those words had come from a man, Lachlan would've struck him down. Instead, he swung his leg over the gelding's head and slid to the ground. As soon as his feet hit the earth, he strode to the woman and unsheathed his sword.

She took a step back and had an arrow nocked in her bow in the time it took him to blink. He was impressed, but his anger didn't allow him to express it. Instead, he held his sword out so she could see the hilt.

"Look," he demanded.

Her amber eyes flicked from his face to the weapon. "MacCullum," she said and lowered her bow. "You could have stolen that. But given the way you carry it and the fury in your gaze, I believe it's yours."

He returned the blade to its scabbard. "I fight for my laird. This was his gift to me for defeating our enemy."

The woman briefly closed her eyes before she put the arrow back into the quiver strapped to the horse. "I really am fine on my own."

"You might know English ways, but you know nothing of ours, lass," he told her and gave a short whistle to the gelding, which walked to him. He gathered the reins in his hands. "I patrol this forest to keep others out."

"Wouldn't it be better to have an army?"

"They make too much noise. I'm quieter on my own."

She gave a nod and once more looked at the tree she'd embraced earlier. "I've always worked on my own."

"You might be able to take some enemies, but on your own, you'd be overrun soon enough."

"Not by men," he thought he heard her say.

Lachlan frowned. "What?"

"Nothing," she hastily replied and swung her gaze back to him. "I need to get through the forest quickly."

"I can do that."

She pressed her lips together, considering him. He saw she didn't want to accept his offer. In her shoes, he probably wouldn't either. But he knew for a fact that there were small bands of enemies wandering the forest, looking for anyone they believed they could take or kill to hurt the clan.

"If you refuse, I'll only follow you."

She snorted. "I doubt it. I'm good at covering my tracks."

"You are no' good enough to make me lose you."

That made her hesitate. "If I agree, how soon can I be through the woods?"

"Two days. I know the shortest routes. If you go on your own, you could be here for days more."

"I doubt that," she stated. "But I am in a hurry."

He wanted to ask where she was headed, but she probably wouldn't tell him, so he didn't bother. Instead, he mounted the gelding. "We better get moving if you're in a hurry."

"Aye," she said and looked at the oak once more.

Then she walked to the tree and placed her hand on it. She leaned closer, and he could've sworn she spoke to it. When she straightened, she kept her gaze lowered while making her way to the mare before climbing onto the animal.

She gave him a nod, and he set off. She didn't stay even with him, instead preferring to remain a little behind. They rode in silence for several minutes while he thought about what he had witnessed her doing with the tree. She had wanted to remain with it a little longer despite being in a rush. What was so important about the tree? It was probably an answer he'd never get.

"I'm Lachlan," he said.

There was a brief pause before she replied, "I'm Synne."

Surely, she hadn't been named that because someone thought her a sin. She was anything but from what he'd seen so far. He wasn't much of a talker. Never had been, actually. Usually, women did all the talking, and he found ways to not answer. Now, he was the one with all the questions, riding alongside a woman who didn't seem to want to utter another syllable.

"Where are you headed?" he asked when he couldn't stand it any longer.

"North."

He was perturbed by her reply, but he wasn't surprised by it. "Any place in particular?"

"Aye."

Lachlan's patience was quickly running out. "If you doona want to tell me, that's fine."

"I don't." Then she sighed. "Actually, I don't exactly know where it's at."

"What's the name of the place? Perhaps I can tell you."

"Trust me when I say that whatever is going on with your clan is safer than where I'm headed."

He glanced back at her. "And the men of your family allowed you to travel alone?"

"I'm a Hunter," she stated with a flash of anger in her eyes. "I don't need anyone, much less a man, telling me what I can and cannot do."

Lachlan was glad that his sister wasn't here to hear that. Men were made for battle. To ensure the safety of their families. Women were the nurturers, the ones who bore the children and kept the home in order. Lachlan didn't set the rules. He just abided by them.

"Besides," Synne continued, "there isn't anyone left to say anything."

He looked at her, but she refused to meet his gaze. Then he saw it, the grief she valiantly tried to keep hidden. She did a good job of it. He might never have noticed had she not said those last words, but now that she had, he was able to see what she fought to keep from consuming her.

"I'm sorry," he said.

She briefly met his gaze. "So will be the ones who took from me."

3

It was a mistake having the Scotsman tag along. Synne knew it, but she also knew that he would follow her if she didn't allow him to accompany her. This way, she could keep her eyes on him.

Yet she had to admit she liked having someone with her. If only Lachlan would stop asking questions. She couldn't tell him what he wanted to know. But the one good thing about the conversation was that it pulled her from her own mind and the constant thoughts circling there.

"I once tracked someone," Lachlan said. "Revenge is no' what you think it is."

"It's exactly what I think it is."

He made a sound at the back of his throat. "You've never sought vengeance before, have you?"

"You ask that because I'm a woman?"

"No need to get testy," he said and met her gaze. "I'm merely pointing out that what is driving you to seek revenge now, willna disappear once you've gotten what you want."

She swallowed and looked ahead. "It doesn't matter."

"Of course, it does. Unless…you doona believe you'll live to worry about it."

Synne didn't bother to reply. She didn't owe him an explanation. He was a means to an end, and that was all.

"Och, lass," he murmured. "You've too much of your life ahead of you to throw it away like that."

She shook her head. "You wouldn't say that if I was a man."

"I would caution anyone with the same words, be they male or female."

Synne cut her eyes to him. "I saw the way you looked at my weapon. There was surprise there. You don't know what to do with a woman who can protect herself."

"Aye, I was shocked," he admitted with a wry twist of his lips. "It isna done here."

"It is where I'm from. Anyone who wanted to learn weapons was allowed to train."

"It sounds like an amazing place. Were there many females?"

"Many," Synne replied softly, thinking of the others.

Lachlan was quiet for a moment. "Doona bury your grief. It will only prolong your healing."

She didn't ask him how he knew. Synne thought she covered her grief well, but apparently, not well enough. "I'll grieve later."

"You're going after someone with anger and loss in your heart, lass. That is a recipe for disaster. You need to have a clear head if you're to win."

"The only thing I need is to reach my destination."

Lachlan pulled his horse to a stop and gazed to the right with narrowed eyes. Synne halted her mare and looked around the forest for potential enemies. There were ample spots for someone to lay in wait or to spring a trap. Maybe it was a good thing the Scotsman was with her, after all.

A few moments later, Lachlan's horse began walking again. Synne looked to the right to see if she could tell what had caught the man's attention, but she saw nothing. Her gaze returned to him and focused on his broad shoulders. Thick sinew and hard muscle was evident beneath the tartan sash, vest, shirt, and breeches he wore.

There was an intensity about him that she recognized since she had been around warriors for most of her life. But with Lachlan, it was different. As if it were ramped up another notch. She hadn't seen him in battle yet, but she imagined that he was a sight to behold.

In the back of her mind, she wished she could see him fight. As soon as the thought came, she regretted it. The last thing she wanted was to run into witches while looking for the Varroki. It was most likely inevitable that the Coven would find her, but Synne shouldn't be hoping for it just to see Lachlan move.

Her eyes drifted lower to his butt. His hips were narrow, his backside firm. She shouldn't be noticing things like that —not when she was on a mission. But how could she ignore the fact that Lachlan was a gorgeous specimen of a man? She'd never tell him that, but it was difficult to look anywhere but at him.

"You doona know me," Lachlan said. "And you have no reason to listen, but I hope you'll heed this advice. Your head and your heart are full of vengeance. It will blind you to things you wouldna otherwise ignore. You shouldna be traveling alone. You need someone to watch your back."

"There isn't anyone."

He sighed loudly. "Then you are riding to your death."

"If you were in a situation where you had no choice but to hunt someone, or death would come to many, many more, would you ignore the call simply because you're grieving or there wasn't someone to go with you?" she asked, turning her head to him.

Lachlan pressed his lips together for a heartbeat. "Nay."

"Neither will I."

He seemed to have nothing to say after that. The silence that followed put Synne back into her head, and it wasn't a place she liked very much. The little time she had interacted with Lachlan had relieved her somehow.

Turning introspective made everything worse. She thought of the worst that could happen and found herself focusing on them and imagining all the horrible things Sybbyl would do to others—as well as thinking about what her death would look like. Her mind didn't allow her to dwell on anything positive. It was all negative, and it brought her already low state of being into a depression that was quickly spiraling out of control.

The more she tried not to think those nasty thoughts, the more they filled her mind until she wanted to scream. Synne squeezed her eyes closed and fought against the demons of doubt that rose up.

"Talk," she bit out. When Lachlan didn't respond, she opened her eyes to find him staring at her. She took a deep breath and tried again. "Please, talk."

He gave a nod and looked forward. "Sometimes, our thoughts can be our own worst enemies. Tell me why you chose the bow for your weapon."

This, she could talk about. Synne was grateful to Lachlan, and she would make it up to him somehow before they parted ways. "My teacher, Radnar, made each of us train with many weapons. He wanted to make sure we could defend ourselves with various tools, not just one."

"Smart man."

"He was a knight. One of the bravest, kindest men I've ever known."

Lachlan's gray eyes swung to hers. "He is one that you are avenging."

It wasn't a question. Synne nodded. "He was like a father to me, and his wife, Edra, a mother."

"Radnar must have been very skilled."

Synne felt a smile start for the first time in days, thinking about Radnar. "He was, but he also recognized that others could teach us, as well. He brought in warriors from all over to add to our lessons. His way worked, although I doubt there would be many who agreed with it outside of our community. He watched us as we trained with different weapons. Most showed skill with at least one, and once he saw which weapon they took to, the training intensified."

"And yours was the bow?"

"I was accurate from my first shot. It's like I don't even have to think about it. I just know what to do."

Lachlan glanced at her weapon. "What were you training for, exactly? I doona think it was just to hunt for food or to protect others. You make it sound as if Radnar was creating an army."

"Radnar and the others taught whoever wanted to learn, for whatever reason they wanted to learn."

Lachlan's brows rose on his forehead. "Lass, I have an uncanny knack for knowing when someone is giving me a line of shite, which is exactly what you're doing now."

"You don't want to know the truth."

"Or is it that you doona want to tell me?" he countered.

She shrugged. "Both."

"There have been few times in my life where there was peace. My clan is large and verra strong, and that makes others uncomfortable, as well as envious. We've been attacked, threatened, and lied to constantly. I tell you this so you'll know there isna anything you can say that I have no' already heard."

"I doubt that," she retorted.

He snorted and looked forward. "Keep your secrets, then."

Synne briefly looked skyward into the gray above her and then blew out a breath. What would it hurt to tell him? She wasn't a witch, and even if he tried to take her, she was positive that she could get away from Lachlan. She didn't want to hurt him, but she would. Normally, she wouldn't dare say anything about witches or the Coven, but there was a war brewing that could threaten everyone, whether they knew of witches or not. So, perhaps now was the time to talk.

"You may discount what I'm about to share with you. Be forewarned that everything I say is the truth. I tell you in case we don't win the battle. You'll need to prepare your clan and as many others as you can."

Lachlan's gray eyes met hers, waiting for her to continue.

"Radnar was a knight, but Edra was a witch. They set up a place in the forest as a sanctuary for anyone seeking to escape the Coven. The abbey was my home, and it was destroyed. The Coven is a set of witches who take whatever they want and kill whoever they wish simply because they have magic. They wanted Edra, but she fought against them and won. From then on, she and Radnar took in abandoned children and gave them a home.

"For years, the two of them went out to hunt Coven members. As the children grew and trained, some of them joined in the hunt. We became Hunters. And we thought we were making headway."

Lachlan asked, "How can someone without magic battle a witch?"

"Edra infused our weapons with magic to give us an advantage."

The Scot, keeping his gaze forward, nodded for her to continue.

"One such Hunter, Leoma, was tracking the Coven when she stumbled upon a man who was after the same witch. He was a lord, and the two of them worked together. They learned the Coven was after the bones of the First Witch."

"How do you know there was a first one?" Lachlan asked.

Synne eyed him, wondering why he wouldn't look at her. "It's how witches came into being. The First Witch, Trea, was Norse. The Vikings revered women who had such power, and Trea had a lot of it. So did her three sisters, but nothing compared to Trea. When she died, she had her followers scatter her bones and burn the rest of her body so her sisters couldn't use her in death. Her sisters began the Coven."

Lachlan remained silent.

Synne licked her lips and continued. "Braith and Leoma found the Blood Skull—Trea's skull—and Braith learned from it that he was its Warden. It wasn't long after that we found the Staff of the Eternal—a weapon containing the thigh bone of the First Witch—but, unfortunately, we lost it. A witch named Sybbyl took it and killed the three elders of the Coven. She now rules, the staff giving her immense power." Synne adjusted her cloak and quickly glanced at Lachlan before she began again.

"But we still have Helena. She is a direct descendant of Trea, and thereby the Heart. Thankfully, Helena fights for us. It isn't enough, though. During the fight, Sybbyl got away and attacked our home, killing everyone inside the abbey, including Radnar and Edra. I was in the forest at the time, unable to get to them to help."

"That's why you're in Scotland now?"

Synne nodded her head. "Sybbyl to locate another bone, but she's also here to find the Varroki, a group of witches and warlocks who have battled the Coven since the First Witch died. They've kept their location hidden. I'm going to them."

"Do you know where to find them?"

"No, but Malene, their leader, said that I would be able to find the way."

Lachlan made a sound. "And you believe her?"

"I do. I know that Sybbyl will eventually find the Varroki, and I know that I'll be there waiting for her when she does."

"It's one woman against how many of these Varroki?"

Synne shuddered. "Sybbyl isn't alone."

"How many witches are with her?"

"It isn't the witches I'm concerned with. It's the Gira."

Lachlan's head finally swiveled to her. "The what?"

"Gira. They're tree nymphs. Their skin looks like the bark of trees, so you pass right by them and don't even know it. Their whispers draw people to them. Once close enough, the Gira take them, locking them inside the tree to torture and eat at will."

Lachlan stared at her for a moment before facing forward again. "That is some tale, lass."

"It's the truth."

4

Of all the things Lachlan had thought Synne might tell him, he'd never imagined it would be about witches and magic. She was so absorbed in her tale that she hadn't yet realized that he wasn't shocked by her mention of magic.

"You'll see soon enough," Synne replied. "If we don't win, the Coven will raze everything you know and love to the ground."

Lachlan swallowed and watched Synne out of the corner of his eye. He didn't reply, not because he didn't have a response, but because he chose not to utter it.

Her mare came to a sudden halt and tossed her head back. "Either you think I'm daft and you're humoring me, or…you already know about the Coven."

He blew out a breath and pulled at the reins to halt his steed. Lachlan briefly closed his eyes before he turned his mount around to face Synne. "I doona think you're daft."

"So, you know."

He gave a single nod. "I know about witches and magic. You can no' live in this land, especially this forest, and no' know."

"What's that supposed to mean?" Synne asked with narrowed eyes.

Lachlan swept his arm around him. "Take a look. This forest is massive. Do you no' think that beings take refuge in such a place?"

"You haven't answered my question."

There was a bite to her words now. She had been distrustful before, but now she was even more so. Not that he blamed her. Lachlan pointed to the side. "There is a Witch's Grove in that direction."

Synne glared at him for a long, silent moment.

He lowered his arm. Then, he spoke the words he'd never said aloud to another soul. "I know because my grandmother was a witch."

Still, Synne said nothing.

"It's a secret kept from everyone," he said. "No one in my clan knows, except for my family."

"Not even your laird?"

"My father is the laird."

If it was possible, Synne's eyes became even icier. Lachlan ran a hand over his jaw. "My grandmother had the gift of healing. No one questioned her knowledge of herbs. Only rarely did she use magic. The last time was when my mother had difficulty while birthing me. My grandmother used magic to try and keep my mother alive, but it wasna enough. She died that night."

"I'm sorry about your mother."

"Mine isna the only one to die in childbirth, nor will she be the last, I wager."

"Did your grandmother mention the Coven?"

Lachlan glanced at the ground and nodded. "About a year before she passed, she got a visit from two women. They wouldna talk to anyone but my grandmother. They didna stay long, but after they left, my grandmother ordered my father to never allow them anywhere near the castle again. A few months later, reports came in of strange happenings. My grandmother said only three words. 'It's the Coven.'"

"Usually, when they come for a witch, asking for them to be a part of the Coven, they kill her if she declines."

"Grandmother was an old, frail woman by that point. Perhaps they knew she wasna worth killing."

"Or she joined them."

Fury rose up in Lachlan with such intensity that it startled him. He fought not to reach for his sword. "If the Coven is what you say they are, she never would've joined."

"Or she would've to save her family."

Lachlan didn't want to believe it. Then again, how could he be sure what Synne told him about the Coven was even true?

"You know about magic. You know about witches and Witch's Groves, and you've even heard of the Coven," Synne said. "There are few places that haven't been hit by the Coven. Their witches thrive on hurting the innocent. It's why we Hunters began. When we hear of such things, we track down the witch or witches and kill them. It's what I've trained for my entire life. And I intend to continue doing it. Because someone has to stop the Coven."

Synne rode past him without looking his way. Lachlan remained where he was, thinking over her words. It was true that many strange and inexplicable things happened to the surrounding clans. But never his people. Could it be because his grandmother had joined the Coven? She had never done anything evil, and he knew that she wouldn't have joined the Coven if they were as Synne said. Then again, he was only guessing. He had no idea what his grandmother had done because she refused to discuss it with anyone.

Lachlan turned his horse back around and nudged it into a canter to catch up with Synne. He slowed the gelding when he pulled up alongside the Hunter. While he hadn't grown up with magic, he'd known his grandmother had…unique… gifts. It wasn't until he was much older that she'd told him she was a witch.

"I understand why you don't believe me about the Coven," Synne said into the silence. "I wasn't keen on taking your word for who you were at first, either."

"Magic isna something that is talked about. When it is, there's always a thread of fear with it."

Synne turned her head to him, meeting his gaze. Her amber eyes held no anger or wariness. "The majority of people don't know about witches. They're the lucky ones."

"I wouldna say that. I knew a witch, and I loved her dearly."

"True," Synne said and looked forward. "I loved a witch. Thought of her as my mother. Edra was an amazing woman, but my life would've been much different had I not known what I do."

Lachlan made a sound in the back of his throat. "Anyone can say that about anything in their lives. I wouldna be surrounded by so much war and death if I hadna been born a male and become such an adept warrior. This is my path. I've accepted it. You must accept yours."

"I thought my path was as a Hunter."

"Why has that changed? Because Edra and Radnar died? You think to stop being what they trained you to be to help yourself and others, simply because their lives were lost?"

Synne cut him a sideways look, her lips flattened. "When you put it that way, nay."

"Stop feeling sorry for yourself. You have a gift, one that they saw in you. It's now up to you to keep others safe from the Coven. And to teach others what you've been taught regarding weapons and witches."

"You make it sound so easy, but I can't infuse weapons with magic to give the Hunters an edge against the Coven."

He lifted a shoulder. "Perhaps no', but there are other witches out there who will want to fight against the Coven. No' all of them will so readily join the Coven's ranks. And did you no' tell me about the Heart?"

"Helena," Synne said and glanced at him. "She could use her magic for the weapons."

"There you go, then."

Synne rolled her eyes while shaking her head. "This isn't something that I can do in a month or even a year. Radnar and Edra spent many years fortifying the abbey and teaching us to become Hunters. We don't have that kind of time. Sybbyl has already attacked us. She's going after the Varroki next."

"Aye. The warlocks."

"And witches," Synne added.

Lachlan patted his horse's neck. "They sound powerful."

"They are."

"But you're worried."

She nodded slowly. "Edra was powerful as well, and she wasn't the only witch there. But…the Varroki are something altogether different. Do you know of them?"

"I've never heard of them."

"They're very secretive."

"They must be if you doona even know how to find them for sure."

She grinned, the movement transforming her face into something ethereal. "I was told to go north. That I'd eventually find them."

Lachlan's brows rose. "You do know we're on an isle, right?"

Synne laughed, the sound going straight to his cock and

making his balls tighten. He'd never heard anything so beautiful before, so sweet. Amber eyes glanced his way, clearly unaware of what she was doing to him.

"Of course," she said. Then she shook her head, a grin still upon her lips. "I've not laughed in days. It feels…odd."

He shifted in the saddle and found his gaze lingering on her no matter how hard he tried to look away.

They rode in silence after that. Lachlan constantly scanned the trees, looking for danger. Synne did the same, but her idea of enemies was something altogether different. By the time he pulled his horse to a stop, the sun was sinking fast. After they had seen to their horses, Synne grabbed her bow and arrows and walked away.

He hadn't been left behind to get firewood since he was a young lad. It made Lachlan grin, but he didn't mind. Synne was a breath of fresh air. At times, he wasn't sure what to make of her, and at others, he was in awe.

The fire was roaring by the time she returned with two hares. They skinned them and set them up to roast. He waited until she leaned against one of the tall pines with a contented smile on her face before he said, "My grandmother spoke highly of those who could converse with plants. You're such a person."

Synne looked at him over the fire. "Why do you say that?"

"It's the look on your face. You seem…happier…when you're touching the trees. When I first came upon you, you were giving that oak a hug."

She scratched her neck and twisted her lips. "I imagine I looked peculiar."

"Nay," he replied. "Content. You looked verra content. And you spoke to it."

"It let me know you were there."

He quirked a brow. "So, you do converse with them."

"Not in the way you think. They don't tell me things with words. More like…feelings."

Lachlan held her gaze. "Tell me more. Please."

5

Few had ever asked Synne what it was like to speak with trees. Everyone at the abbey had accepted her gift without question. The Hunters had been curious but rarely wanted to know anything more. Not having to describe it made it difficult for her to put it into words now.

"You doona have to," Lachlan said when she paused.

Synne shook her head and stretched her legs out toward the fire to heat her feet. "I'm trying to find the words."

"You were doing good before," he replied with a half-smile.

That made her grin and glance down at her hands. If she didn't know better, she'd think he made her nervous. But that was ridiculous. He was just a man.

A handsome one with eyes that seemed to spear her.

She shook off that nonsense and settled back against the oak, promising herself that she wouldn't move again. "I feel safer amongst the trees. For as far back as I can remember, the need to be near them, to touch them, was present."

"Did you always live in or near a forest?"

Synne's gaze dropped to the dancing flames. "I'm not

sure. I don't know what happened to my family. Edra and Radnar found me wandering the woods when I was very young. I don't know if I was abandoned or taken or something else. I was alone, and then I wasn't. Edra tried many times to see if she could help me determine what had happened, but not even magic could give me answers."

"So, you turned to the trees," Lachlan surmised.

"They've always been a constant in my life." Synne reached back and put a palm against the bark. "They've given me shelter, hidden me high in their limbs against enemies, alerted me when danger was near, and let me know when I was safe." She paused and frowned as she met Lachlan's gray eyes. "They also prevented me from getting to the abbey when Sybbyl attacked with her Gira."

Lachlan blew out a breath and studied her. "You have a special relationship with the trees. They wanted to make sure you were no' harmed."

"I could've helped my friends."

"Or you could've been killed along with them. As much as you hurt now, it's apparent that your destiny lay elsewhere."

She shrugged her shoulders and fiddled with the edge of her cloak. "I feel like I let my family down."

"You're fighting against the Coven. That isna letting them down. For all you know, perhaps Edra made sure you couldna get to them. She wanted to give you a chance."

"Finding them…" She looked away and swallowed, unable to finish the sentence.

"Aye. I know that feeling," he said in a soft voice as he looked into the fire. "It's happened to me as well, and it's no' something you ever forget. You learn to live with it, though."

Synne found her gaze drawn to him. No warrior could survive battles and not have wounds and scars, both visible and invisible. She wanted him to talk more about it so she could learn more about him. But, in truth, he didn't need to. It was there on his face, in his voice.

She hadn't meant to take them down such a dark road, and it was better for both of them if they pulled themselves out quickly. Synne cleared her throat. "As I said, the trees don't give me words as you and I would exchange, but more a…feeling. It's difficult to describe. It's like it passes from them into me."

"Do you have to be touching them?"

"I always have before."

"I saw you hesitate to come into the forest. For someone who loves it so much, you didna want to venture inside."

Synne looked up at the branches above her and saw the darkening sky through them. "It's the Gira."

"Do the trees no' warn you of them?"

"Aye, they do."

He raised a brow. "I'm no' understanding, lass."

Synne looked at him and drew in a breath. "It makes no sense, I know. The Gira terrify me in ways I can't explain. When the forest warned me of their approach near the abbey, I froze. They can be killed, and while they have magic, I shouldn't be more afraid of them than I am of the witches."

"It does little good to be angry at yourself for emotions you can no' control."

"I'm a Hunter. I *have* to control such things."

His gaze was steady as he stared at her. "How many times have you encountered the Gira?"

"Once."

"When they attacked your friends?"

"And I couldn't fight against them."

Lachlan was silent for a long moment. "Are you sure you've no' encountered them before?"

"Trust me, I'd know if I'd faced them before."

"What else are you afraid of?"

Being alone. She didn't say the words aloud, though. It had taken her years to get past that, only to find herself alone once more. Was she destined never to have a family? Maybe there was something wrong with her.

Lachlan leaned to the side and propped himself on a forearm. "There's nothing wrong with being afraid. No matter how many times I go into battle, my stomach feels as if I have bees buzzing around. Then the fighting starts, and I forget about it."

"I have a healthy dose of respect for witches. I know how powerful they can be, especially Sybbyl. Do I fear them? No. Nor do I fear death."

"Just the Gira, then."

Synne nodded once, hating to admit it.

"No one has such a fear without it being warranted."

"What are you saying?" she demanded with a frown.

He tossed a pebble into the fire. "Only that there's a reason you're afraid of the Gira. Was it the stories someone told you?"

"We were taught with facts."

Synne didn't care that her words were laced with anger. She shifted and turned the rabbits to cook on the other side before she settled back against the tree.

"What did the trees tell you about me?" Lachlan asked.

Her gaze slid to him to find him looking into the fire. The red-orange glow danced on his face as he seemed enthralled by the flames. She loved looking into fire, as well. It was mesmerizing, just as listening to a river or a roaring waterfall soothed her.

"They told me that someone was near," she finally answered. "There was no dire warning attached, so I didn't get the sense that they thought you'd do me harm."

"My duty is to protect the lands of my clan. I'm in the forest to patrol it and look for enemies. Had you been an enemy, I would've struck you down," he stated without preamble.

She understood the ways of a warrior. While other women might have been appalled by such talk, she knew it put Lachlan and her on equal ground. "And had you been a witch with the Coven, I would've struck *you* down."

They shared a smile.

Silence fell between them as the fire crackled. The quiet of a forest might unnerve some, but Synne had always enjoyed it. Then again, the trees had been able to warn her if danger approached. Others didn't have such a gift. And when anything could be hiding behind a tree, she could see why some stayed away.

It wasn't long before the hares were done. Both she and Lachlan ate, lost in their thoughts. Except Synne found her mind drifting to the Highlander. He hadn't put her down for knowing how to use a bow or for wearing pants. He hadn't been condescending about her relationship with the trees, her training as a Hunter, the witches, or anything. She was used to that with the men at the sanctuary, but she had come up against others in the outside world who didn't share those views. It made her never want to leave the abbey, because she didn't feel as if she should have to defend her way of life to anyone—especially a man.

And the fact that men thought they could rule women completely made her equally angry. It infuriated Synne to watch women kowtow to such men. Then again, those women hadn't been given the same opportunities that she had. They came from two different lives, and if she were in their shoes, she would most likely act the same way.

Lachlan acted more like Radnar than other domineering men. She liked that. Otherwise, she would've dropped him on his arse.

"I have a feeling that smug smile is somehow about me," Lachlan said.

Synne shook her head even as she swallowed her chuckle. "Tell me about your family and clan."

"My father is a good laird, but he's aging. I had an older brother who died in battle several years ago. After my mother died, my father remarried, and I've a sister and a brother from that union."

"You're the eldest, then?"

"Aye."

"So, you'll take over as laird."

He nodded. "Aye."

"Do you have a spouse and children of your own?"

"No' yet, much to my father's exasperation," he said with a chuckle. "What about you?"

Synne shook her head as she swallowed.

"Is it no' allowed?"

"To marry? Of course. Edra and Radnar allowed us to make our own choices. Leoma married Braith."

Lachlan paused in eating as his brow furrowed. "He's the Warden of the skull."

"Blood Skull," she corrected. "That's right."

"Are other Hunters still out there?"

She licked the grease from her lips. "A few. Leoma and Ravyn that I know of. And Helena. Other Hunters were out tracking witches, and I let them know to go to Leoma if they made it back to our forest and found everyone gone."

"Why did you no' stay with Leoma or find Ravyn or Helena?"

"Because I'm going to stand with the Varroki against Sybbyl and the Coven."

"Are the others no' joining you?"

She set aside the bone she'd cleaned of all meat. "Aye, but they're also trying to locate another bone of the First Witch."

"You said the last piece was Helena, so no' a bone at all. Are you sure the rest are bones?"

Synne shrugged and reached for more meat. "Sybbyl can't be allowed to get more of the bones. She's already taken out the three elders of the Coven."

"You said she couldna get the Blood Skull or the Heart. Those are two powerful objects. Surely, they could help you stand against her."

"Right now, they could. If Sybbyl gets her hands on more bones, that might not be the case."

"Do you know where another relic is?"

Synne lowered the meat and looked at him over the fire. "Aye."

"Where?"

"Scotland."

6

Lachlan was awake well before dawn. What little sleep he'd gotten was filled with dreams of his grandmother talking of magic. And Synne.

He turned his head to look at her. She slept on her side, facing him with her arm curled beneath her head. His gaze lingered on her face, taking in her beauty. The women he knew were hardy. They had to be. But Synne had a different kind of strength. Lachlan had never encountered another female who understood what it was like to be in battle. Synne did.

She was steady. Tough. She dared anyone to question who she was both as a woman and as a warrior. And damn if he didn't find that insanely attractive. He wanted to deny the feelings he felt within him, but he couldn't.

The time he'd spent with her yesterday had proven that there were bigger things for him to be concerned with than a war with another clan. He wanted to go with Synne and fight alongside her. His father wouldn't be happy about that, however. But Lachlan didn't care. They couldn't pretend this war didn't involve them. But if Sybbyl won, then it would be about them.

Truth be told, he wanted to spend more time with Synne. She could take care of herself, but it was always nice to have someone watching your back. That's what he'd be for her. She had a grand destiny. She hadn't crossed his path for nothing. His grandmother used to tell him that nothing happened without reason. He was taking that to heart now. Synne had come into his life and had told her story because he was meant to be a part of it. Of that, he was sure.

Convincing her might not be so easy. And he didn't want to even think about his father. Yet this was something Lachlan had to do. For himself, for Synne, and for his clan.

He blew out a breath and looked at the sky above him. He'd been unable to sleep during the night as he went through every emotion swirling inside him. He was tasked with keeping his clan safe. Helping Synne was on that same path. However, it meant he'd have to leave the clan.

To remain behind, to leave it to Synne and whoever the Varroki were, was ignoring the oath Lachlan had taken to make sure he did everything in his power to keep his people from harm. And the Coven was undoubtedly a group that everyone should be wary of.

Then there was Synne. From the first moment he'd seen her outside of the forest, he'd been unable to look away. While the trees didn't speak to him, his instincts kept him out of trouble. And they hadn't warned him that Synne was an enemy. Then, he'd approached her and found his life altered forever.

Now, he wished he'd asked his sister if she had been able to do magic since it came from his father's side of the family. After his grandmother had died, the word *magic* hadn't been spoken again. Lachlan should've brought it up, he should've talked to his father about his grandmother and all the things he hadn't understood. But he hadn't. He wasn't certain why he'd resisted, but he regretted it now. And regret was something he strove never to experience.

Both the horses suddenly raised their heads, their ears pointing forward. Something had gotten their attention. Lachlan strained to listen, but he didn't hear anything. He stared at the animals, waiting to see if they shifted their focus. When they didn't, he quietly rose and grabbed his sword as he hurried to Synne. Her eyes were already open when he reached her.

He put his finger to his lips and drew his sword out of the scabbard. Synne was on her feet in an instant, moving behind a tree with an arrow already nocked and pointed in the direction of where the horses looked. He glanced at her, his gaze lingering on the long, golden braid of her hair before he focused on finding what had startled the horses.

Lachlan moved soundlessly to another tree and peered around it, trying to determine what was out there. Their mounts didn't act as if it were a predator, but they also hadn't looked away.

When he glanced back at Synne, she was no longer there. Something out of the corner of his eye got his attention, and he raised his gaze to find her scaling the tree with such ease and quickness that he couldn't look away. Suddenly, she was far above him, situated on a thick branch with her gaze forward. She was as still as a statue, as silent as a ghost. He forced his eyes away from her and back on the matter at hand, but it was one of the most challenging things he'd ever done.

He cleared his mind. One by one, the sounds around him faded until he heard it—footfalls. Two sets. Whoever it was didn't speak. But they also didn't move as warriors would if coming to attack. They took even steps as if someone were taking a stroll, coming right to Synne and him.

They—along with the horses—were concealed, but for how much longer? The two interlopers were on foot, while he and Synne had mounts. This was his clan's land, and he would face whoever it was. Lachlan took a breath. Before he could move, an arrow landed inches from his foot.

His head jerked upward to Synne, who was staring at him. She gave a single shake of her head. He frowned, wondering how she'd even known what he planned. Then he realized his hand was on the tree. It must have somehow told her. But…that meant the tree knew what he was about.

He looked at the trunk skeptically. He didn't have magic. How could it know what he was thinking?

Synne doesn't have magic.

Even after his inner voice stated the fact, Lachlan had a difficult time accepting it. Because if he believed that, then it meant that the trees had always known what humans thought and felt. That indicated they likely screamed out in pain while being cut down, and only their kind had heard it.

He closed his eyes to see if he could feel anything. To his surprise, a heartbeat later, it seemed as if warmth penetrated his palm and ran up his arm to spread throughout his body. His eyes snapped open as he looked at the bark.

"Thank you," he whispered.

It might have been his imagination, but it didn't matter. Lachlan had felt *something*. It was too bad his grandmother wasn't alive. He would've loved to talk to her about this. She could've likely shared a font of information with him, had he but asked.

But that was something to consider at another time. Right now, someone came their way. Lachlan glanced at the horses. The two were pressed against each other, their gazes still locked on whoever approached. Lachlan peered around the tree and saw a flash of a pale brown cloak. A moment later, two women came into view. Their hoods were pulled forward, blocking their faces. They walked through the snow as if the cold didn't affect them, and given the wet hems of their cloaks, it had no doubt penetrated their shoes as well as their gowns.

They halted and looked around before looking at each other. Wordlessly, their heads swiveled back to Lachlan. He couldn't see their eyes, but he knew they were looking at him. They were female, but there was something altogether different about them. He didn't need Synne to tell him that these were witches.

He'd never fought one before. Then he recalled that Synne had arrows infused with magic to help in her fight against the Coven. His sword had no magic in it. All he had was his skill, but he wasn't sure that would be enough.

Perhaps his turmoil regarding whether to go with Synne or not would be taken out of his hands. If he had to sacrifice himself so she could get away and fight the Coven, then so be it. He might not be able to defeat the witches, but he could sure as hell keep them occupied long enough for Synne to take them out.

"We know you're here, Hunter."

The voice came from all around them, the English accent clear. Lachlan didn't know which of the women had spoken, but they were far enough away that they would've had to shout for him to hear. He eyed the one in the tan cloak before his gaze moved to the one in the dark green one. He saw something spark in the former's palm. It looked…yellow.

"Show yourself now, and we'll end you quickly."

Lachlan was beginning to hate that voice. He glanced up to look at Synne, but she was gone from her perch. He hadn't even realized she'd moved.

The witches began walking toward him once more. As he watched, he saw that when the snow became too deep, it was suddenly and inexplicably moved aside to allow the women to walk. The fact that he was seeing magic shouldn't surprise him, but it did.

"You'll never survive the Coven. You're now the one being hunted," the witch announced.

The laughter that followed sent a chill running down Lachlan's spine. He glanced at the trees around him, searching for Synne. Then he saw her. She was moving from tree to tree in a fashion he'd never witnessed before. It was almost as if she were floating in the air, she made it look so easy. And the trees… If he didn't know better, he'd swear they were bending to help her.

As Synne made her way behind the two witches, Lachlan turned to the horses. The ropes tethering them were now loose. Both animals were moving slowly away. Lachlan's gelding looked at him before disappearing behind some trees. He wasn't sure what to make of that, but once more, there wasn't time to think about it.

"One Hunter. You can't possibly think to defeat us."

Something told Lachlan to look for Synne again. When he did, he saw she had two arrows nocked. She gave him a nod. He then stepped from behind the tree and faced the women. "You two sure talk a lot."

"Who are you?"

He shrugged, trying to determine which of them was speaking. "Does it matter?"

"You aren't the Hunter."

Lachlan smiled. "You're on MacCullum land, which means, you're trespassing. You have one chance to leave."

"Leave? We're not going anywhere without the Hunter."

"I'm the only one here."

"Lies."

The word was hissed. It enveloped Lachlan to the point where he felt suffocated by it. He tried to move, attempted to get his sword up as the witches approached, but he couldn't.

He was the strongest warrior of his clan, but he couldn't even save himself against two witches. This is what awaited them if the Coven came.

Lachlan wanted to look at Synne, but he didn't. He kept his eyes on the witches. As they neared, he tried to see their faces inside their hoods, but only darkness met his gaze. As dots flashed in his vision, he knew he was dying. He glanced at Synne to see her pull back her arm, ready to loose the arrows. That's when he smiled at the witches.

One hooded head leaned forward as if trying to determine what he was grinning at. In the next instant, both witches jerked as the arrows found their marks. Lachlan drew in a much-needed breath as their magic ceased, and the two fell forward.

He bent to turn them over when suddenly the bodies began to disintegrate. He jumped back as they became ash, leaving only their clothes behind.

"We need to get moving," Synne said as she walked past him and released a low whistle.

Lachlan watched as her mare and his gelding trotted to them. "Did your arrows do that?"

"My arrows killed them, but when witches die, they burn from the inside out and turn to ash," she told him as she readied her mare. "We need to go."

He nodded and straightened as he began saddling the gelding. He thought back to his grandmother and now understood why his father hadn't let him see the body. "Should we no' do something with the clothes so no one will know what happened?"

"More witches are coming. There isn't time for that." She mounted and looked at him. "You need to get to your clan. Keep everyone out of the forest. They're after me, but they'll be happy to kill anyone in their way—as you experienced."

Lachlan put his sword in its scabbard and threaded his

arm and head through the strap so it lay against his back. Then he was atop his horse. "Thank you for saving me."

"You were my diversion. I should be thanking you. Now, if you'll point me in the right direction, I'll lead the Coven away from here."

"Nay."

She blinked. "Nay?"

"I'm coming with you."

He couldn't be serious. But the longer Synne looked into Lachlan's gray eyes, the more she realized that he was. "You can't come with me."

"Aye, lass, I can."

"Your clan needs you."

"And you need someone to watch your back."

She blew out a breath. "I'm trained for this. I can handle myself."

"I'm no' saying otherwise. What I'm telling you is that you need fighters against the Coven. I'm a good warrior. I can help."

Synne had to admit it would be nice to have someone with her. She and Lachlan worked well as a team, and if the Coven were coming after her, she would need all the help she could get.

"I'll no' let you down, lass," Lachlan said when she didn't answer him.

She licked her lips and looked at what was left of the two dead witches. "We got lucky this time. Next time, we might not."

"That's the way of battle."

"While that's true, you aren't used to battling witches. Then there's your clan. You can't just leave without telling them, and I need to find the Varroki."

Lachlan smiled. "I willna be taking time to speak to my father, nor will I be leaving without telling them. I've another plan."

Synne wished she were strong enough to say that she would be fine on her own, but she not only wanted Lachlan with her, she also *needed* him. All this time, she'd thought she was strong enough to be a Hunter on her own, but she wasn't. Why hadn't Edra and Radnar told her? Why hadn't they pointed out her weaknesses so she could work on them?

She knew it was unfair to be angry with them, but she couldn't help it. She was mad. At the world, at the injustice of what the Coven had done, at…everything.

"Synne, we can do this," Lachlan said in a soft voice.

She swung her eyes to him and gave him a nod. Synne didn't try to speak because the words wouldn't come. They were lodged in her throat as she fought back tears for the family she'd known that was now gone.

"Follow me," he told her.

Synne didn't look back as she nudged her mare into a trot. She and Lachlan didn't speak for another hour as they traveled through the forest. No matter how hard she looked, she didn't see any more witches. She took every opportunity to touch the trees as she passed. None of them alerted her to danger. Still, she didn't let her guard down.

She'd believed that after Sybbyl had destroyed the abbey, she would be safe as she found her way to Blackglade. Sybbyl had no way of knowing how many Hunters there were, so the witch couldn't know if all of them had been killed in her attack or not. How then were witches after her? No matter how Synne looked at it, she couldn't figure it out.

Then she realized that it was a moot point. Sybbyl had a bone of the First Witch. That gave her more power than any other witch in the Coven. That meant there was likely no end to what she could do. Which didn't bode well for Synne, Leoma, or Helena.

Or the Varroki.

Synne thought about Malene. She was the Lady of the Varroki and supremely powerful in her own right. So much so, that Synne believed Malene could take out the Coven and Sybbyl by herself. But Malene didn't see it that way. The Varroki had begun as a way to fight against the Coven, and they would continue in that vein until the very end.

When Lachlan finally slowed, Synne pulled herself from her thoughts. She came up alongside him as he halted his gelding. Their gazes met as their knees brushed. Something electric and energizing passed between them. It made her heart skip a beat, but if Lachlan felt it, he didn't show it. So, she didn't say anything.

But she couldn't stop thinking about it.

"One of my clansmen is stationed just over that rise. I'm going to tell him what we're doing," he told her.

Synne shifted in the saddle. "How much are you going to say?"

"Enough that he knows this is important. I'm no' daft enough to mention witches or magic, but the words I pass to my father will get the point across."

"The forest has been quiet."

Lachlan looked past her and nodded. "You expect another attack soon."

"I do."

"Hmm," he said after a moment. "Me, as well."

They continued on, and once they crested the steep rise, she spotted the man standing guard with his horse a few yards away. Lachlan waved, and the man waved back. As they approached, Synne spotted the man's dark blond hair, and the wariness of his gaze when it landed on her.

"Alan, I need you to take a message to my father," Lachlan said without dismounting.

Alan's brown eyes narrowed on Synne. "Who is she?"

"Synne. I'm guiding her across our land, and I'll be taking her farther north."

Alan's gaze jerked to Lachlan as he frowned. "North? We need you here."

"I'm aware of the upcoming battle with our enemy, but a bigger foe is coming this way. Listen to me carefully, because I need you to tell my father these words exactly."

Alan stood there for a moment, a muscle in his jaw ticking. Then he bowed his head slightly. "I'm listening."

"I'm fulfilling my duty to protect our clan as I've vowed. Grandmother knew about this, and it's finally come. Keep everyone close to the castle. What's coming doesna care who we are. They'll kill without hesitation."

Alan repeated the words verbatim.

"Good," Lachlan told him.

"Let me come with you," Alan said and glanced at Synne. "You could use another sword."

Lachlan moved his mount forward until he could lay his hand on Alan's shoulder. "You've been my friend for as long as I can remember. There's no one else I'd rather have by my side, but the clan is more important right now. I need you to watch over them in my place, help my father and the others. I ask this of you because I know I can trust you."

"What are you no' telling me?" Alan asked.

Synne wished it was as easy as speaking the truth, but not everyone knew about witches and magic. If the wrong person was told, she and Lachlan could be burned alive. She had shared with Lachlan on a whim, but also because she knew that if it came down to it, she could handle herself and get away. Both she and Lachlan could overpower Alan as well, but there were more lives at stake. The clan—*all* clans, actually—needed to be warned.

"A lot," Lachlan answered. "Trust me."

Alan bowed his head. "I always have."

"Thank you. I doona know when I'll be back. You might see strange things in the forest. Doona go after them."

Synne flattened her lips because Lachlan was making things worse, not better. She caught Alan's attention. "While you might not want to, I would advise alerting neighboring clans, as well."

The way Alan looked at her reminded Synne that she wasn't Scottish, and she'd just announced that to him by speaking. Just when he'd been about to let all questions drop, his gaze sharpened because she hadn't been able to keep her mouth shut.

Lachlan straightened and gave her a hard look before he looked back at Alan. "Synne didna bring this to us. It was already headed this way. She's only trying to stop it."

"A woman?" Alan asked with scorn.

Lachlan's expression hardened as he glared at his friend. "Aye, a woman. She saved my life this morning. Heed my words, Alan. I doona want to learn that the clan was attacked and people killed simply because Synne is a *sassenach* and a woman."

Alan looked away and swallowed. "Fair point." He blew out a breath and met Lachlan's gaze. "If you doona return to us, your father will never forgive me."

Lachlan smiled and clicked to his horse. Synne watched him before her gaze slid back to Alan. She glanced at the ground. "Everyone I knew and loved, as well as the home I had, was destroyed by what's coming."

"Then why no' face it?"

Lachlan stopped and turned to look back at her. Synne stared into his gray eyes that were as steady as his hand. Radnar would've liked him. No doubt, Radnar would've taken Lachlan in and shown him everything he knew.

Her gaze slid to Alan. "I intend to face it. That's why I'm going north. Others ready to fight are waiting for me."

"Then you two better get moving," Alan said with a nod. He turned and strode to his horse before mounting it. He spun the animal around and raced eastward.

Synne then nudged her horse to start moving.

"We've got another day of riding to get across my clan's land," Lachlan told her.

"And how much farther north can we go?"

He lifted a brow as their horses walked side by side. "Depends on how fast we travel and what we run across. Clans doona like others crossing their lands. We're constantly at war with each other for one thing or another."

"Sounds exhausting."

He chuckled. "It's life. I've never known anything else. Most times, the wars are settled by one laird offering a daughter up for marriage."

"I can't believe women agree to that."

"They doona have a choice."

She snorted and rolled her eyes. "Of course, they do. They have a brain, a mouth, and they can think for themselves. How would you like to be offered up to a woman as a way for a war to end? A woman you might detest."

"I doona think I'd mind if that woman was you."

She looked at him to see him grinning. Despite her ire, she found herself smiling in response. "You have to admit, you'd hate having that choice taken from you."

"Sometimes, the choice is out of a man's hands, as well. I'm well aware that if I doona choose my own wife, there's a chance my father will offer me to one of his enemy's daughters as payment for a truce. When two clans are bound by marriage, they become allies. There is strength in numbers."

"It's ridiculous."

"Perhaps, but we're going to be crossing some of those allies' lands on the way north."

Synne wrinkled her nose. "If you ever have children, don't make them marry someone they don't want to. No one deserves that kind of life."

"It's no' always bad. My mother was such a bride, and she and my father fell in love. It can turn out all right."

"Perhaps," she admitted. "But I wager that more times than not, it doesn't. You doom a woman to a life of misery, while a man can find himself a mistress if he wants."

Lachlan made a sound in the back of his throat. "Women do that, as well."

"Aye. They do." She flashed him an apologetic smile. "I'm sorry. I grew up with vastly different beliefs, and just because I agree with mine, doesn't make yours wrong."

"It doesna, but I admit I like hearing different views. It makes me think, and it makes me consider that the way we've done things in the past isna always right or wrong. It's worked, but it might no' always work. And since I've a sister who is terrified she'll be offered up as a wife to one of our enemies, I'd like to tell you I'd never do that. But if it means an end to the war, if it means a truce and allies? A laird must take into account more than just one person. He must consider his clan."

Synne nodded slowly. "I hadn't thought of it that way. You do have a point."

"I think we both do."

They shared a smile, and Synne was happier than ever that Lachlan was traveling with her. He wasn't just a warrior, he was intelligent, as well. He would push her mentally and physically. Radnar had always said that a good warrior realized they never stopped learning. That there were always more skills out there to acquire.

"I'm glad you're here, Lachlan."

"Me, too, lass."

Somewhere in northern Scotland

The magic of the Witch's Grove moved over Sybbyl, wrapping her in a blanket of comfort. The wood was dense with ancient trees that the Gira used as camouflage, watching her as she stood in the center of the clearing. She was close to the Varroki. And soon, she'd find them and wipe them from existence.

Her fingers tightened around the Staff of the Eternal. Within the wood was the ancient thigh bone of the First Witch. The moment Sybbyl had touched the staff, she'd felt the power running through it. And that power was now hers.

She smiled as she looked at the weapon. It didn't matter that it wasn't pretty. Power didn't need to be. It only mattered how that ability was used. And no one could use it like she could. She'd proven that when she decimated Edra and the Hunters the witch had trained to kill.

The very thought of Edra hunting her own enraged Sybbyl. It's why she'd taken such pleasure in killing the witch. She had dared to think she could stand against the Coven.

Sybbyl had wanted Edra gone for years, and that was when Sybbyl was only part of the Coven. Now that she ruled it, she would make sure no one could ever rise above her.

"There's the Heart."

Her smile dipped at the voice in her head. She ignored it as she had for days, but it was growing louder and louder. At first, she'd thought it was her conscience rearing its head and sowing self-doubt, but she had quickly realized that wasn't the case. Then, she'd thought it might be remnants of magic from the elders she'd killed, but once more, she determined that wasn't the case either.

There was only one explanation—it was the staff.

Sybbyl had wanted to ask the Gira if the bones of the First Witch could speak. Yet, every time she tried, she couldn't get the words out. The Gira followed her because of her magic and the fact that she ruled the Coven. No one— absolutely *no one*—could know that there was even the slightest chink in her armor. Especially the Gira.

The nymphs were particularly…vicious. They were great as allies, but if they ever turned on you, it was horrendous. They usually kept to themselves rather than aligning with any person or group. Still, there had been a handful of scenarios throughout history where they had chosen a side. While they had been allies with chosen witches, those witches had made great leaps in power. But when the Gira decided to sever that tie, the witches died brutally.

Sybbyl wasn't going to be like those witches. She was smarter than that. She had worked her way up in the ranks of the Coven to take her rightful place as the leader. The idea that the Coven needed three elders was ludicrous. That stemmed from the First Witch's sisters, who had all wanted control and nothing more.

But Sybbyl was nothing like any of the witches who had come before her. She was something altogether different.

Edra and her Hunters had discovered that. So would the Varroki. And once Sybbyl had another of the First Witch's bones, she would be able to easily thwart Helena.

Just thinking about the witch made Sybbyl furious. She should've been able to defeat Helena already, but the witch's magic was more potent than any other's. It was why Sybbyl had wanted her in the Coven. She hadn't realized that Helena was a direct descendant of the First Witch, but it soon wouldn't matter. Sybbyl knew that another bone was in Scotland, and she was going to find it before she turned her attention to the Varroki.

The bones wanted to be reunited. They had always called out to one another, but only those possessing magic and holding one of those bones could hear it. Sybbyl let those opposing her believe they were more powerful, but it was an illusion. Soon, she'd show them and everyone else that she was untouchable.

Then, every living thing on the planet would bow before her.

The idea of such power made her smile as she closed her eyes and imagined her future. It would be glorious, her castle massive and utterly magnificent. Once she ruled, there would never be another burned alive because of ignorance. Anyone with magic would have power. And those without…well, they would get a taste of what it was like to be hunted and to live in fear.

Something fell upon her cheek. Then her nose. Sybbyl opened her eyes to see the flurries of snow swirling around in the air as if some invisible hand controlled them. She watched them for a while, her mind emptying. The longer she stayed in the Grove, the more her magic was renewed. And with the Staff of the Eternal in her hand, it doubled.

"You're the illusion. Nothing you have will be enough."

She jerked to the present. The message was one voice, not

the many of the Gira, so she knew it wasn't them. Her gaze slid to the staff.

"*Afraid? You should be.*"

"I'm the leader of the Coven," Sybbyl replied.

The voice laughed, the sound raspy and low. "*You're terrified. Just like you were as a little girl. You hold power before you like a shield, hoping no one can see your knees knocking.*"

"Nay."

"*I can see inside you. There is no lying to me.*"

Sybbyl stopped arguing. There was no need to continue. She knew the truth, and she felt the power of the staff. The scared girl she used to be had been gone a long time. She knew her place, and it was right where she was. She'd known that she would be queen eventually. And here she was.

She pushed her magic into the staff and asked, "Where is the next bone?"

The flurries fell quicker, swirling around each other to land in an arrow that faced southeast. She frowned because it had initially pointed north. Had she traveled so far that she now had to backtrack? Or was someone moving the bone?

That was a definite possibility. Had a Hunter found the relic? No. If that were the case, the staff would've told her. Wouldn't it?

The laughter that rang in her head made her want to hit something. She took a deep breath and promised herself that she would ignore it. Sybbyl waited several moments to see if the voice had anything else to say. When it didn't, she focused on the location of the next bone. She wasn't quite ready to leave the Grove yet. There was something so peaceful about it that it made it hard to leave. But go she must.

She had to get that bone from whoever had it. There was no other option. If Braith, as Warden of the Blood Skull, came after her along with Helena, Sybbyl would need more than just the staff and the Gira.

"You have more enemies."

The Varroki. How could she forget? Not that Sybbyl was too worried about them. They stayed hidden for a reason.

"How easily you forget Jarin."

She gritted her teeth at the mention of the warlock. The fact that he had refused her advances was something she'd never forget or forgive. But he had also fought against her and alongside Helena. Then, he'd professed his love for Helena, and that was more than Sybbyl could take.

She lifted the staff and slammed the end of it into the ground in anger. The Varroki had warlocks. The ones who'd survived her attack would be used by witches to ensure that magic continued for future generations. The rest would be killed if they didn't join the Coven.

Sybbyl debated whether to gather the black mist that allowed her to travel over long distances. She hadn't yet learned how to pinpoint a specific location, and it used up a lot of magic. There was a chance that she might have to battle Helena or even the Varroki when she found the next bone, so she needed to conserve her magic. That meant she was walking.

Without a word to the Gira, she started in the direction the arrow in the snow indicated. The moment she exited the Grove, she felt its loss. The more time she spent in a Witch's Grove, the more she wanted to stay. They were known sanctuaries for witches for a reason. Not only did others stay out, but they also gave witches solace and peace, two things they rarely found out in the cruel world.

Since she'd acquired the staff, the properties of the Groves had benefited her tenfold. She wasn't as happy anywhere else as she was within the confines of those sacred places. Yet, if she were to complete her plans, she needed to leave the Witch's Grove and travel.

The idea of possessing a second bone of the First Witch made it easy for Sybbyl to leave the Grove. Only a handful of Gira followed her, but it didn't matter. They could stay behind for all she cared. Then again, the nymphs did come in handy at times. If they wanted to help, she wasn't going to stop them.

As she moved through the forest, each step brought her closer to her destiny. There wasn't anything she feared, no one to deter her from attaining her goal of ruling all. She smiled, knowing that she was doing the right thing. No one who had come before her or after would ever know, without a doubt, that they were on such a sure path.

Sybbyl found a road and traveled it. A few hours later, she came upon a small village. She walked through it alone and didn't hold back her smile when she saw men, women, and children darting for cover. They might not know what she was, but they knew enough to be fearful. That's just what she wanted.

As she neared the outskirts of the village, four burly men stepped in front of her with menace in their eyes. The Gira remained with the trees, but Sybbyl didn't need them against men without magic, who thought they could make her cower.

"A beautiful woman such as yerself shouldn't be travel'n alone," the largest of the men said.

The other three smiled and leered at her.

Sybbyl raised a brow. "I'm not alone."

"Ye must be touched in the head," another said. "Look at 'er. She be wear'n a crown."

The men laughed and, behind her, others joined in. Sybbyl returned their smiles. "You should be on your knees before me."

Their laughter grew, but she didn't mind. It was a great place to show everyone her power and what awaited the world. Sybbyl felt the magic of the staff mix with her own. She held up her hand, palm out. The ancient spell formed in her mind. Before the staff, she would've had to say the words. Now, she just had to think them.

As soon as the spell was complete, magic shot from her hand in red light toward the four men, straight into their hearts. They screamed in pain, a sound that was cut off suddenly as they fell to the ground, unmoving.

Sybbyl then turned to the crowd behind her. "Anyone else want to laugh at my crown?"

One by one, the townspeople dropped to their knees, their gazes downcast. Satisfied, she slowly turned and resumed her walk, stepping over the dead men.

9

Lachlan was pleased with the amount of ground he and Synne had covered that day. What didn't sit well with him was the fact that they hadn't encountered anyone else.

He felt Synne's gaze as she brushed her mare, and he scanned the surrounding area. They had chosen a secluded spot for the night, making it difficult for anyone to spot them. However, it also hampered their view and hindered their awareness of anyone approaching. But he had purposefully remained in the forest for Synne and her connection to the trees. Tomorrow, they wouldn't be so lucky.

"Does it ever stop snowing?" she asked from behind him.

Lachlan glanced at her over his shoulder and shrugged. "It's Scotland."

"Since I've never been here before, I'm not sure what that means."

"It means that the winters are harsh. The farther north we go, the worse it'll get." He turned and looked at her clothes. "We might need to get you a warmer cloak."

"I'll be fine. It's better if we steer clear of any villages."

That made him frown. "Why?"

"The last thing I want is to bring a witch to a village. The Coven is tracking me. No one else needs to be killed."

Lachlan flattened his lips as he realized the truth of her words. "I didna think of that."

Synne finished with her horse and came around to stand next to him. "We made up a lot of time today. At this rate, we could find Blackglade sooner than I'd hoped."

"Those witches found you quickly. Do they use magic to travel?"

"The stronger ones do. Sybbyl can transport places with the staff. Other witches?" She shrugged. "I can't say for sure. I've no idea how they found me, and it doesn't matter. We need to remain on guard no matter what."

He gave her a dry look. "That much is obvious."

That made her smile, her amber eyes crinkling at the corners. "Are we still on your clan's land?"

"Near midday, we crossed onto Campbell land." Lachlan walked to his gelding and removed his saddle and bridle. The horses were tied to a tree to keep them close. He rubbed his hands over his horse to brush the day from the gelding's winter coat and met Synne's gaze. "Any tips for the next time we run into witches?"

"Don't underestimate them."

Lachlan snorted. "I assumed as much. What type of magic can they do?"

"Anything. Everything," she answered with a shrug. "Some can do a little of all, while others can only do specific types of magic. One of the witches that attacked us this morning had yellow that sparked in her palm."

"I saw that."

"Not everyone can. Her magic was yellow. Had she done more, you would've noticed it more."

That made him frown. "So, magic can be seen?"

"Sometimes. Helena's magic is purple. She can use it so

that it sinks into a person like coils and kills them. Great when battling other witches."

Lachlan finished with the horse and nodded. "That would come in handy."

"If you're with me, the witches of the Coven will assume you're a Hunter. That's good because they'll be wary of you."

"The two this morning were no' wary," he pointed out.

Synne twisted her lips. "They wanted us dead. They didn't care."

"Then neither will any others."

She blew out a breath and looked off to the side through the trees and the blanket of snow that covered the ground. "Everything is changed now. I need to remember that. For so long, we were the ones doing the hunting. Now, Sybbyl has changed that. They're hunting us. I'd hoped she would believe all the Hunters had been killed at the abbey."

"Was there a list of the Hunters, perhaps? Maybe she saw that."

"Anyone at the abbey would know how many Hunters there were. Leoma, Ravyn, and I are the only ones I know of who weren't inside. Then there's Helena. As well as Asa."

That was the first time he'd heard that name. "Who is Asa?"

"Another witch who lived with us. She can speak to animals, and she was the one who marked our skin."

He wanted to ask what exactly Synne meant about marking her skin, but he was too caught up in the fact that Asa could speak to animals. "Can you find Asa?"

"Unfortunately, no. She wasn't at the abbey, though. And she rarely leaves."

"Did Sybbyl take her, perhaps?"

Synne's face scrunched up with exasperation. "Asa never would've allowed that to happen. She'd die first."

"You speak of Sybbyl's power with the staff. Is there a chance that she was able to take Asa prisoner?"

"Of course, there's a chance, but I don't see that happening. I know you're asking questions, and I'm doing a poor job of giving specifics. But Asa hated the Coven as much as Edra and Helena. Few witches were able to get away from the Coven once discovered. The Coven gives the witches they encounter two choices. Join or die. Those who refuse the Coven are generally killed instantly. There are a few—Edra and Helena—who managed to get away. There are even more, like Asa, who remained hidden from the Coven."

Lachlan shook the snow from his head. "The Coven wanted to swell their ranks with members. The more witches they have, the stronger they are."

"Exactly. Witches hid anyway because regular folks feared them. Once the Coven began searching for more members, they had to make a decision: remain where they were and hope the Coven didn't find them, hide, or stand and fight, knowing they could die."

"Anyone can die at any time," Lachlan said. "Yet, it was smart of the witches to hide those who didna want to join the Coven. Because anyone they found who refused would be killed, which meant one less witch to stand against them."

Synne nodded, smiling sadly. "That's why Edra and Radnar began training us. At first, it was simply so we could take care of ourselves, but also so we'd recognize a witch and be able to protect not only ourselves, but others, as well. The more we trained and learned, the more we wanted to hunt the Coven as Edra did. That's when our training intensified. Edra and Radnar said that if we were going to face witches, we needed the skills to do it since we didn't have magic."

"You have magic."

Synne laughed wryly. "I don't, even though I wished for it."

"You converse with trees. I'd call that magic."

She cocked her head to the side. "Radnar said the same thing."

"Why did you no' believe him?"

"I thought he was humoring me."

"Do you know of anyone else who can speak to trees?"

She shook her head.

Lachlan smiled. "It's magic, lass. Plain and simple. It might no' be the kind you wanted, but it's magic."

"I can't do anything else, though."

"You can do more than most of us."

"For so long, I've been caught up in the fact that I wasn't a witch, that I never thought of it that way. Edra always kept me in the forest near the abbey. Only when Coven members came close did I get to fight. It used to anger me terribly that she didn't let me loose as she did the others."

Lachlan walked to her and brushed a snowflake from her cheek. "Edra understood your connection to the trees and kept you there to foster that."

"I think she did. Why didn't she tell me that when I asked?"

"The same reason a mother or father doesna always give their child direct answers. So the child can learn."

Synne shook her head and briefly closed her eyes. "I wish I would've realized this sooner."

"You know it now. That's what counts."

She didn't answer him, lost in her thoughts. Lachlan looked around again. The forest was silent. Usually, he loved it like this, but the knowledge that the Coven was tracking Synne put him on edge. To those with an untrained eye, there weren't any signs of animals, but he had grown up in the forest and knew how to hunt.

"I'll be back with some food." He glanced her way to find her nodding her head.

Lachlan walked deeper into the forest. He was soon swallowed up by the trees. When he glanced back, he couldn't see Synne or the horses, just as he wanted. Though his tracks were easy to spot in the snow, there was nothing he could do about that. Luckily, with the way the snow was falling, it would soon cover his path.

Would that be enough to stop the witches? Probably not. He wished he had known to ask his grandmother more questions while she was alive. There was much he could've learned from her to ready him for this day. Then again, how could he have known he would be fighting against a coven of witches?

It took him longer than he wanted to find food. When he returned to the camp with a pheasant in tow, a fire roared in greeting. But there was no sign of Synne. His gaze immediately moved up to the branches around him. That's when he spotted her sitting upon a thick limb with her eyes closed and her hand on the tree.

He didn't call out to her. The trees had no doubt told her of his approach. Instead, he made use of the time and cleaned the bird to get it ready to roast over the fire. Once that was seen to, he scouted the area, looking for fresh tracks —be they animal or human. As far as he could discern, nothing had disturbed the snow.

When he got back to the camp, Synne was waiting for him. She didn't look up as she turned the bird over so it didn't burn. He removed his sword and scabbard from around his body and set it against one of the trees and then drank deeply from his waterskin.

"It's not too late for you to return to your clan."

His head jerked in her direction. "Why would you say that?"

"Because you have a family." Her gaze lifted to his. "I've lost mine, but yours is still alive."

"No' all of your family is gone. And I'm here *because* of my family. I'm fighting to save them."

"The Varroki are powerful, but none more than Malene. Despite that, there's no guarantee that we'll win."

He drew in a breath and glanced at the ground. "Lass, there's no guarantee with anything in life other than taxes and death. Everything else is a draw. I know that each time I wake up in the morn. I understand that every time I face an enemy on the battlefield. Whether it's a weapon, disease, old age, or magic that takes my life, I will die. What I willna do is stand aside and let others fight battles for me."

"I don't want you with me because I'm a woman, and you don't think I can handle myself."

He gave a loud snort. "I might have thought that upon our first meeting, but that notion was quickly dispelled. I promise you that. Why no' tell me what's really bothering you."

She refused to hold his gaze then and looked away. "I don't want to let anyone down."

"Do the best you can, and that willna happen."

"You make it sound so simple."

"Because it is."

10

She didn't want to let anyone down, but that's precisely what Synne was worried might happen. Lachlan had told her to do her best. What if her best wasn't good enough? What if—?

Synne halted her thoughts. She wouldn't go down that road, questioning Edra and Radnar and anyone else who had taught her at the abbey. No, her problem was with herself. The fear that had never really left, the one that had been inside her for as long as she could remember. Had her parents abandoned her? Had there been something wrong with her that'd made her unlovable? Was that why they hadn't wanted her?

Some of that apprehension had faded in the years she'd spent at the abbey. She had even thought it might be gone for good. But the destruction of the sanctuary had that fear rearing its ugly head, and there was nothing she could do to make it go away. It was there, and she was beginning to believe that it always would be.

"You killed those two witches this morn," Lachlan said as he checked the pheasant.

Synne nodded and cleared a spot of snow so she could sit

next to a tree to lean back against it. "That was only two of them."

"Two more than I've ever had attack me. You make light of a serious situation. You were trained to fight against the Coven. Trust what you've learned."

"You're right, I know."

Lachlan sat between two roots protruding from the ground that he'd cleared of snow. "You're still grieving. And you will be for a while. Even killing Sybbyl and everyone in the Coven willna stop that."

His words, spoken with such conviction, made her stop and think. "You went after someone for revenge."

"My father warned me what would happen if I did, but I refused to listen to him. Just as you are no' listening to me now."

"I'm listening," she argued.

He gave her a half-smile that made her stomach flutter in a way that had never happened before. It shocked her so much that it took her a moment to hear the words he spoke next.

"You're listening, but you are no' accepting my words. There's a difference."

She swallowed, still confused by the way her body reacted to him. "Maybe."

He sat back and closed his eyes. He sat there in silence for a moment before he lifted one leg to plant his foot on the ground and then rested his arm on his knee. "It was for my eldest brother."

She couldn't look away from him. His words, spoken so softly she almost didn't hear them, hit her square in the chest. He had mentioned an older brother who had died, but she hadn't asked him how.

Synne drew her cloak tighter around herself and waited for him to continue. The silence stretched on for so long, she began to think that he had gone to sleep. Finally, he spoke again.

"My parents met once before they were wed. Nine months after the wedding, my brother was born. It was another eight years before I came along. Nathan was loved by everyone. He was kind and smart and good at everything. Everyone wanted to be his friend, but he was my brother." Lachlan suddenly smiled without opening his eyes. "We were verra close, despite the years that separated us. If Nathan did something, I had to do it, as well. He was always there to get me out of trouble, and many times, he took the blame for me."

Synne heard the love for Nathan in Lachlan's voice. It made her eyes fill with tears to hear him talk in such a way. She hadn't had siblings, though none of the children Edra and Radnar had found had family. They became each other's family. Still, it was different than having someone always there from the moment you were born, looking out for you.

Lachlan drew in a long breath and then released it. "Then, my mother's clan asked for aid when they were attacked. My father readied his men and answered the call. Though there were plenty of men left behind to guard the castle, Nathan still wanted to go. Da agreed. I was furious. I even went so far as to try and sneak in with the others, but at only ten summers, I stuck out." Lachlan's eyes opened, but he looked into the fire, not at her. "Nathan came to me, but I refused to talk to him, much less answer him." Lachlan swallowed hard. "He didna come home."

Synne had the urge to go to him and touch him to give him comfort, but she stayed where she was. "I'm sorry."

"It happens," he said with a shrug. "For the next few years, I trained harder than anyone else. Each time I picked up a weapon, I saw the Frasier clan. I begged my father to retaliate. He told me they had been defeated and that everyone had lost someone in the battle. That wasna enough for me. When he refused to go after them, I tried to leave one night with a small band of my friends. My father, along with his strongest warriors, were waiting for us. Nothing was said as they herded us back to the castle. Only when we were alone did Da caution me about revenge and letting it consume me.

"Still, I didna listen. A few months later, I snuck out again. This time, I went on my own, and no one was there to stop me. I made it to the Frasier's and got inside the castle. It was easy," he said with a frown. "So verra easy. It wasna until I had the blade of my dagger at the laird's throat that I realized where I was and what I was about to do. There was no fear in the ruler's eyes, but next to him in bed, his wife clutched at his arm, silent tears rolling down her face. That's when it dawned on me that I had no idea who had killed my brother. I couldna blame an entire clan, nor even the laird for something that'd happened in battle. That night, I nearly began another war because I couldna stop my revenge."

"What did you do?" she asked.

His gray gaze finally slid to her. "I said nothing to him as I climbed off the bed and strode from his chamber. I walked out the front door of the castle, fully expecting somcone to stop me. No one did. No' even at the gate, which they opened for me. I found the horse I'd tied off near the castle and rode home. The next morn, when I came downstairs, my father was absent. A few hours later, he found me and told me that the Frasier laird sent a missive. He'd known who I was, and it was he who had let me go. I'd thought I had the upper hand, but it turned out the laird had a blade to my ribs that I hadn't even known about. I might have gotten into the castle, but he could've stopped me from getting out. Instead, he let me return home."

Synne's brows rose at the news.

"Turned out he'd learned of Nathan's death and feared that someone might come seeking retribution. He had a description of me, so he knew instantly who I was and why I was there."

"You could've killed him."

"And he could've killed me. Because of my inability to accept what had happened, I nearly sent two clans back to war."

Synne looked up and away. "I'm sorry about your brother, but I'm glad you're here. Contrary to what you think, I am listening to what you have to say. The Coven has to be stopped." She glanced at her hands before returning her gaze to him. "I'm glad I get to be a part of that because they killed those I loved. They destroy everything in their path. Grief, anger, resentment, and even determination drive me. I fight for everyone I lost, and I fight for those still living."

He nodded slowly. "I only told you my story to caution you no' to let your revenge blind you to everything else."

"There's a difference between the Coven and the clan you went after."

"Aye. I lost a brother. You lost a couple who were surrogate parents and a home. No' to mention all your friends."

Synne wiped at her nose and looked away. "I wish I could find the next bone. I'm not sure it would do much good, though, especially if Sybbyl or any of the Coven finds me before I reach the Varroki."

"You could destroy the bone."

"I'm not sure that would work," she said to him.

He shrugged. "Has anyone tried?"

"The thigh bone is integrated into the staff, though I suppose it could be burned. But, no, to answer your question, no one has tried to destroy it. Same for the skull."

"If you find the next relic, would you destroy it given a chance?"

Synne considered his words for a moment. "If I knew I could get it to the Varroki, then no."

"Why no'? Who cares whose hands it lands in? You believe the Varroki are right. The Coven believes they're right to hold it. Why no' take it out of the equation altogether?"

She couldn't answer him, and that didn't sit well with her. "No one has spoken of destroying the bones. I know the body of the First Witch was burned, and her remaining bones scattered, but now that you mention it, why didn't they grind them up or throw them into the sea?"

"What I want to know is why so many are here if the bones were scattered."

"Radnar asked that same question. Edra couldn't answer him. No one that I know of can. But I have a theory."

Lachlan raised his brows and lowered his leg to cross his ankles. "And that is?"

"The First Witch was Norse. The Vikings revered witches, and many settled in England and Scotland when the Norse invaded. I couldn't tell you why there seems to be a large number of witches here. Legend says the First Witch's followers or descendants went in all directions to scatter the bones. But because there are so many witches here, it could be why the bones, over time, somehow found their way to this isle."

"Are there no' witches in other countries?"

"I don't know."

"It could be that the bones were scattered as well as the First Witch's followers were able. Maybe they began that legend to throw anyone off looking for the bones. Still, maybe the farthest they could go was Scotland and England."

Synne had to admit Lachlan had a point. Everything she knew about the First Witch came through stories, and she knew how easily they could be twisted and embellished with each retelling. Without knowing the truth, it was hard to determine what to believe.

"Where did the First Witch die?" Lachlan asked.

Synne shrugged. "The legend says Norway."

"Regardless, what we know is there is another bone in Scotland, and the Coven wants it. You might want to find it, but perhaps it would be better to get to the Varroki first. Perhaps they can help locate the bone."

It was on the tip of Synne's tongue to argue about finding the bone, but that was just her pride talking. She had to get to the Varroki. The longer she took to reach them, the greater the chance she would be caught by the Coven. She wanted to find a bone because the others had, and she wanted to do something for Edra and Radnar. But it didn't appear as if she would be the one to find the bone. And, honestly, she was fine with that.

Because she was going to take part in the defeat of the Coven.

Two more days of travel passed. Synne's feet and hands were numb, and she was tired. Her sleep had been disturbed by dreams that dissipated the moment she woke. But they bothered her, nonetheless.

There hadn't been any talk of going to a village since that first time, but now she was hoping they'd stumble upon one just so she could have a bath, wash her clothes, and get warm for a night. The cold had settled into her bones so deeply, she feared that she would never feel warm again.

She glanced at Lachlan, who had worn a perpetual frown for the past day. "What's wrong?"

"It's no' normal."

"What isn't?"

"That we've no' come across anyone."

She looked behind her and then to either side. "I understand that we're crossing over several clans' lands, but it is vast out here. I'd get lost between the mountains and many glens. It'd be easy to hide."

"Easy, aye. But we're no' hiding, lass."

Synne looked at the gray sky, wondering if the sun was even out. It had yet to stop snowing. "Frankly, I'm glad we've not run into anyone. We don't have to explain ourselves to people or try to talk them into letting us pass."

"While that is nice, it's no' normal. Patrols are always on the borders. Always."

She was about to discount his words with another argument, then she took a moment and set aside her discomfort and irritation of the weather to really hear what he was saying. That made Synne sit up straighter. "What would cause the clans to not patrol?"

"Fear."

"Fear like the Coven instills."

His gray eyes met hers. "Aye. I know you doona wish it, but we need to find a village and get some answers."

"I understand," she said solemnly.

Internally, she was shouting for joy.

She could have a nice long bath, sit by a fire, have her clothes washed so she didn't smell like her horse, and eat a warm meal with some ale. It sounded heavenly.

For the next several hours, Synne passed the time thinking about scrubbing her hair and being able to feel her toes again. She didn't ask where Lachlan was taking them when he diverted their route. He knew this territory, she did not. But she wasn't so lost in thought that she didn't pay attention to where they were or what was around them.

The moment the village came into view, she nearly let out a whoop of excitement.

"We'll set up camp on the outskirts. I willna be long," Lachlan said.

Her head snapped to him as her mouth opened, but no words came out as she attempted to find an argument for going with him.

Lachlan kept a straight face as he said, "Unless you'd like to accompany me. Perhaps we can find a room for the night. That is, if you think it would be safe."

"I think it'll be fine," she replied a little too hastily.

He finally smiled and chuckled. "You've been shivering for days. Though you have no' complained. I did warn you the winters were harsh."

"More than I'm used to," she grumbled. "I think you're right about a warmer cloak."

He was still smiling when he said, "Come on. We'll be inside before you know it."

True to his word, they had the horses stabled and found their way into the pub in short order. The moment they were inside, Synne sighed at the warmth. While Lachlan asked about rooms, she looked around at the many faces, some who looked their way, and some who didn't.

Lachlan glanced at her and jerked his chin as he walked away. She followed him to a back table. A tankard and a pitcher of water were set on the table as well as two bowls of food. She didn't look at him as she grabbed the ale and took a long drink.

She felt his eyes on her, but she didn't care. That's what he got for assuming she didn't like ale.

"Well, then," he said and motioned to the serving woman for another ale. "I suppose I should ask next time."

Synne nodded as she spooned the stew into her mouth. "You should. This is delicious."

He ate his stew slower, seemingly not affected at all by the cold. She was envious that the weather didn't bother him. She was used to snow and the cold, but during English winters. Scottish ones were another creature altogether.

With her belly full, she sat back and leisurely drank her ale. The tavern was loud, like any other. There were the drunkards who spilled more from their tankards than what got into their mouths. The old men who sat together, eyeing those they didn't like and grumbling about one thing or another. Then there were the ones who had ducked into the place for some food and drink but otherwise wanted to be left alone. Those could generally be found in the corners.

"Everything looks normal," she said.

Lachlan made a sound in the back of his throat. He finished off his ale and set his tankard down. "Looks can be deceiving. Our room is the third on the left. I've asked for a bath for you. It should be ready by now. I'm going to find you another cloak and see what I can learn from those in the village."

Synne pulled out her coin purse and handed it to him. "Take what you need for the cloak."

"I've got it," he said. "Keep that for later."

"Thank you."

He flashed her a smile and got to his feet. "I'll be back."

Synne didn't even wait until he was gone before she rose. The idea of a bath was too tempting to resist. She grabbed her tankard and took it up the stairs to the rooms. She entered the third to find a servant girl with red hair and a face full of freckles filling a wooden tub full of water, steam rising from the surface.

"Thank you," Synne told her.

Synne set aside her bow and arrows after the servant had left, then removed her cloak and tossed it onto the bed. Then she took off her boots and undressed before getting into the water.

It felt so good, she sighed in contentment. Her feet were full of pinpricks, they were so cold, but it didn't take long for them to warm up. She lounged for as long as she dared before she unbraided her hair and scrubbed it as well as her body. The last thing she wanted was to stay too long and have the water cool, so she was shivering again. It was bad enough that she would have nothing to put on when she finished with the bath.

Regardless, she felt like a new person when she stood.

12

With a new cloak for Synne in hand—as well as information
—Lachlan made his way back to the tavern and up the stairs.
He was surprised that Synne hadn't been angry to learn there
was only one room for the night, and they'd be sharing it.
Then again, she wasn't like other women he knew.

That didn't mean he didn't feel the attraction. It meant he
fought it.

And it was a losing battle.

He'd kept quiet at the meal because he wasn't sure if he
should room with her. When they traveled, she slept on one
side of the fire, and he on the other. This was a room. With a
bed. Why that should be any different, he didn't know. But it
was. Staying with her meant tempting himself in ways he
wasn't sure he could handle.

Lachlan paused by the door and listened. There was no
sound of sloshing water, so he assumed she was finished with
her bath. He opened the door and stepped inside to find
Synne standing in the tub, her blond hair wet and hanging to
her waist while her body was outlined by the fire in front
of her.

Dimly, he heard someone coming up the stairs. He softly closed the door behind him as his gaze took in her back and the outline of her hips. His mouth went dry, and his cock hardened. Blood pounded in his ears as the fire crackled to fill the silence.

There were many things Lachlan wished to do. The first was to go to Synne and pull her into his arms for a long, slow kiss. Then he wanted to run his hands over every inch of her body before he had her screaming in pleasure as he gave her orgasm after orgasm. He'd never wanted someone as fiercely or as fervently as he did Synne.

It was laughable that he'd thought he had been managing his attraction thus far. He realized it had all been an illusion. He'd lusted after her since the first moment he spotted her outside the forest. Once he spoke to her, it had never entered his mind to leave her side.

His hand tightened around the cloak he'd bought for her. He craved to taste her lips, wished he were holding her.

Hungered to know her body.

She looked at him over her shoulder. They stared at each other, neither speaking. The cloak dropped from his numb fingers, falling with a soft whoosh to the floor. In the next breath, he saw Synne shiver from the cold air. Lachlan slowly walked to her, their gazes never breaking. When he reached her, he bent and retrieved the towel that had been left near the fire to warm. He opened it wide and waited.

Seconds ticked by before Synne turned her back to him once more and allowed him to wrap the towel around her. Then he held her hand as she stepped from the water to stand near the hearth. Being so near to her, he saw the beads of water on her skin and ached to lick them.

She didn't release his hand as she turned to face him. He didn't know what to say, or if he should say anything. He'd never sought out female companionship, but Synne wasn't like others. That was partly what made him long for her as he did. Her beauty was just an added benefit.

His gaze lowered to her neck and shoulders. That's when he saw that there was something on her skin. The shadows had kept him from seeing it before. As if sensing his interest, she shook her head to move her wet hair and leaned her head back so he could see better.

Below each collarbone was a boar's head, one facing the other. Intricate knotwork extended out and up over her shoulders to disappear onto her back. Lachlan reached out and touched her skin. It was smooth, but the design was beautiful. Synne then turned around and lifted her long length of hair so he could see that the ink extended all the way around her back in one smooth design.

"The Norse believed that animal spirits, called *fylgia*, accompanied their gods. The boar was the *fylgia* of Freya, the goddess of love. It was called Hildisvini, or Battle Swine, and was always with Freya in wars. I dreamed of boars often. A few years later, I found one injured and saved it. Asa told me that the boar was my *fylgia*, and gave me this tattoo," Synne explained in a soft voice.

"I've never seen anything like it."

She dropped her hair over one shoulder and dropped the towel so he could see her entire back. "This is a Yggdrasil in Norse, or the Tree of Life for the Celts."

Lachlan was awestruck by the branches and roots that twisted into more knotwork while the design took up her entire back. "Amazing."

"This is a symbol of the connection between all things in the world. As above, so below. Nothing can die, and every-thing is in a constant state of unending transformation."

Lachlan was mesmerized. "Do you have more?"

Synne turned to face him and held out her left arm to show the underside and the ink there. "This is a Web of

Wyrd, but it's also known as Skuld's Net. It connects the past, present, and future. It's said that the Web of Wyrd was woven by the Nornir, the Shapers of Destiny. It's constructed of nine staves and all the runes."

"Meaning?" he asked while looking at the symbol, which was the length of his middle finger and half the width.

"Meaning the Web of Wyrd symbolizes all the possibilities of the past, present, and future." She gently pulled her arm from his hand and stepped back so he could get a view of her.

Lachlan's breath lodged in his throat when he saw her body. Pert breasts with pink-tipped nipples that were hard. Smooth, creamy skin. His gaze traveled down her stomach to the indent of her waist and the flare of her hips. His perusal halted when she shifted slightly so he saw the outside of her right thigh. Upon it was a circle with runes that looked a little like a compass.

"It's a Vegvisir and means *that which shows the way*. It's the Viking compass that provides necessary assistance as well as guidance to return home unharmed."

He wanted to know what each rune meant, but he was too drawn into her words and by her beautiful body. Before he could ask a question, Synne shifted to show her other thigh. This one he knew.

"The ouroboros," he said, looking at the snake eating its tail. "The emblem of wholeness or infinity. Life, death, and rebirth."

Synne smiled at him. "It's the symbol we Hunters use."

When she didn't say more, Lachlan had a difficult time keeping his hands to himself. He wanted to touch her, hold her, feel her warmth against him. It took everything in him not to reach for her.

But Synne didn't attempt to cover herself. In fact, she stood as if waiting for him. He searched her eyes for any hint that she might want him, and to his surprise, he found it. His hand rested on her hip, and just as he was about to pull her to him, a knock came from the door.

"Sir?" called the young serving girl. "I've got water for yer bath."

His head jerked toward the door. He was about to tell her to leave when Synne pulled away from him and walked to the bed.

She slipped beneath the covers and jerked her head to the door. "I've had my bath. It's time for yours."

Lachlan drew in a steadying breath and strode to the door to unlock it. Two girls walked in with buckets as they began hauling out the old bathwater. He picked up the cloak from the floor and hung it near the door. Then he began removing his weapons, cloak, and boots. He glanced at Synne to see that she looked comfortable amid the blankets.

"Thank you," she said and motioned to the cloak with its fur-lined hood. "It looks very warm."

"You're welcome, lass. It'll serve you better than what you have."

They stopped talking until the girls were once more gone with the rest of the dirty water. Then Synne asked, "Did you find out anything?"

He nodded and put a finger to his lips, letting her know it was something for when they were fully alone. Before too long, new hot water filled the tub. Lachlan had to admit he was looking forward to scrubbing the grime from his body. He barred the door once the girls were gone for good, then stoked the fire, adding another log to it.

"Two villages west of here encountered a woman wearing a black crown," he whispered.

Synne's gaze intensified as she sat up, pulling her knees to her chest. "Sybbyl. Helena told us she wears a crown of onyx now."

"She killed four men without so much as touching them, then bade the villagers to bow before her."

"Is she still there?"

"She left after."

"Without any more destruction? That's odd."

Lachlan shrugged and unbuttoned his vest. "From what was said, she didna seem to be looking for anything."

"Trust me, she's looking."

13

Synne forgot what she was saying when Lachlan removed his shirt. He was talking, saying something important, but his voice was drowned out by the wild thumping of her heart at the sight of his bare chest.

Broad shoulders, thick arms, hard sinew. It wasn't her first time seeing a man's chest, but Lachlan's form stole her breath. Ever since he'd walked in on her naked, she hadn't been able to stop thinking about her body against his.

Of his mouth on hers.

Of his hands on her skin.

Of his hard body sliding against hers, into her.

Her lungs burned, and she suddenly realized that she hadn't been breathing. She drew in a deep breath, but her eyes never left his body. She squeezed her legs together as a rush of longing filled her. She should be brushing out her hair and plaiting it instead of staring at Lachlan. But she'd been sure he'd been about to kiss her before they were interrupted. Had it all been her imagination?

Her thoughts skidded to a halt as he removed his breeches. The way he was angled kept her from seeing his cock. And then he lowered himself into the water with his back to her.

"I think we should keep heading north. What about you?"

She blinked. Bloody hell. She hadn't been paying attention at all. "Sure."

He turned his head to look at her over his shoulders. "That's all you have to say?"

"You know this area."

"Aye. But you know the…well, what's following us."

She didn't blame him for not wanting to say the word aloud in such a place. Despite the noise from below, there were ears everywhere.

He shrugged after tossing water on his face. "I doona think we have much choice. A good night's sleep and some warmth will do wonders for you. We'll head out at first light."

"A sound plan," she agreed.

Synne watched as he used the bar of soap to wash his hair and then his body. All the while, she knew the best thing for her would be to leave in the middle of the night, head off alone. Lachlan had an entire clan counting on him. It was selfish of her to want him as a traveling companion when he was needed elsewhere. Even though he could be useful against the Coven.

She quietly rose from the bed and dropped to her knees near the wooden tub. Her hand reached out and stopped his as he struggled to wash his back. She had been freezing for days, but since he'd walked into the chamber, she had been on fire.

With slow, steady movements, she washed his back, pushing him forward so she could reach it all. Then she rinsed him. Suddenly, he grabbed her hand and pulled her around so he could see her.

She met his gray eyes, her heart missing a beat at the flagrant desire she saw there. Synne moved a lock of black hair from his face with her free hand and let it trail down to his thick beard. She gave him a soft smile.

In one move, he was on his feet as he pulled her up beside him. He yanked her against him, holding her tightly. His arousal, thick and hard, lay between them. "Lass, I want you."

"I want you."

Three simple words was all it took for his mouth to be on hers. His kiss was soft and insistent, gentle yet unyielding. His hands splayed across her back when she parted her lips and let his tongue inside. He held her as if he feared she might disappear with his next breath.

And she clung to him, afraid that this was all just a dream.

He didn't break the kiss as he stepped out of the tub and turned them to walk her backward to the bed. Lachlan gently laid her on the bedding, the mattress dipping when he leaned a knee upon it. She ran her hands over his thickly corded back, her body aching for him. She'd heard others talk of lying with a man, but she had never imagined it could feel this good.

Lachlan's hand reached between them and cupped her breast. She liked the way it felt when he massaged it. A gasp of surprise—and pleasure—tore from her when he found her nipple. The feeling was so intense that she was rocked by it. And she wanted more.

He deepened the kiss and found her other tight bud, making her moan in pleasure. Before she knew what she was doing, she ground herself against him. The sound of his groan caused her blood to run hot in her veins.

Then he was gone, kissing his way down her throat. She was about to tug him back up for more kissing when his lips once more wrapped around a nipple. She forgot everything, including her own name, as she gave herself to the pleasure Lachlan gave her.

But the more he did, the more she wanted. An ache began low in her abdomen that intensified with his teasing. The more she rocked against him, the more the sensation grew.

She whispered his name when he slid a hand over her sex and found her clit. He swirled his thumb around it, sending her teetering on the edge of…something. Before she could reach it, his finger slipped inside her. Synne bit her lip, loving the feeling of something within her. She never imagined that a finger could feel so good.

"Lass," he whispered in a desire-roughened voice.

She forced her eyes open to look at him, praying that he didn't stop moving his hand. He said nothing, simply looked at her. She let her lids close again and sighed in contentment. It all felt so wonderful. She wanted to do this always with Lachlan.

Her eyes flew open once more, and her back arched when his mouth latched on to her sex. His tongue teased her clit while his finger continued moving inside her. Suddenly, she was back on that precipice once more. Then, she tipped over the side.

Her body jerked from the force of the climax. It ripped through her, flinging her into an abyss of ecstasy. She was helpless to do anything but ride the waves of bliss that took her higher and higher.

She heard Lachlan say her name, felt him move over her. His hand was gone, replaced by something larger. It slid inside her, and she gasped as another wave of pleasure washed over her. Her arms were around him. She wasn't sure how or when that had happened, but she didn't care. She felt too good to worry about it.

"Hold on to me, lass," he whispered. "Cling to the pleasure."

He didn't need to tell her any of that, she was already doing it.

That's when she realized that his cock was inside her. She had wanted to see it, touch it, but that would be for later. Now, he filled her, stretching her. And it felt delicious. He found her mouth and gave her a fiery kiss at the same time he thrust hard.

A sharp pain went through Synne, but it was gone as fast as it had come. Then she got to enjoy the feel of Lachlan inside her. His hips pumped slowly at first, but gradually, he increased his tempo. Sweat soon covered both their bodies, their breaths mixing. He gave a final thrust before pulling out, his seed spilling on her stomach.

Minutes ticked by before their breathing quieted. Lachlan looked at her and then shifted to run a hand down her cheek. "Lass, you've gifted me with something special. Thank you."

"You knew I was a virgin?"

"Aye. I felt the barrier."

Synne licked her lips.

"It's nothing to be embarrassed about," he told her. "I feel honored to have been chosen by you."

She met his gaze and cupped his face. There were so many things she wanted to say, but she couldn't get the words out. Besides, she wouldn't know how to even begin. Everyone at the abbey had been her family, but more times than not, she was by herself in the forest. Not because she didn't like people, but because the trees understood her.

"Did I hurt you?" Lachlan asked.

Synne shook her head with a smile. "Very little. I'd heard it could be painful."

"You should've told me. I would've been angry had I hurt you."

He was a considerate lover, just like Edra and Asa had urged her to find. They had cautioned her that many men didn't care about a woman's pleasure. Not so with Lachlan. She hadn't even thought about that. All she'd known was that her attraction to him was something she couldn't ignore.

"Stay here," Lachlan told her as he rose. He found the towel and brought it to her to clean her stomach.

Then, with a gentle hand, he began cleaning between her legs. Synne sat up and took the cloth from him. She'd known there would be blood, but she hadn't expected so much of it. She finished cleaning herself and was soon pulled back against Lachlan, who had gotten into bed.

"Are you worried about Sybbyl?" he asked.

"I'll be worried about what she and the Coven will do until they're gone."

"She was close."

"How many days ago did that occur?"

"Yesterday."

Synne didn't like the sound of that. She settled more comfortably against Lachlan and rested an arm over his washboard stomach. Her gaze lowered to his now flaccid cock. She couldn't wait to see it hard, but that was for later. "The fact that she's close does make me edgy."

"Should we leave now?"

"Traveling at night wouldn't be wise."

Lachlan made a sound in the back of his throat. "When is it ever safe to travel when witches are near?"

He had a point. Synne shrugged. "Did you discover which direction Sybbyl was headed?"

"They said she continued west, but she could've doubled back or changed directions. You said she wants the next bone and the Varroki. Which do you think she'll go after first?"

"Another bone would give her more power." Synne blew out a breath. "If I had to guess, I'd say she'll go after the bone before the Varroki."

Lachlan put his free arm behind his head. "Sybbyl was traveling alone. At least no one saw anyone else with her."

"That doesn't mean anything. The Gira could've been near. I've trained for most of my life to fight witches, but I don't stand a chance against Sybbyl on my own."

He kissed her forehead. "We'll get to the Varroki."

She let him make that promise, even knowing he couldn't keep it.

14

Blackglade

Clouds were gathering overhead. The sea churned. It was a sign that a storm was coming, but this was something more than just the weather, and Malene understood that.

She stood atop the tower, looking toward Scotland. Behind her, thunder rumbled. The Living Heart was within the walls of Blackglade, guarded by the most fearsome of Varroki warriors—Jarin. Helena and Jarin were now mated, their love intertwined. Their child would arrive in a few months. Malene sincerely hoped that Sybbyl and the Coven were dealt with by then.

The truth was that Malene was worried. After what had happened at the abbey, she knew the Varroki had to be prepared. Edra had been a powerful witch, but she hadn't had the Staff of the Eternal nor an army of Gira at her disposal. Everyone at the abbey had known it was only a matter of time before the Coven found them. But losing Edra and Radnar was a particularly painful blow. Because of them, however, there were other Hunters out there. They would make their way to Leoma and Braith, thanks to Synne.

Malene thought of the blond Hunter, who preferred the company of trees. She hadn't wanted to leave Synne on her own, but she'd sensed that it was Synne's destiny. Regardless of whether or not the Hunter found her way to the Varroki or was caught by the Coven, it was a path Synne had to walk. Malene couldn't help her, no matter how much she wanted to.

"You're still debating your decision."

The sound of Armir's deep voice behind her made her heart race. She wasn't sure when she'd fallen in love with him, only that she knew without a doubt that he had her heart. If only she had the courage to tell him.

She blew out a breath as he walked up beside her. "I am."

"Synne is strong. Stronger, I wager, than even she knows."

"She's also fragile. She lost her family. The fact that Edra kept her out of the abbey to keep her alive will be difficult for Synne to bear."

Armir's long, golden blond hair was gathered into one thick band with leather straps every few inches, holding it together as it hung down his back. The sides of his head were shaved with tattoos of various runes showing. His pale green eyes swung to her. "The same magic that chose you as leader of the Varroki told you that Synne had to make her own way here. There's a reason for that."

"I know. I don't have to like it," she snapped. Then, instantly, she regretted it. "I'm sorry. I'm not angry with you."

"You're irate with the situation."

It had been Armir who'd found her when she was a little girl and brought her to Blackglade. The magic there chose young girls to be Lady of the Varroki, closed away in the tower to try and control the magic they didn't understand. She hadn't asked for this life, and she hadn't wanted it. At least, at first.

Then, she'd embraced her path. She gave in to the magic and felt the blue radiance in first one hand and then the other. Most Ladies of the Varroki didn't last longer than five years. She was on her fifth year and was the only one who had the blue radiance in both hands. The magic within her was something she didn't fully understand or know how to control. But that was part of why she had come so far. She wasn't trying to control it.

Blackglade hadn't been her birthplace, but it was her home now, and the people were hers. She would fight to the death to protect them.

"We'll win."

She met Armir's gaze and forced a smile. "If we don't, it'll be the end of all of this."

A muscle ticked in his jaw. "That won't happen."

"As strong as you are in both magic and physically, you can't fight Fate if it has chosen to end us."

He looked away, fury sparking in his eyes. "Take a look around you. A hard look."

Malene frowned but did as he asked. "All right. What am I looking at?"

"That," he said and pointed to one of the stone columns bent inward because of her. Then he pointed to the next and the next. "That. That. And…that. What do you see?"

"I know what you're doing," she stated instead of answering. "You're pointing out the strength of my magic. You forget that I didn't even know I was doing that."

"It doesn't matter. You did it. You also used the travel spell to take us across a tremendous distance. That isn't done," he pointed out.

She threw up her hands. "I'm not giving up on the

Varroki or Blackglade, if that's what you're thinking. I'm merely pointing out that something could happen."

"And we could win!"

The wind took his shout, but she heard it just the same. For a moment, she nearly went to him and put a hand on his chest. Until recently, his position, like many others in the Varroki, had kept him celibate. She had changed that.

And a part of her had hoped he would come to her. She should've known he wouldn't. Just as she hadn't gone to him.

She ensured that the Varroki numbers stopped dwindling because it was happening at an alarming rate. Now, with the threat of the Coven and Sybbyl, it was a double hit to the Varroki. Armir had always stood so strong, though. When she raged against destiny for choosing her, when she screamed to return home, he had remained steady and calm.

Now, it was her turn to be that for him.

"You're right. We could. And we will," she said. "I'll do whatever it takes to make sure that happens."

The anger left his face in a blink. "Not at the expense of your life."

She smiled without answering, but she was prepared to do just that if it meant saving Armir and the others. She might not be able to have him, call him hers, but she could ensure that he and the Varroki continued on.

"Malene."

"I heard you."

He moved to face her, his eyes boring into hers. "You've harnessed much of the power within you, but that doesn't mean you're invincible."

That made her laugh. "I never said I was."

"If you claim to love the Varroki so much, then think of them."

It was all she could do not to snap at him. She kept her gaze outward, hoping she might get a glimpse of Synne. "I've done nothing but think of every Varroki." Her eyes swung to him. "Including you."

"They…*we*…need you."

Malene smiled, wishing with all her might that his words were true. "If the Varroki have proven anything, it's that they don't need anyone."

"Why else would the magic send us out searching for young girls to lead us?" he argued. "The tribe needs you."

"Young girls who have no idea of the magic inside them. Pliable children. Young ladies who are taken from their homes and thrust into a new world that they don't want anything to do with. None of the Ladies of the Varroki lasted longer than ten years."

"You will." His chin lifted in defiance.

If only he knew that part of that was because of him. But she wouldn't—*couldn't*—tell him that.

"You're the one the prophecy spoke about. You're the Lady of the Varroki, the one who will lead a new generation, take us in a new direction," Armir continued. "You have the blue radiance in both hands."

Malene took a deep breath and looked back across the land. She didn't react to his mention of a prophecy, though she wanted to. She would have to find out what was said, but she suspected that the statement had accidentally slipped from Armir. To push him now would alert him of that, and he would probably refuse to answer any questions. Instead, she continued their conversation. "I have already taken the Varroki in a new direction. I've given you and everyone here a way to continue. I hope I get to see where it leads, but I'm fully aware that might not happen."

"Don't give up."

The words were spoken in a whisper. Never before had she heard Armir plead for anything. Her gaze snapped back to him. He was close enough that she could touch him. The ends of her hair lifted in the wind, reaching for him as her hands couldn't.

Their eyes locked for a long minute.

"I'm not. I never will," she told him.

For a heartbeat, Malene thought Armir might say more. There was something in his pale green eyes that she hadn't seen before. She wanted to know his thoughts, to hear the words he wouldn't let pass his lips.

But the moment slipped by, and her chance was gone in a blink.

"Have you searched for Synne?" Armir asked.

Malene shook her head. "I've put it off, afraid of what I might learn. But I came up here to do just that."

She didn't look at him as she walked to the center of the tower. The magic rushed through her, and soon, blue light shone from both palms. She raised her hands above her head as the spell fell from her lips. Wind swirled violently, causing her skirt to whip around her legs, and her hair to slap at her face.

Malene ignored it all as her mind focused on an image of Synne. The magic pushed against her, while at the same time, it pulled. When her legs could no longer hold her, she dropped to her knees, refusing to end the spell until she had the information she sought.

Suddenly, something flashed in her mind, and she saw Synne in a tavern, but the Hunter wasn't alone. She was with a Scotsman. The black-haired warrior looked determined and more than capable. The image of the pair faded as the spell allowed Malene to see a wider view of their location. The moment she had it, Malene began to lower her hands, but something dark and malevolent on the edges of her vision stopped her.

A voice in the back of her mind cautioned her not to look any deeper, but too much was at stake for her to ignore it. Malene shifted her focus to the sinister energy, knowing it came from Sybbyl and the Coven. The instant Malene looked at it, she was enveloped by blackness. It stole her breath, choking her.

In the background, she heard a woman's evil laughter.

"Malene!"

The sound of Armir's voice pulled her out of the spell. His arms held her tightly as she dragged in much-needed air. He held her against him, smoothing her hair out of her face. She turned into his chest and remained there until her heart stopped racing.

Armir said nothing, simply held her. She knew that had he not been there, she may not have come back from the brink of death. She also knew that the only one who could've reached her was Armir.

"Please, say something."

"They're in Scotland," Malene said as she opened her eyes to look up at him.

Blond brows snapped together. "They?"

"Synne has a warrior with her."

"Someone sent by Braith?"

"A Scot."

Armir digested that information. Then he asked, "What happened?"

"I felt something malevolent. I thought it might be Sybbyl going after Synne. It's why I looked at it."

"It wasn't after Synne, was it?"

Malene swallowed and shook her head. "I know it was foolish and thoughtless not to protect myself before I looked."

"Very," Armir said in a biting tone.

"It won't happen again."

He said nothing as he stood and helped Malene to her feet.

She stopped him before he walked away. "Thank you."

His pale green orbs held hers for a heartbeat, then two. Finally, he bowed his head and walked away.

Malene watched him. The stakes had just been raised, but Sybbyl was foolish if she thought that Malene wouldn't prepare herself and the Varroki for the war that was inevitably coming. Too much was at stake.

Especially her heart.

15

The sky was still dark when Lachlan and Synne mounted their horses and rode out. The night had passed too quickly as he held her in his arms. He hadn't wanted it to end, but there had been no way to stop time.

Neither had said much as they rose and dressed. When they left the tavern, no one but the owner and servants were awake. In no time, the two of them were headed out of town.

Lachlan pointed their horses north and wondered how much farther they'd get before they encountered more witches. He hoped his clan was faring well. They were a strong people, and had good numbers, but that probably wouldn't matter to the Coven if they set their sights on them.

Synne handed him a portion of bread. Their gazes met briefly as they shared a smile. He gave a nod of thanks and took a bite. Then he nudged his horse into a gallop. He didn't want to be out in the open any longer than necessary. Synne kept even with him as their mounts' hooves ate up the ground.

They alternated between walking and galloping the horses until midday when they stopped to rest. Once again, they had encountered no one on their journey. The weather was dreary with overcast skies that promised more rain or snow later, but for the moment, none fell.

While the horses drank from the loch, Synne filled the waterskins. Lachlan eyed the shoreline. Across the large body of water, he spotted a small herd of red deer, drinking. They soon picked up his and Synne's scents and ran away. The smooth water was undisturbed. At any other time, he would've said it was a serene place. The fact that there wasn't another soul in sight made him wary, however.

"You feel it," Synne said as she straightened and handed him his skin.

He frowned. "Feel what?"

"The darkness that's falling over the land. You can't see the evil, not yet. But it's approaching. Others might be using the weather as a reason to stay indoors, but the truth is that they can feel what's coming, and they want to hide from it. It's what I'd be doing if I could."

"You're a fighter. You wouldna hide."

One corner of her mouth lifted in a half-grin after she'd taken a long drink of the cold water. "It's a lot easier to hide and think someone else can take care of the issue than face it head-on. A part of me wanted to run away after everyone had been killed at the abbey. I almost did, too. Then I thought of what Edra and Radnar had lived for, what they had given to all of us. I knew then that I had to face what was to come."

"You're stronger than many of the warriors I know."

Synne chuckled as she shrugged. "Some might call me stupid."

"My father once told me that it isna the size of someone who makes them a warrior. It isna even how many people they've killed or battles they've been in. What makes a warrior is that they will stand when no one else will. That they put others before themselves. You are such a warrior, and I'm honored to know you."

Her smile was beautiful as her amber eyes softened. "No one has ever given me a greater compliment."

"I merely speak the truth. When this is all over, return with me to my clan. I'd like my family to meet you, especially my sister."

"I'd like that."

Neither mentioned the fact that they might not come out of this alive. They had to think of the future, or else it would be easy for fear and doubt to take hold and crush even the mightiest of warriors.

They ate oatcakes sitting near each other on the trunk of a fallen tree. Lachlan couldn't take his eyes from Synne. She had plaited her hair in braids on either side of her head that came together in one plait in the back. He remembered the wavy length of her golden tresses spilling over his hand and arm as they slept. He couldn't wait to hold her again.

That's when he realized that he wasn't just fighting for his clan's survival. He was fighting for Synne, for a future with her. Lachlan didn't stop and think of what kind of future they could have if she was a Hunter and he eventually the laird of his clan. That problem was for another day. All he knew was that he wanted her more than he'd ever wanted anything in his life.

With Synne, things made sense. Which was odd since he was trying to find a secret group of warlocks and witches that lived in northern Scotland. It was as if being with her had opened up a part of his life he had closed off after his grandmother died, something he was supposed to have known about. Now, he knew and was doing his part.

Lachlan didn't know what made him turn to the side. His eyes saw nothing, but his instincts screamed that danger was near. He reacted instantly by wrapping his arms around Synne and pulling her with him to the ground.

An instant later, splintered wood and snow dropped around them. Lachlan looked to where they'd been sitting and saw a long, thick limb embedded in the tree.

"Witches," Synne whispered and jumped to her feet.

She raced to her mare and grabbed her quiver of arrows while he unsheathed his sword and turned to face whoever was out there. Yet no one showed themselves. Lachlan wasn't stupid enough to believe they were gone.

He glanced at Synne and jerked his chin to the side, letting her know that he was going around. She nodded and disappeared behind some trees. With his feet crunching on the snow, Lachlan moved slowly to the left for several paces before he altered course and headed deeper into the woods.

Synne was certain that it was a witch, but wouldn't they show themselves? The two he'd met a few days ago hadn't hesitated to come at him. Why was this one hiding? It could be more than one. Or it could be the Gira. But Synne had warned him that there would be whispers from the Gira. There was nothing but eerie silence. Synne was right, then. It was witches.

Every step took him farther away from his gelding—and from Synne. He was attempting to draw out whoever it was in the hopes that Synne could release an arrow or two and take them out as easily as she had the first two. But his conscience warned him that it likely wouldn't be as simple as it was the first time.

Minutes ticked by with nothing. No sound, no movement from anyone or anything other than Lachlan. Finally, he halted and listened. Even the wind had stopped. The silence was deafening. He searched the trees for Synne, but he couldn't spot her. She was adept at hiding, whereas he was used to flushing out his enemies. If only his weapon could hurt witches like Synne's could.

He continued walking, picking his way through the forest to try and avoid roots and stumps hidden by the snow. The hairs on the back of his neck stood on end. He turned, but before he could lift his sword, he was thrown backward through the air. His breath was knocked from his lungs when he hit a tree and was held several feet off the ground.

The woman walked into view then. She held out her hand as if that were the only thing holding him. She had gray hair with some brown left in it, and her face was lined with age. He struggled to get air even as he realized that with the impact, his sword had fallen from his hand. He glanced down to where it lay half-buried in the snow.

The witch laughed. "Even if you had it, it wouldn't do you any good. You Hunters are so full of yourselves."

It took him by surprise to hear her Scottish brogue.

She eyed him before looking around for Synne. "Where's the other one?"

Relief went through him when his lungs finally eased, and he was able to draw in air. He glared at the witch, not intending to tell her anything.

"She'll come out soon enough," the witch said with a smile.

A second later, pain flared through Lachlan like fire. He ground his teeth and squeezed his eyes closed to fight the agony of his limbs being pulled slowly from their sockets. The more he held back his cries of pain, the more the witch tortured him.

In a blink, the pain vanished, and he was falling. Lachlan barely realized it before he landed with a jarring thud. He blinked and reached for his sword. His fingers closed around the hilt, and he used the tree to climb to his feet. That's when he saw the old witch touch her shoulder where her cloak had been torn. Lachlan hurriedly looked around and saw the arrow embedded in a tree twenty feet behind the witch.

"That was your one shot," the witch said as she advanced on Lachlan.

He locked his gaze on her and raised his sword. The witch then rose several inches off the ground and came at him. The sound of more arrows launching buzzed through the air, but the witch easily deflected them. Lachlan didn't want to die, not when he hadn't helped Synne make it to Blackglade or fight against the Coven.

Not when he hadn't experienced a future with her.

He peeled back his lips and released a battle cry as he swung his sword at the same time the witch reached him. The blade didn't cut through her. However, it did stop her attack on him.

Confusion filled her faded blue eyes. She redoubled her efforts, but nothing happened. Lachlan wasn't sure what was going on, and it didn't matter. He was alive, and he was going to make the most of that fact.

He pushed the witch away from him. This time as he pointed his sword at her, she didn't slow as she came for him. A look of utter bewilderment filled her face when she was stopped once again. She coughed, blood pouring from her mouth before her eyes rolled back in her head and she fell sideways.

Lachlan moved his sword with her since she was impaled upon it. He used his foot to pull it free of her body as Synne ran up. They stood together as the witch turned to ash.

"What happened?" Synne asked.

Lachlan shrugged and looked at his sword. "I'm no' sure."

"Your blade killed her."

He looked into Synne's eyes and shrugged. "I doona know how. I was going to give you time to get off another shot. Next thing I knew, my sword stopped her."

"You did more than stop her. You killed her. No weapon that isn't spelled by a witch can do that. Maybe your grandmother spelled it."

It wasn't something he had ever thought about before, but since the sword was part of his family history, it was possible. "I feel much better about fighting witches now."

Synne's smile was huge as she placed a kiss on his lips. "It certainly shifts the odds in our favor."

"But she was able to cast aside your arrows. How was she able to do that?"

The smile faded from Synne's face. "I don't know, but I don't like it. I always hit my mark. Always. She was old, so she probably had strong magic, but that shouldn't matter."

"We survived our second witch attack. Let's get moving before more arrive."

"Good idea."

Lachlan took one last look at the ashes of the dead witch before he cleaned the blood from his sword and sheathed it.

16

The scene of Lachlan killing the witch stayed with Synne long after they rode away. For the rest of the afternoon, she replayed the entire battle over and over in her mind, from when Lachlan had pulled her to the ground, to when she stood next to him and the witch's ashes. And nowhere in those recollections could she figure out why her arrows had missed their mark or how he'd managed to kill the witch.

The most likely scenario was that his grandmother, a witch herself, had spelled his sword. It had belonged to her son at the time, so it would make sense that she would want to make sure the weapon could take down a witch should any come to their clan. But why wouldn't she have told Lachlan's father or Lachlan himself?

Maybe she had, and Lachlan's father didn't feel the need to pass on that bit of information to Lachlan.

While Synne knew the mystery of Lachlan's sword was likely solved, that didn't stop her from wanting to know all the details. She'd always been that way. If there was a puzzle of any kind, she wanted it explained.

More pressing, however, was the fact that she hadn't found her mark with the witch. Sure, one of her arrows had grazed the old woman, but since Synne had been aiming for the witch's heart, it should've done more than just graze her.

None of her arrows had ever failed to go where she wanted. Never. Now it had happened seven times in one day. How? Synne searched her mind, becoming more anxious and upset as the hours passed. Then, out of nowhere, she heard Edra's voice in her head.

"Never underestimate a witch. You don't know their power, and each one has something different. Know your strengths and weaknesses, because there will come a time when you'll have to use them instead of your bow and arrows."

Synne was ashamed that she had forgotten that early lesson, but at least she remembered it now.

Lachlan slowed his gelding to a walk. Synne gently tugged on the reins, and her mare quickly relaxed to a canter. She glanced at Lachlan to find him watching her. "What?"

"You've been pensive all day. You're still thinking of the witch."

It wasn't a question, and she didn't treat it as one. "I am."

"You've really never missed with your arrow?"

She shook her head. "Never. Today was a first, and I honestly didn't think it would bother me as much as it has."

"Could the witch have used a spell?"

"Anything is possible. I was just thinking about something Edra told me when I was young. She said that I should never underestimate a witch because each of them has different powers. She also told me that I should know my strengths and weaknesses because I might not always be able to use my bow and arrow."

"Edra was right."

"I forgot that today. Had your sword not been spelled, you'd likely be dead. And I probably would be, as well."

He shook his head and patted his horse's neck. "Doona think like that. We won. Look at what you did right and what you did wrong. That's what a warrior does each time they come from a battle because each one is a learning experience."

"I know that everything you're saying is right, but I keep thinking how close we came to dying."

Lachlan's eyes slid to her. "If you hang on to that, fear will begin to grow. If you are afraid like that when you enter battle, you've already given your enemy the win. You can no' think about anything but your goal—defeating your enemy in any way possible. Most times, it's going to be with your bow. Other times, it'll be with your wits or whatever else you have at hand. You have a skill with the bow I've no' seen the likes of before. Whether that old witch used a spell, or there was something else at work, doesna matter. You're a skilled Hunter, taught by a great witch."

"You didn't even know Edra," Synne replied with a smile.

"I may no' have met her, but by the things you've told me, she was a great woman and witch. She took in orphans, gave all of you a home, taught you about the evil in the world, and also gave you the skills to keep yourselves and others safe. I doona know many who would do what she did, all while knowing that it was only a matter of time before the Coven found her."

Synne drew in a deep breath and released it as she gave a single nod. "Edra was all those things and more. So was Radnar, and every other warrior and witch who lived at the abbey and made it their home. They gave me a purpose."

"You chose your path. They just made sure you knew how to handle yourself while on that path."

"If I come out of this battle alive, I want to pick up

where Edra and Radnar left off. I've told all the Hunters to go to Leoma and Braith's castle. Since Braith is the Warden of the Blood Skull, the castle is well fortified by Leoma's magic, as well as the skull's. It will likely be the base, but I want to teach others, to pass on everything I've learned."

Lachlan smiled at her. "I think that's admirable. I wish there was something like that in Scotland."

"We Hunters travel all over. Many don't return to the abbey for months as they're out tracking one witch or another, but I don't know if any have come to Scotland. Surely, they have. But then there are the Varroki."

He grunted. "I'd think it would be beneficial to Hunters to have many such locations for training and such. You do have a point regarding the Varroki being here. So, they hunt witches, as well?"

"They're witches and warlocks who dole out justice to other witches. Until recently, everyone thought only women could have magic. Then we met Jarin. He's one of the Varroki warriors who helped Helena. They're going to have a child together."

"The Living Heart of the First Witch, and a Varroki warrior. That child is going to be extremely powerful."

Synne chuckled. "It certainly will."

"I can no' imagine Sybbyl would allow the bairn to live."

The smile fell from Synne's face. "Sybbyl wanted Jarin for herself. When he refused all of her advances, she grew furious. And when she learned that Helena was carrying Jarin's child, Sybbyl knew that she had no other choice but to kill it and continue trying to turn Helena to her side."

"She has another option," Lachlan pointed out.

"What is that?"

"Wait until the child is born and take it, converting it to her side. Be it male or female, it'll be another descendant of the First Witch."

Synne stared between the mare's ears. "I didn't think of that."

"You make it sound as if you made a horrible mistake."

"I did," she snapped and looked his way. "I should've thought of that. I'm sure the others did."

"They probably did, especially Helena and Jarin. But just because you didna, doesna make it a mistake. It means that your mind still believes in good things. Trust me, you doona want to always think the worst as I do."

She swallowed and glanced away. "Aye, but you're always prepared for the worst. I'm not. That puts me at a disadvantage. A grave one when dealing with those like Sybbyl."

"You're doing yourself a disservice. It's your ability to see the good in others, to only think of the positive, that sets you apart from everyone else. You may no' see the evil or expect it, but you react well when it comes at you. That's no' only because of your training, but also because of your instincts."

Synne turned her head forward, considering his words as the horses walked. "I appreciate the compliments, I really do, but I must ask. If you had a choice, would you rather always think the worst, or see the good in others?"

"I should've known you'd ask this," he said with a smile in his voice. Then Lachlan sighed loudly. "In my position as the son of a laird who will one day be laird, I think I'd like a bit of both. I'd like to be able to hope for the good, but also expect the worst so I could prepare my clan."

"A mix," Synne replied softly. "I like that. I would like a mix, as well." Her head turned to him. "How do I do that?"

Lachlan shrugged, his lips twisting. "It's simple. When you see someone or a place, think of the absolute worst things that could happen and how you'd react to them. For example, look around. What do you see?"

"Craggy mountains topped with snow. Wide-open spaces coming since we're about to leave the forest, and gray skies."

"All right. Now, what do you think when you see all of that?"

Synne looked around, thinking. "I feel safe in the forest with the trees, but out in the open, I won't have to worry about the Gira. The mountains will give me an advantage when I crest one, so I can have a great vantage point. And as for the weather, I believe it'll hold off for a while longer."

"All positive thoughts, which can do a lot for a person. I'm no' degrading it at all."

She met his gaze. "I see your point. Now, tell me what you see."

His lips flattened for a heartbeat. "In the forest, I see multiple hiding places for my enemies to wait to attack. The undulating terrain within the forest also makes it difficult to spot enemies until the last moment."

"True." Why hadn't she thought of that? Because Synne knew that she could climb the trees and converse with them for her safety. Lachlan couldn't.

"Outside of the trees, there is nowhere for us to hide. We could be spotted from leagues away. The glens offer more shelter, but also allow enemies the advantage of higher ground in an attack. The top of the mountains is better, but then there's the fact that everyone can see us."

Synne nodded, listening intently.

"Then there's the weather as you mentioned. The snowfall that will most likely come sooner than I can find shelter. I hope it's thick enough to cover my tracks to thwart my enemies, but that will take time. If it's rain, it'll dampen the sound of anyone coming toward me. That leaves me with shelter for the night. I need to cover a lot of ground, but finding the right place to bed down to keep out of sight is paramount. If I find it early enough since I doona know this way, I'll take it instead of traveling."

Synne was silent for a long moment. "Everything you

mentioned is guessing how an enemy would come at you instead of what I did, thinking only of getting to my destination."

"I didna even go into the details of the various ways I'd react if attacked."

"I think it's a very good thing you're with me," she said with a smile as she looked into his gray eyes.

He gave a nod, his lips softening. "I do as well, lass. Though no' because I think differently than you. I'm glad I'm with you because I like you. And I like being with you."

Her smile grew as she looked away. "No one has ever said anything like that to me before."

"That surprises me. A woman of your beauty and skill would be snapped up in a heartbeat in my clan. You'd have men falling at your feet, begging you to choose them."

She chuckled at the thought. "No man has ever fallen at my feet nor begged me for anything."

"There were men at the abbey, aye?"

"There were," she replied and looked at him. "Many knights from all over. We also had a blacksmith and a man from a foreign country I'd never heard of."

"Younger men?" Lachlan prompted.

Synne shrugged, knowing what he was asking and uncomfortable with it. "Some Hunters, like Leoma, used their beauty against men to get information they needed about witches. I never wanted to do that, and Edra never made us do anything we didn't want to do. I preferred my solitude with the trees."

"So, there could've been men interested, and you didna know."

"I suppose."

"But you were no' interested in them?"

She shook her head. "Nay." Then she turned her head to him. "I could admire a man, think of him as handsome. I saw many training shirtless and appreciated the sight, but it wasn't until you that I felt anything other than friendship for any of them."

Lachlan's smile was slow and heart-stopping. "Lass, you do know how to say all the right things."

17

She would feel better if she were in a Witch's Grove. But Sybbyl didn't have that luxury. Instead, she was in this infernal cold, looking for the next bone. The small cottage she'd commandeered would have to do. The only thing that made it bearable was the fact that anytime she came across people, she had them on their knees in short order.

The fear in their eyes left her giddy. Even without speaking, the villagers were terrified of her. Children cried, women shook, men wouldn't lift their gazes from the ground. Yet there was always a handful who thought they could put her in her place. She showed them quickly enough who held the power. It was a heady experience, and one she'd never get tired of.

There was just one issue. There was no sign of the bone. And each time she asked the staff to give her directions, the bone was nowhere to be found. Almost as if it were moving on its own.

Sybbyl snorted. No, it wasn't doing that. Some*one* was moving it.

A sound caused her to jerk her head to the side. She

winced from the pain that shot through her. She had tried all different kinds of spells, but nothing healed the wound on her neck—or the one on her wrist. The injury on her neck was deep, which could be the reason it was taking so much magic. However, that didn't explain the one on her wrist. It wasn't nearly as bad, but it wasn't healing either.

Both had been caused by Helena during their battle. Sybbyl could ignore them if she remained still, but when she moved, the pain was excruciating. It hadn't let up, and in fact, she was beginning to think it was increasing. That, along with the fact that they weren't healing, worried her. She kept it to herself because she knew the moment she got the second bone, she would be able to heal herself.

The Staff of the Eternal should've healed her. Perhaps it hadn't because it was up against the Heart of the First Witch. But two against one was all it took. Her wounds and the fact that she was eventually going up against the Varroki is why Sybbyl searched for the bone now.

Her thoughts halted as she heard the sound again. Sybbyl raised her hand and, with a flick of her wrist, opened the door. Before it stood Avis. Sybbyl had befriended her because she'd seen Avis's potential.

"My queen," Avis said as she bowed her blond head, now soaked from the rain and snow.

"How did you find me?" Sybbyl demanded.

Avis's brown eyes glanced toward the fire near Sybbyl. "Word is spreading about you. I simply followed the rumors through the villages until I found you."

"If you came all this way, it must be important. Come in and get warm."

The young witch hurried to step inside and closed the door against the wet and cold. She shivered as she removed her soaked cloak and hung it on a peg to dry. Then she walked to the fire and stuck her hands out to warm them. "Three witches are dead."

Sybbyl made sure that neither of her wounds was visible, then she looked at Avis. "Where?"

"Scotland."

"Who were they hunting?" Sybbyl asked, but then again, she already knew the answer.

"A Hunter."

Sybbyl's eyes narrowed. "Did all three attack at once?"

"Twins were the first victims. The second was an old witch. Every one of us is out looking for Hunters and other witches to bring to the Coven."

"Then how do you know it was a Hunter they sought?"

"The twins picked up a trail and told the Coven they were after a Hunter. When they didn't report back, those near the location went to check and found their ashes."

Sybbyl raised a brow. "And the old witch?"

"Her remains were found two days from the twins', directly north."

"And you believe it's the same Hunter?"

Avis nodded. "I do. It makes sense."

"Perhaps, but it doesn't matter. Soon, I'll have the second bone and will go after the Varroki."

"What if this Hunter is headed to the Varroki?"

Sybbyl threw back her head and laughed. "Who cares? It doesn't matter if one or one hundred Hunters join the Varroki. They're all going to die."

Avis smiled, glee shining in her brown eyes. "It's going to be glorious."

"Aye, it is."

"How close are you to the next bone? Can I come with you?"

Her eagerness was endearing, but the elders' folly in letting Sybbyl near them when the Staff of the Eternal was found had gotten them killed. She wasn't going to make the same mistake with Avis. "I have something else I need you to do."

"Anything," Avis replied.

"Track whoever is killing my witches. I don't care if it's a witch or a Hunter, kill them."

Avis bowed her head. "I'll see it done."

"Now," Sybbyl demanded when the witch remained.

There was a bit of hesitation as if Avis thought to argue. But in the end, she walked to her cloak. Once the drenched garment was back on her shoulders and fastened, Avis pulled up the hood. Without looking back, she said, "And after I've killed whoever it is I search for? Where do you want me?"

"Gather the Coven," Sybbyl said with a grin. "Once I have the next bone and head to the Varroki, I'll need every witch to stand with me."

"And we'll do it gladly."

Sybbyl stared at the closed door long after it had been shut. Avis had said all the right words, but Sybbyl wasn't sure if the witch actually meant them. So what if she was back out in the weather? Other witches were, as well. None of those Sybbyl had served had allowed her any luxuries as she earned her place in the Coven. Neither would she with any of her witches.

Alone once more, Sybbyl pulled back the sleeve of her gown to look at her wrist. She held the staff with her wounded arm and once more tried casting a healing spell using her own magic as well as the staff's. Once more, nothing happened.

Sybbyl set the staff aside and tried the same spell again with only her magic, but there was no change. Then she had the staff in hand once more. This time, she tried to use the staff without her magic, but it was impossible. In order to access the magic of the staff, a witch had to use her own powers. But there was a real possibility that the staff could heal her if only Sybbyl could stop using her magic.

A part of her thought to call Avis back and see if the witch could use the staff. The moment the thought went through her mind, Sybbyl disregarded it. There was no way she would put the Staff of the Eternal in anyone else's hands. It was hers. If she handed it to anyone, then she didn't deserve to wield it. She had worked too hard for too long to claim her destiny to give it up simply because a couple of wounds were paining her.

She had suffered much more than this. At that thought, she squared her shoulders and looked into the fire. The wounds weren't affecting her magic or her ability to use the staff. They were an annoyance as well as a sign that she could be hurt. She would make sure they were kept covered so no one could see them. But she wouldn't stop looking for a solution to heal them. She had magic. It was meant to heal her, and she would find out why that wasn't happening.

"You know why."

That damn voice again. It had been days since she'd heard it, and Sybbyl wasn't happy it was back.

"You can't ignore me. I've proven that already."

"What do you want?" Sybbyl snapped.

"Merely pointing out a fact."

"That I know why my wounds aren't healing?" She gave a loud snort. "If I knew, I wouldn't keep trying different healing spells."

"Admit the reason."

"Nay." Sybbyl hated that her voice rose because she lost control of her emotions at the prodding of a stupid voice in her head.

"In your head?" The voice laughed. *"I'm not in your head."*

"You are."

The staff warmed in her hand. "*Are you sure?*"

"Stop it." This time, Sybbyl kept her voice controlled, but she felt anything but calm.

The voice laughed again.

Sybbyl looked around the cottage. The voice was in her head. It had to be in order for it to know what she was thinking.

"*How…naive. I'm part of the First Witch, the most powerful to have ever walked this Earth. You hold a part of me and push your magic into the staff.*"

She swallowed. "When I use the magic of the staff, I'm allowing you inside me."

"*From the first moment you touched me. I know all your secrets, Sybbyl. All your fears.*"

She didn't respond to that. Instead, she asked, "Tell me why my wounds aren't healing."

Silence met her words.

After squeezing her eyes closed for a moment, she asked, "Will you please tell me why my magic isn't healing the wounds?"

"*You hold a relic, a piece of me. The Heart is living, breathing, and holds more magic than a single bone. The Heart wants you dead for what you've done, and she made sure to put that in her magic when the two of you clashed. There is nothing you can do to heal yourself.*"

"I refuse to believe that. Magic can heal anything. I'll find the right spell. Sooner or later."

Thankfully, there was no answer. Sybbyl leaned the staff near the hearth and used a spell for food. Once she had eaten her fill, she found a bathing tub and snapped her fingers, filling it instantly with hot water.

With the fingers of her good hand, Sybbyl swirled the water, using magic to infuse it with healing properties. Then she disrobed and stepped into the tub.

18

The weather hadn't held. The new cloak Synne wore was better than her old one, but even it couldn't keep the rain from her. But it wasn't just rain. It was snow mixed with rain. She'd never seen anything like it before.

"It happens," Lachlan replied when she asked about it.

Even the horses seemed irritated at the turn of the weather. Their progress slowed because of the sleet. Synne didn't know how much longer she could stand being in it, but it wasn't as if she had a choice. They were out in the middle of nowhere without any shelter. Where could they go to get out of the storm?

A shout from Lachlan ahead of her had Synne lifting her face to see what he was doing. He waved at her and nudged his gelding into a gallop. Synne leaned low over her mare and said, "Let's go, girl."

The horse quickly followed, and it wasn't long before Synne saw what Lachlan had shouted to her about—a cave. It wasn't easy to get to, and they had to dismount to lead the horses up to it. But once inside, it was large enough for even the horses to take shelter.

"Get out of your clothes," Lachlan told her as he hurriedly removed the saddle from his mount.

Synne ignored him and busied herself with her mare, but her fingers were so numb, it took twice as long as usual. Finally, Lachlan was there, pulling her hands away to do it for her. She then began to undress, but the moment the cold air hit her skin, she was shaking even more.

"I don't think this was a good idea," she told him.

He ignored her and set about digging through his bags for something. When he turned to her, a thick, wool blanket in the MacCullum plaid was draped around her. She smiled her thanks and sank down on her haunches to cover as much of herself as she could.

"I'll be back," Lachlan said as he headed toward the cave entrance.

She immediately stood. "Where are you going?"

"We need a fire."

"There's no wood."

"Peat. I'm going to find peat. I willna be long."

With that, he was gone. Synne looked at her sodden clothes laid out to dry and wrinkled her nose at the thought of putting them back on, so she remained. The horses stood huddled together, their heads down, and their eyes closed. She could sleep as well if only she could get warm. Why anyone would want to live in such a climate was beyond her comprehension. She couldn't function in such conditions.

Her eyes snapped open when she heard someone approaching. Before she could even think about getting to her bow, Lachlan called out to her. Then he was back inside, pulling out a large mound of peat from his cloak and vest.

She watched as he quickly created a pile of it and got it lit. The first crackle of the fire brought a smile to her face. It wasn't long before the flames were high, and heat reached her. But Lachlan wasn't finished. He put his bag near her and then removed his clothes. She eyed his large body once more, and this time, she was able to lower her gaze to his cock. Even flaccid, it was impressive.

"Keep staring, and there will be another way we can warm ourselves," he said with a smile.

Synne grinned and opened her blanket. The moment his chilled skin touched hers, her teeth chattered together. Lachlan then took the cover and unfolded it even more, creating a large enough section that they could lay on it and cover themselves.

"This is better," she said when they were chest to chest, their body heat melding.

"Much. I think we should always sleep like this."

Synne nodded. "I agree. I didn't think I'd like to sleep with someone, but I find that I enjoy it very much. Your chest makes a nice pillow."

He chuckled softly. "And I verra much like holding your soft body against me."

"Does everyone sleep like this?"

"I doona know. I think if they doona, then they're missing out."

She lifted her face to him. "Agreed."

His lips met hers for a soft kiss. "Are you getting warm."

"Aye. Finally."

"You worried me. I swore you were turning blue."

She snuggled against him, shifting her legs so she could warm another part of them. "I confess that I don't particularly enjoy the cold, but I've never had it affect me quite like this."

"You're used to a milder winter than we have up here."

"I'm doubly glad you found me a better cloak."

He rubbed his hands up and down her back. "Aye. Me, as well."

She heard the worry in his voice, however. "I'll be fine. I promise."

"When I think about you making this trip alone, I can no' fathom it."

"I would've survived. It's what I do. It's what we all do. We have something that must be done, and we put one foot in front of the other until it is."

He kissed the top of her head and released a deep breath. "I know you're capable. I just…"

"Worry," she finished.

"Aye."

"I don't want to be a burden."

"Nay, lass," he admonished. "No' like that. I worry because I care. Deeply."

She let his words linger between them for a moment. "Because we were together last night, and you were my first."

"Nay. I'd feel this way regardless if we had shared our bodies or no'. You're special, Synne. But you're verra special to me."

That made her smile. "I care about you, too."

The warmth soon had Synne drifting off to sleep. She didn't know how much time had passed when Lachlan shifted and caused her to wake.

"Hungry?" he asked.

"Aye."

He extracted his arms and moved the blanket just enough that he could sit up and reach for his bag. There, he took out some oatcakes and a waterskin. He gave her the food and tended to the fire.

Synne watched him, wondering what life would be like if it was just the two of them. The current situation had thrown them together, but Lachlan had *chosen* to come with her. He'd joined her on her mission. Would they get on well if they had met under different circumstances? Would he even want her if they had met differently? Would she want him? Would they have argued or passed each other as if neither existed?

"What are you thinking about?" he asked when he returned to the blanket.

Synne sat up, keeping the cover around her with one arm free. "If we had met under different circumstances."

"I doona understand."

"You approached me because I was in your forest. If we had been in a village, would you have spoken to me? Would I even have looked at you?"

He gave a nod. "Ah. I see. To answer your question, I absolutely would've gone up to you."

"You can't know that," she said with a smile.

"Aye, I do. You snagged my attention in an instant. I couldna look away. I still can no'."

Synne leaned her head on his shoulder. "I like this. I don't like being cold, but I like being with you. A lot."

"Hearing that makes me happy."

With Lachlan and the fire, Synne was soon warm. It wasn't long before she was once more drifting off to sleep. She didn't care when Lachlan wrapped his arm around her as he lay down. She fell asleep on his chest, a smile on her face.

Synne was startled to find herself in a forest. She couldn't remember where she had been, but she knew it wasn't this place. It was warm, as well. That seemed...odd, but she couldn't quite put her finger on why.

She turned in a circle, looking around. There was nothing about the woods that seemed familiar. And yet, she had a feeling that she knew this place. She couldn't pinpoint why no matter how hard she tried.

The forest was an old one. Large trees with twisting,

gnarled branches hung over her head. The ground was littered with moss and ferns. In the distance, she heard the gentle sounds of a brook. But what caught her attention was the silence. There were no birds, no animals. Nothing.

Unease rippled through her. Her heart began to pound, and her hands grew clammy. She needed to hide, but where? All around her, she saw nothing but trees. She rushed toward a moss-covered boulder and tried to climb it. She slipped, skinning the palms of her hands when the moss fell away.

Synne ignored the wound and managed to get atop the rock. But still, the fear wouldn't relinquish its hold. She scanned the woods, searching for…someone. There was someone out there. She knew that with the same certainty that she knew they would help her. She just needed to wait for them.

She drew her knees up to her chest and tried to calm her racing heart. There was a tree near, and she might be able to jump the distance and grab hold of its limbs. She was always trying to climb trees, and she had yet to accomplish the feat. But up high, she would be able to keep out of sight of whatever was out there.

As she looked at the tree, it appeared as if the bark moved on its own. That wasn't possible, though. But the longer she stared, the more she was sure of it. Then, suddenly, eyes stared back at her.

Synne opened her mouth to scream, but no sound came out as the full shape of a woman with skin that looked like the bark of the tree faced her. The woman's hair, piled atop her head, even appeared to be bark. The fact that she had blended in so well with the tree that Synne hadn't seen her had icy fingers of fear clawing at her.

Then the tree-woman held out her hand to Synne. She didn't move, too afraid to run away, scream, or even take the being's hand. Synne hadn't known such a creature existed.

The being moved the hand closer as soft whispers filled the air. Synne couldn't hear what was said, but it did nothing to calm her. The being wanted her, but why? Synne was nothing like her. Besides, she was waiting for...

She never finished the thought as the sounds of someone running toward her caught her attention. Synne turned her head to look. She saw a woman with long, blond hair holding her skirts and running as fast as she could. Behind her was a man with light brown hair, bellowing something.

Just as Synne thought she was about to hear him, the whispers grew louder. She slid from the boulder to go to the couple. She knew them. That's who she had been waiting for. Now that they were there, she'd be safe.

The man let out a shout as he was suddenly grabbed by another of the tree-creatures. Synne cried out when he disappeared into the tree. The woman glanced over her shoulder, but she never stopped running to Synne. That's when Synne decided to go to her. She had barely gotten up to a run when the creatures grabbed the woman, as well.

Synne halted, tears flowing down her face as she screamed, her hand outstretched for the woman, who kept reaching for her even as the being dragged her to the tree.

19

"Synne. Synne!" Lachlan yelled as he tried to wake her.

He'd been pulled from sleep by the sound of her screaming for her mum and da, but it was the terror in her voice that made his heart clutch.

"Synne," he said again as he pulled her thrashing form into his arms "It's all right. I've got you. You're safe. You're safe, lass."

He stroked her, calming both her and himself. He wasn't sure how long he held her before he realized that she had stopped moving and was no longer screaming. Lachlan glanced down to see her clutching his shirt as if he were the only thing keeping her there.

Only then did his heart begin to calm. He'd never seen someone have a nightmare like that before. His sisters had had their share of scary dreams. Even he had experienced night terrors before. But nothing close to what he'd just seen with Synne. Whatever she'd seen had clearly been horrifying. The fact that she had called out to her parents made him wonder if it had something to do with what had happened to them.

He pressed a kiss to her forehead and held her tighter. Lachlan didn't ask about the dream. She might not remember it, and he didn't want to drag her back into whatever had scared her if she did. The fire was dying, but he didn't want to release Synne to stir it. They remained as they were until a chill traveled through Synne. Then, he had no choice but to get the fire going once more.

"I'll be right back," he whispered.

Reluctantly, she released him and huddled in the blanket. She wouldn't look at him directly. Her gaze remained on the fire, watching the flames grow until the red-orange glow shone on the cave walls.

Lachlan slid beneath the blanket and held out his arms. Synne immediately turned to him. He let out a little sigh of relief. It meant a lot that she'd gone to him. Maybe in a few days, he'd ask about the nightmare. For now, he'd simply hold her.

"It's been a long time since I've had that nightmare," she said, her voice soft and breaking as if it took everything she had to get the words out.

He rubbed his hand up and down her back. "Tragedies can sometimes dredge things up."

"I'd forgotten I'd ever even had them."

Lachlan imagined a young Synne, found by Edra. He might not have known the witch, but if she was half of what Synne said, then there was no way Edra would have stood by and done nothing as Synne suffered night after night. Because if he were capable of magic, he'd make sure that Synne never experienced another nightmare again.

Synne sniffed. Lachlan smoothed back the strands of hair that had come loose from her braids. The fire crackled, and one of the horses blew out a loud breath.

"Edra stopped them," Synne stated in a whisper.

Lachlan nodded. "Aye. I believe she did."

"Now that she's…gone…so are the spells she used."

"Perhaps the Varroki can help you once we reach Blackglade."

Synne was silent for a long time. Then she said, "Nay."

"What?" he asked, taken aback by her refusal.

"I need to face this."

Lachlan put a finger beneath her chin and turned her face up to his. "Lass, I'm no' sure that's wise. You were screaming. The fear I heard in your voice was…" He shook his head. "I can no' even find words. And then you kept calling for your—"

He halted then, realizing what he'd been about to say.

"Calling for who?" she asked.

He debated whether to lie or not, but in the end, he decided on the truth. "Your parents."

Synne's gaze took on a faraway look. "She had blond hair, like mine. He had light brown hair. Their faces are faded," she said as her brow furrowed. "I can't even see their eyes. They were running to me, trying to get to me. All these years, I didn't know if they'd abandoned me or not, but they didn't." Her gaze returned to him. "I know what happened to my parents."

"It was a nightmare, lass. I'm no' sure you can believe what you saw."

"It wasn't just a nightmare. I was reliving what happened." She licked her lips, a tear falling from the corner of one eye. "They were killed, Lachlan. By the Gira."

His breath left him in a whoosh, as if he'd been sucker punched in the gut. "But…they didna take you."

"Nay," she said with a small shake of her head. "I don't know why. One reached out to me, trying to get me to take her hand, but I wouldn't. I saw them take my father first. My mother fought them with everything she had. It took three of the Gira to get her. She kept screaming my name, her hand reaching out to me. I ran toward her, trying to get to her."

"Do you remember anything after that?"

"Nothing. My memory is blank until Edra brought me to the abbey. I don't know if it was days, weeks, months, or years between."

Lachlan sighed. "At least you know the truth about your parents now."

"What happened to them, aye. But I doona know where we lived, who they were, why the Gira didn't take me, or even what forest Edra found me."

"You didna ask where Edra found you?"

She shook her head. "It never seemed to matter. Especially when the nightmares stopped, and I could live normally."

"You know witches. Surely, there is a way to find the answers."

"Maybe," she said and ducked her head.

He felt her lashes rubbing against his chest as she closed her eyes. Lachlan listened to her even breathing, but he knew she wasn't asleep. He couldn't stop thinking about how she had said one of the Gira wanted her. It had reached out a hand to Synne instead of taking her as it had her parents.

Could it be because she could communicate with the trees? She told him that Gira used the trees as camouflage, which meant they needed them. Or it could be as simple as they didn't take children.

Though, he doubted that. If the Gira were as bloodthirsty as Synne made them out to be, it wouldn't matter what age their quarry was. They'd take whatever came their way.

"I want to know why it wanted me," she suddenly said.

"That is certainly a question that needs an answer."

She opened her eyes, her lashes brushing against him

once more. Then she shifted her head to look at him. "At least I finally know why I've been so terrified of the Gira. I believed I'd never seen one before. Now, I know that isn't true. I've seen several of them. And, as strange as this might sound, the one that was nearest to me that day, the one who held out her hand, didn't seem…frightening. I was scared, and since I'd never seen such a creature, I didn't go to it. But it could've taken me like my parents were taken."

"I was just thinking about that myself. It is verra strange that they left you, but then I remembered that you can speak to trees."

She twisted her lips. "I suppose that could be it."

"Please tell me you are no' thinking of finding a Gira to ask them. Can they even converse?"

"Their whispers are enough to draw people to them, so I think they can speak."

"Did they talk to you?"

She wrinkled her nose and shrugged. "I cannot remember. Some things are so vivid, while many others aren't."

"Is this the first time you've had the nightmare since the abbey was attacked?"

Her gaze dropped. "Not exactly. I've had the start of the dream several times, but I was able to pull myself awake as if I subconsciously wasn't ready to see it."

"Maybe you were no'. Perhaps that's why you had it tonight."

She pulled his face down and gave him a kiss. "I'm glad you were here."

"Me, too."

"Was it bad?" she asked with a frown.

"I couldna wake you at first. I didna like seeing you so terrified."

Synne closed her eyes and yawned. "I don't like to be scared."

Silence fell once more, and it wasn't long before she was dozing. They had several hours before dawn, but Lachlan couldn't find sleep again. His gaze moved to the sword that lay next to him. He was thankful that his grandmother had spelled it, but like Synne, he had many questions about his past that couldn't be answered.

Some might say that was for the best. But Lachlan was of the mind that the more information someone had, the better off they were. He might not like all that he had learned, but that didn't mean it wouldn't be useful later on.

Inverness was two days' ride east of their current location. Synne only knew to go north, and while there was much more land that met coastline to the east of them, he suspected that the Varroki were farther north near the Orkney Isles. That area was as remote as it got, and that was saying something since most of Scotland was isolated.

It had been years since he'd taken the journey with his uncle, but Lachlan knew he could find the way. If Synne's only instructions were to head north, then there had to be someone, somewhere, waiting to lead her to the Varroki. At least that's what Lachlan hoped. Otherwise, they could be searching for years to find this place.

The hours passed slowly as he went over the route in his head. The rain and snow had stopped, for the moment, anyway. When dawn finally arrived, Synne stirred and rolled onto her back to look at him. He gave her a smile, and she returned it easily. The nightmare, as horrid as it had been, had also seemed to give her answers. What he worried about now was if it would have lasting effects on her. From what he could see, that wasn't the case.

"I'm all right," she told him, guessing his thoughts.

He rolled toward her and covered her mouth for a slow kiss. "You let me know if that changes."

"You looking out for me?" she asked with a grin.

"Aye. Have a problem with that?" he teased.

She shook her head. "Not in the least."

"Good. Unfortunately, our clothes willna be dry."

"Thank you for ruining my morning by reminding me I'll be cold throughout the day."

He chuckled and rose to his feet. Lachlan tested her clothes first. "They're only slightly wet."

"In this weather, that means they're freezing."

He twisted his lips. "Aye. Mine are worse than yours."

She held out her hands. "No time like the present to get moving."

In short order, they were clothed once more. Lachlan looked at her as she fastened her vest that clung to her body, molding to her breasts. He had thought to wake her by making love to her, but that had been before the nightmare. Perhaps tonight they'd get the chance to share their bodies once more.

"You're leering," she told him with a smile.

He shrugged. "You are beautiful, and I know the taste of your body. I can no' help it if I want more."

She walked to him and rose up on her toes for a kiss. "I've never met anyone who talks to me the way you do."

"Do you no' like it?"

"I like it very much. Please don't stop."

He reached out an arm and dragged her against him. "Then I never will."

They smiled at each other and shared a quick kiss. Then they were readying the horses and gathering their items to leave.

"Ready?" he asked.

"Not at all."

Lachlan chuckled as he grabbed the gelding's reins and walked the horse from the cave.

"How much farther until we reach water?"

He pointed to the east. "Two days' ride that way." Then he pointed to the west. "A day and a half that way." Then he pointed north. "About four days hard riding."

Synne mounted her mare and gathered her cloak around her. "Then we better get moving."

2 0

The weather held for the rest of the day, allowing Synne and Lachlan to cover a lot of ground and eat up some distance. Just as the days before, they encountered no one. Synne was beginning to prefer it that way because it was easier than having to second-guess if the person was part of the Coven or not.

After such a long journey, Synne was glad that one more day was behind her. The fact that she still had several more didn't make her feel that great. She was exhausted from the travel and the lack of sleep from the night before. She couldn't wait to be in Lachlan's arms once more, but she wasn't at all keen on having the nightmare again. Although, there was a chance that she might see more than last time. Still, watching her parents being murdered wasn't something she wanted to relive.

She was the one who found the boulders that she pointed out to Lachlan as night approached. They checked them out and found a hidden spot that would keep them shielded from view.

When she dismounted, Lachlan approached her with a

deep frown marring his forehead. He cupped her face in his hands and grunted.

Synne quirked a brow. "What was that about?"

"You've dark circles under your eyes."

"That happens when I don't sleep well."

"We should've stopped sooner."

She rolled her eyes. "I'm not a wilting flower. I can handle hardships."

"Aye, but we both need to be at our best. Witches have already attacked us twice. I suspect more will be coming."

He had a point. She'd been so wrapped up in thinking about her nightmare and wanting to get to the Varroki, that she had all but forgotten about Sybbyl and the Coven. That was dangerous. Things like that were what got people killed.

"You're right," she admitted.

He flashed her a smile and gave her another kiss. She was really coming to love those. He'd given them to her all during the day, for seemingly no reason. And she really, really liked it.

"Would you be offended if I took your bow to hunt for food?"

She put her hand on her hip. "While I stay here and tend to the horses and start the fire?"

"If that's a problem, you can hunt. But the snow is deep."

She scrunched up her face.

"That's what I thought," Lachlan said with a laugh.

She handed him her bow and a quiver of arrows. After another kiss, he was gone.

That night, she and Lachlan took turns keeping watch. Even with their location, both realized that they had been lucky the night before. They needed to be more aware of… everything. Lachlan took the first watch, and Synne had gone immediately to sleep after filling her belly. It felt that she had just closed her eyes when he woke her.

Synne then took her turn. The hours crept by with nothing out of the ordinary until she woke Lachlan again. She got another few hours before it was her turn to keep watch until dawn. It wasn't snowing, but the temperature had dropped so that even the little warmth from the fire disappeared before it reached her.

Lachlan and the horses seemed unfazed by the weather. Synne hated that she was so cold, but she couldn't change that. So, she had to deal with it. She glanced over at Lachlan, who was sleeping with his arms folded over his chest as he lay on his side. The thought of sliding her body next to his for warmth had her itching to do just that.

If she had magic, she could remove his clothes and have her way with him. She smiled at her fanciful thoughts. The time they'd gotten to share had been amazing, and she knew that wouldn't be their only time together. Right now, however, they needed to keep their focus on staying alive until they found the Varroki.

Just thinking of them had her wondering why Malene and Armir hadn't given her better directions. It wasn't as if she would tell the Coven where they were located. Besides, Sybbyl already knew about them.

Synne wrapped her arms around her middle beneath her cloak and shivered. She was coming to hate the cold. She had only been traveling for a couple of weeks—first from the abbey to Braith's castle, then from there to Scotland—but it felt as if she might never reach her destination.

Snow crunching got Synne's attention. Both horses jerked their heads up, their ears pricked toward the sound. Synne silently nocked an arrow and pointed it between the gap in the boulders while she waited to hear the noise again.

She heard it again, this time closer. Then she heard the squeak of the rabbit right before she saw the animal. She lowered her bow as relief poured through her. She briefly closed her eyes. When she opened them, a woman stood before her in a black cloak, the hood pulled up but still showing her face. Synne knew in an instant that she was a witch.

"Raise the bow, and I kill him," the witch said and lifted her arm toward Lachlan.

Synne glanced over to see Lachlan's sword hanging in mid-air over him with the tip hovering over his heart. Synne slid her gaze back to the witch. "What do you want?"

"You."

"What are you waiting for?" Synne demanded. "Kill me."

The witch raised a brown brow. "I never said anything about killing you."

That took Synne aback. She lifted her chin. "Are you with the Coven?"

Instead of answering, the witch said, "Many are on your trail, Hunter."

"I know. Three witches who came for us are dead."

At this, the witch looked at Lachlan. "He's a formidable warrior. I can see why the two of you have teamed up."

"What do you want, if you don't wish to kill me?" Synne asked.

The witch smiled, showing even, white teeth. "I'm not the one who wants you."

"Sybbyl can go to Hell. You can kill me now because I'm not going anywhere near the Coven."

"For one with such knowledge, you know very little."

"What's that supposed to mean?"

"Exactly what I said," the witch replied.

Synne blew out a breath. "I'd like it if you would actually answer a question."

"I have. I told you I'm not here to kill you, and that I'm not the one who wants you."

"Then who does want me?"

"Someone who can help."

Synne narrowed her gaze on the witch. "Then bring them here."

"That would be…difficult. I've come a long way to find you. What needs to be said has to be done with only you."

"I'm not going anywhere without Lachlan."

The witch regarded her for a moment and then nodded. "Ah. I see."

"What do you see?" Synne asked with a frown.

"Much more than you, obviously." The witch cut her brown eyes to the bow with the arrow still nocked.

Synne slowly took the arrow out and placed it back in her quiver. "You can lower the sword now."

"I will once you're gone."

"And where am I going?"

"To the one who requests your presence."

Irritation filled Synne so that her words were laced with it when she said, "And where is that?"

The witch pointed behind her. "Follow my footsteps."

"I'll follow you."

The witch shook her head. "Actually, I'll remain here with the warrior. You're safe, Synne. I know you won't believe me, but it's the truth."

"You're right. I don't believe you."

She didn't want to go, but she also didn't want Lachlan to die. The fact that the witch had crept up on them in such a location made Synne furious with herself. How had she let that happen? She looked at Lachlan then walked until she was even with the witch.

With her head turned to the side to look at the woman who threatened Lachlan, Synne said, "If he's harmed in any way, I won't rest until I hunt you down and kill you."

"No harm will come to him. Or you," the witch replied.

Synne didn't believe a word the woman said. She glanced

at Lachlan once more, wishing he'd wake, but the witch must be keeping him asleep. After inhaling a deep breath, Synne swung her gaze to the witch. "What is your name?"

Her brown eyes lowered to the ground briefly. "Time is running out. You must move quickly. You do want to win, don't you?"

"Anyone who knows who I am would say that." But Synne also couldn't deny the sensation that time wasn't on her side at the moment.

Without another word, she walked past the witch and quickly found the footsteps in the snow. She almost tried to climb the boulder to get a better vantage point, but she didn't. There were no trees about to give her an idea of what to do, so she wasn't sure what prompted her to keep walking.

The footsteps were easy to follow. They took her up the mountain and down the other side. That's when Synne spotted a small grove of trees. The trail of footprints led her straight to them. Just before she entered, she thought about the Gira. The witch could be part of the Coven. If that was the case, then why hadn't she just killed Synne? After all, the witch had crept up on them and taken them unawares.

Maybe the witch hadn't killed her because it was Sybbyl who was waiting for her. Synne wouldn't mind that. She was ready to face the leader of the Coven—even if it meant her death. Thanks to Lachlan, her anger didn't rule her as extensively as it had before, but it was still there. She needed to control it, or it would definitely lead to her death.

But what if the witch wasn't part of the Coven? What if it was someone else who awaited her? Like the Varroki? No, it wouldn't be them. The Varroki would've taken both her and Lachlan to their city.

The moment Synne stepped into the grove, there was a shift in the air. It wasn't filled with anger or evil, but instead…peace. She immediately felt the tension ease out of her shoulders. Synne kept her guard up because it could all be an illusion. Witches were good at those.

She reached the middle and turned in a circle, looking for whoever it might be. A red squirrel scampered along a tree limb, chattering before it froze when the animal spotted her. Then, with a twitch of its tail, the critter continued on its way.

There was no sound, only movement that drew her gaze to the left. Synne stared at the tree. Then, slowly, lids opened, and she found herself staring at a Gira.

21

Lachlan came awake instantly. His eyes flew open, and he instinctively knew there was an enemy near. He reached for his sword, but it wasn't next to him. His head swiveled, and he saw the woman standing at the entrance with his blade. The tip of the weapon was in the ground as it spun around and around, but she wasn't touching it. She wore a black cloak with the hood down, showing brown hair laced with copper that disappeared beneath the collar.

"About time you woke," she said without looking at him.

His gaze scanned the area. "Where is Synne?"

"Otherwise occupied at the moment."

"Witch, I'd caution you to watch your words."

Her eyes slowly lifted to him. Brown eyes with a hint of yellow stared at him flatly. "You're awfully confident without your weapon."

"I doona care if you've magic or no'. I learned to fight with whatever was around me."

"I know."

That took him aback.

She exhaled loudly and grasped the sword by the hilt.

"Your grandmother was a witch. Did you really think no one else knew?"

"I thought it was kept to just my family. What do you want?"

"I'm not here for you. I came because someone wished to talk to Synne."

"Who?" he demanded, taking a threatening step toward her.

The witch wasn't cowed. Instead, she quirked a brow. "I kept you asleep while Synne and I spoke. I even held your own weapon over you to get her to do what was needed."

Lachlan narrowed his eyes at the woman. "Why do you tell me this?"

"Because I tried to tell Synne that no harm would come to either of you. I understand why neither you nor she can believe that, but it's the truth. If I wanted her dead, I could've killed her and then you."

He might want to deny it, but the fact was that she could've murdered him. That wasn't to say she Synne wasn't dead.

"She isn't far," the witch continued. "Synne will be back before you know it. Until then, I need you to understand that you have to pick up the pace of your journey."

"What do you know?" he pressed.

She glanced away and licked her lips. "I know that time isn't on your side."

"How can I believe anything you say? You could be with the Coven."

At that, the witch's nostrils flared as anger flashed in her eyes. "Don't ever say that again."

"Then help us."

"I'm doing everything I can."

Lachlan snorted. "Standing here talking to me is all you can do? I need to see Synne. Now."

"You'll see her when she's finished."

"Finished with what?" he asked in a low, deadly tone that usually got his men moving instantly.

She rolled her eyes. "Men. You're all the same. When you don't get your way, you resort to that tone."

"Someone I care about could be in danger. What would you do in my place?"

"I'd do whatever I needed."

Lachlan quickly covered the short distance between them and grabbed his sword before she knew what was happening. He put the blade against her neck and stared down at her. "You were saying?"

"Impressive," she said with a smile.

He frowned, noticing that she didn't seem worried at all. But why would she? She was a witch. She could probably kill him with just a thought. He lowered the sword and took a step back. "Why did you no' defend yourself?"

"Because I knew you didn't intend to kill me."

"You couldna know that."

"But I did." Her gaze shifted away.

Lachlan was close enough that he could still kill her if he wanted. Just as he knew that she could kill him. Neither of them made a move. He wasn't sure why she held back, but her words disturbed him greatly. He'd said nothing to make her believe that he wouldn't harm her. Yet, he hadn't planned on it.

The witch pressed her lips together and met his gaze once more. "I'm sure Synne told you that each witch has some magic that they can do better than any other."

"And yours is knowing if someone plans to harm you?"

She smiled as if she found his words humorous. "That would come in handy, but nay, that isn't the case."

"Then what is it?"

"It isn't important."

He narrowed his gaze at her. "Are you being purposefully evasive?"

"I've spent my life hiding from those who would burn me and those who wish to use me. I've learned to keep much about myself a secret. It's better that way."

"My grandmother was safe in my clan. You could find one."

The witch gave him a flat look. "Your grandmother was safe because your family led the clan. Had she been anyone else, what do you think would've happened?"

"You doona know that for sure."

"Neither do you. The facts are the facts. I don't like them, but I accept them and adjust things to suit me."

Lachlan still wasn't sure what to make of this witch, but if she wasn't with the Coven, she could be a great asset. "I'm joining Synne to fight against the Coven. Come with us."

"Just you and a Hunter against the Coven? No, thank you," she said with a snort.

"It isna only the two of us." Lachlan didn't elaborate more. If the Varroki wanted to stay hidden, then he would aid them in that endeavor.

The witch cocked her head to the side. "Who else?"

"There are more Hunters, and the Heart of the First Witch." He could attest to that for certain, and it didn't matter who had that information because the Coven no doubt already did.

At the mention of Helena, the witch's gaze sharpened. "Is that a fact?"

"You doona seem surprised with the knowledge that the bones of the First Witch are being found."

The woman shrugged. "There have been rumors for months."

"The bones were supposed to stay hidden."

At this, the witch smiled, shaking her head. "That was

never going to be possible. Too many witches want power to not look for the bones. It was inevitable that they would eventually be found."

"Then someone should've done a better job of destroying them."

"Did you ever think that perhaps the First Witch ordered her bones scattered because she knew what was coming? Did you not think that she did it on purpose, putting the bones where they needed to be for when the time came?"

"When what time came?"

The witch shrugged. "Take a look around. It hangs in the air like mist you can't see. It seeps into your skin. You eat it, drink it, breathe it. You're a warrior. I know you feel it."

"Aye," he answered. "It's the tension before a war."

She barked a laugh. "It's evil rolling across the land, and it is infecting everything."

"If you feel that strongly, tell me why you are no' fighting?"

"Who says I'm not?" she retorted.

Lachlan opened his mouth to reply when her head snapped to the side. He watched her stand as still as a statue for a long moment. Then, she looked his way.

"Don't tarry," the witch warned. Her gaze darted to his sword. "And no matter what you do, don't lose the sword."

"Wait, why?" he asked when she whirled around.

When he followed her through the narrow gap between the boulders, she was gone. As if she had vanished into thin air. Lachlan quickly forgot about her as he thought about Synne, but still, the witch's warning to get moving prompted him to saddle the horses before he went out looking for his Hunter.

22

This couldn't be happening. And yet, there was no denying it. Synne had her bow drawn, and an arrow nocked in the next heartbeat.

The Gira simply stared, not at all fazed. The lips of the nymph moved, curling in a soft smile. "I'm glad you came."

The voice wasn't a whisper, but full and robust. Synne was so taken aback by it that she could only blink. "If I'd known what awaited me, I wouldn't have."

"I know," the Gira said, her golden eyes lowering to the ground for a heartbeat. "Nevertheless, you're here now."

"I can change that."

"I hope you don't. There is much I've wanted to tell you."

Synne snorted and lowered her arms as she spun around and began walking away. "You have nothing that I want."

"It's about your parents."

Those four words stopped Synne in her tracks. Was it a coincidence that she had dreamed of her parents last night only to meet a Gira today? Synne wasn't sure. But what she did want to know is why her parents had been killed, and she hadn't.

She inhaled deeply, then faced the Gira.

There was no delight on the nymph's face. Instead, Synne thought she spotted…regret.

"Why now?" Synne demanded. "Why have you sought me out now?"

"I've been trying for years, but Edra's magic is strong. She kept you from seeing the past in your nightmares, and that also ensured I couldn't get to you."

Synne couldn't stop the fury that pulled at her face or filled her voice. "I say that's a very good thing."

"It was," the nymph admitted. "Because I couldn't get to you, the other Gira couldn't find you either."

"Why does that matter?"

The Gira swallowed and moved her head, her hair of twigs reaching skyward. "It might be best if I start at the beginning. My name is Asrail. For many moons, I was the queen of my people. Until my son fell in love with a mortal, and I found a witch who used magic to turn him human."

Synne's knees grew weak as she took in the words. "How do I know you aren't lying?"

"You don't," Asrail replied. "The Gira are anywhere trees are. My children were all over, so I knew it wouldn't be noticed that my son wasn't around. And it worked. Perfectly. Until I learned of you. I stayed away, despite wanting to know you. I'd only seen your parents from afar over the years. But the knowledge of you made me incredibly happy."

Synne hungered to hear more and yet dreaded it at the same time.

Asrail's sorrowful eyes filled with tears. "The Gira believe themselves above any other being, and by not only allowing but also helping my son become human, I committed a sacrilegious crime in their eyes. When they found out where I was and saw my son—and you—they demanded your death as well as that of your parents. I wasn't going to let that happen. Your mother and father attempted to talk to them. That's where they were that day. They left me to watch over you because they knew I wouldn't let anything happen to you."

She suddenly smiled, her gaze softening as she let her memories fill her. "Your father had a way with words. He had a commanding presence, and he was well-liked." Her smile faded as she blinked and focused on Synne. "That was the only reason I wasn't there beside him. I should've known that the Gira didn't want to listen to anything that he or your mother had to say. They attacked, but they forgot how skilled my son was. He may have looked like a human, but he was still very much a Gira. He was the reason they initially got away."

Synne waited for Asrail to continue, but silence filled the air. She then cleared her throat to find her voice. "What happened then?"

Asrail gave a little shake of her head as if pulling herself together. "You sensed that something was wrong. I called to you, but you ignored me at first. Then, you went to the boulder. I was so close to you, but I didn't want to grab you. I needed you to take my hand."

"My parents… They almost reached me."

The nymph nodded her head solemnly. "They were close, aye."

"I saw them get taken."

Asrail closed her eyes and turned her head away for a long moment. Then she looked at Synne. "I had to make a choice. I could've saved you or your parents. Not both. I chose you."

"What?" Synne demanded in a hoarse voice. "You were the queen! You could've saved us all."

"I wish that were true, but it isn't. If I had been able, I

would've given my life for all of you. Allowing my son to follow his heart turned the entire Gira race against me. The few I knew who would stand with me chose not to out of fear. I watched my son be killed before my very eyes. I watched the woman he'd fallen in love with devoured. You were next."

Synne raised her brows, desperate to know the rest. "Finish. Please."

"I stood between them and you." Asrail moved away from the tree to show that her left arm was missing. "They came at you for weeks, trying again and again, to get to you. I used every bit of magic I had to move us, but they continued locating us. That's when I realized that I had to let you go. They were following me. I'd seen the witch, Edra, take in a child before, so I made sure that she was near when I left you in the forest. Even as young as you were then, you heard the trees. They let you know that Edra was safe. I was already far away when I looked back to see the witch set you on her horse and ride away."

Synne wasn't sure how she was supposed to feel knowing that she was half-Gira, or that her grandmother had saved her from certain death. She put her hand on the tree and slowly lowered herself to the ground, dazed.

"When I heard that the Gira had joined Sybbyl to attack the abbey, I went in search of you," Asrail continued. "I held out hope that you were alive, and I knew there was a chance you were going to the Varroki."

Synne's gaze jerked to Asrail. "You know of them?"

"Of course," she replied with a soft chuckle. "The Gira know much, but we share very little. We could've told the Coven about the Varroki long ago, just as we could've told the Varroki where the elders of the Coven were at any time."

"Why didn't you choose a side?"

Her wooden brows lifted. "My child, we did choose a side. Our own."

Synne couldn't fault them for that. "And now? Are you still with the Gira?"

"I was banished. When they realized that I had left you somewhere so they couldn't find you, they attacked and left me to die. But I wasn't about to give up that easily. I had you to watch over. The Gira can heal themselves with the help of the trees, so I found a place to hide and healed while biding my time until I could speak with you again."

"I'm not sure I can believe you."

"I know, and I understand that. I expect nothing from you. I wanted to speak with you and tell you what happened. Explain that I'm the reason your parents are dead."

Synne shook her head, tears threatening to spill for people she barely remembered. "They were killed because they dared to love. It wasn't your fault or mine. Whether it happened that day or not, it would've happened eventually. You know that."

"I warned your father what the Gira would do if they discovered him and your mother. He said he didn't care. That even one day with her was better than none at all. She told me the same thing. Who was I to stand in their way? Your mother loved him for who he was, not what he was. I've never seen two people more in love than they were. My heart rejoiced that he'd found his soulmate, even when I knew it would all end badly."

"If what you've told me is true and you did save me, thank you."

Asrail smiled as a tear rolled down her cheek. "You are of me, child. I would do anything for you."

Could it be true? Did Synne have family? She'd never thought to call a Gira family, but there was a part of her that knew the story Asrail told her was true. She had no memories of her time with the Gira, but that could be because she had shut them out as she grieved for her parents.

"Don't ever stop listening to the trees," Asrail warned.

That got Synne's attention. She rose to her feet. "I won't, but I'm not always around them."

The nymph grinned. "You don't have to be. Put your hand to the earth. The roots of trees run miles underground. They can tell you things from leagues away. It's how I knew where you were. And it's how I know a witch is coming for you."

"She's not the first."

"Sybbyl isn't far away. If she learns where you are, she'll alter her course."

Synne snorted loudly and returned her arrow to her quiver. "I'm no one to her. What's one Hunter? Besides, she'll come searching for the Varroki after she finds the next bone."

Asrail's brows drew together as she studied Synne. "Is it possible that you don't know?"

"I can't answer that since I don't know what you're referring to."

"Elin wasn't sure you knew."

Synne raised a brow. "That was the witch's name? Elin? And what wasn't she sure I knew?"

Asrail started to answer, then stopped as she looked away as if concentrating. After a heartbeat, her head snapped to Synne. "Our time is up. The Gira are on their way. Go, find your warrior and continue on your path to the Varroki."

"Wait," Synne said and rushed to Asrail, taking hold of her arm. Synne was taken aback to realize that the skin felt just like the bark it resembled. She looked into her grandmother's eyes. "I'll get to see you again, won't I?"

"If I have anything to say about it, you will," she replied with a smile.

"And the Varroki? I don't know where to go other than north."

"Keep heading that way. They're waiting for you. The moment you get close, one of them will find you. Now, go."

Synne tightened her grip. "Not until you tell me what it is that Elin doesn't think I know."

23

One moment the footsteps were there, and the next, they weren't. Lachlan wished he had magic of his own because he was fast losing patience. How was he supposed to find Synne if her footsteps had been erased? And it had nothing to do with the snowfall because none fell.

He thought about shouting for her, but Lachlan realized that their enemies were probably closer than he realized. He turned in a circle from where he'd last seen the footprints and tried to figure out where Synne might have gone. All he could hope for was that a witch hadn't taken her, because if they had—

His thoughts halted when he spotted someone running toward him from atop the next hill. It took him a second to comprehend that it was Synne. Elation swept through him until he realized that she was running as if someone were after her.

Lachlan didn't hesitate to jump atop his horse and grab the reins of the mare before he nudged both horses into a run to meet her. Synne said nothing when he reached her. She shot him a smile and leaped upon the mare's back before they turned their mounts north. As they rode away, he looked back over his shoulder and glimpsed a grove of trees. Just as he was turning back, he could've sworn that he saw a part of a tree move, but it was most likely his imagination.

"What happened?" he asked.

Synne shook her head. "I don't know where to begin."

"Did you encounter a witch back there? Is that why you left in such haste?"

"I was told one was coming for me." She met Lachlan's gaze. "And Sybbyl isn't far."

He shrugged, having figured that himself. "All right."

"I was told we needed to keep heading north. When we get close to Blackglade, a Varroki will find us."

Lachlan frowned. "You got a wee bit of information to be sure. Can you trust this source?"

"Aye."

"How can you be certain?"

Synne slowed the mare and maneuvered the horse around stones, her gaze on the ground. "Was the witch there when you woke?"

"Aye. Who is she?"

"I think her name is Elin. For some reason I've yet to discern, she's helping Asrail."

Lachlan's frown grew. "Is Asrail another witch?"

"Not exactly."

"Lass, are you being purposefully irritating?"

Synne blew out a breath and glanced at him. "I'm just not sure I'm ready to tell you what happened."

"Because you doona think I can handle it?"

"Because I'm still coming to terms with it."

Ah. Now that made much more sense. Before Lachlan could ask another question, Synne clicked to the mare, and the horse started galloping again. It was another grueling day of travel, but Lachlan didn't care. He'd felt the need to put some distance between himself and their enemies from the moment he woke.

A few clouds dispersed enough that he caught glimpses of blue sky. Not that he expected them to get lucky and have the snow or rain leave them alone for long. And he didn't mind being behind Synne at all. He quite liked that she took charge whenever she wanted. Whoever she had spoken to must have had a lot to say because Synne still hadn't said anything to him.

When noon came, he pulled on the reins near a river and whistled to Synne. She looked back at him and nodded before halting her mare and dismounting. Lachlan landed on the ground beside her and dropped the reins so the gelding could drink. He then searched his bags for the waterskin and two of the last remaining oatcakes. He tossed one to Synne, who smiled her thanks.

When he found a rock to sit on and dusted off the snow, Synne sat next to him. She picked at the snack. He didn't pressure her to speak since it was obvious that she had a lot on her mind.

"I met my grandmother."

He slid his eyes to her as he turned his head, surprised by her words. "I didna know you had one."

"Neither did I until this morning. She's…she's not what I expected."

"Family rarely is." He swallowed his bite of oatcake. "How did she find you?"

Synne finally met his gaze. "The trees."

"So, that's where you get your ability."

Synne nodded before a single tear slipped free and fell down her cheek. She hastily wiped it away and sniffed. "I don't know why I'm crying."

"You found family you didna know you had. There's no

reason no' to rejoice in that or feel grief for no' having your parents around."

"You're right."

He flashed her a smile and teased, "I usually am." That made her chuckle, which was what he wanted. "Why did she no' come with us?"

"I want to tell you, but I don't know how you'll react."

"My grandmother was a witch, lass," he said with a smile. "I think I can handle it."

Synne blew out a breath and faced him. "Asrail is a Gira. She was once their queen."

Lachlan waited for Synne to start laughing to let him know that she was jesting, but it never happened. That's when it hit him that she was being serious. "A Gira? The beings you're scared of?"

"Do you remember the dream I told you about?"

He cocked an eyebrow at her. "The nightmare, you mean?"

"Aye. I told you there was a Gira reaching for me."

"Did this Asrail tell you that it was she?"

Synne slowly nodded. "My father was her son."

Lachlan honestly didn't think he could be shocked any more, then Synne left him reeling. "Her son? But…how?"

"Asrail found a witch to help my father turn human so he could be with my mother. They hid for a long time, but then they had me. Asrail said she stayed away, but when she found out about me, she wanted to see him and me. Other Gira followed her without her knowledge. They learned the truth and demanded our deaths and that my grandmother step down as queen. My father and mother attempted to talk to them while Asrail protected me. When the Gira turned on my parents, it was Asrail who stepped between them and me. She hid me for a while before she realized that they would keep tracking her. She knew of Edra, and left me near her so I could be found. Eventually, the Gira caught up with Asrail. She was attacked and lost her arm. They left her for dead, but she fought her way back, and has been searching for me ever since."

Lachlan ran a hand down his face. "That is quite a story."

"It is. I think I took it about as well as you are."

He looked at her and the tense moment eased as they shared a laugh. Lachlan covered her hand with his. "You believe her story?"

"I can't explain why, but aye, I do."

"You need to trust yourself."

"And if I'm wrong?" she asked.

He shrugged. "We'll deal with it. Listen to what she told you. If she gives a warning, heed it. But always give yourself an out."

"Think about the worst."

"Well, more accurately, take it all in stride. Believe her if you must but also be prepared that it might be lies. Then, you'll be pleasantly surprised if it *is* the truth."

Synne turned her hand so their palms brushed, and their fingers twined. "How will I ever know? That's the first time I've spoken with a Gira."

"Maybe we'll find another."

"Asrail told me that they've known of the Varroki but didn't tell the Coven. Nor did they tell the Varroki where the Coven elders were. She said the Gira chose themselves, not a side."

Lachlan twisted his lips. "That was probably a smart move."

Synne was silent for a moment as she looked at their joined hands. "Asrail was nice."

"She warned you about the witch and told you where to find the Varroki?"

"Aye," Synne said and looked into his eyes. "Why?"

"She didna have to do that."

Synne worried her lip with her teeth. "That wasn't all she told me."

"Oh? What else did she say?"

Instead of answering, Synne's gaze moved away as her face lined with worry.

"Lass, what is it?" he pressed.

"I've not just been thinking over the fact that I'm part Gira, and that's how I communicate with trees. There's something else I've been thinking about, trying to determine if it's even possible."

Lachlan chuckled and shook his head. "From what I'm learning, anything is possible."

"You said your grandmother was a witch." Synne's head swiveled back to him, her amber eyes watching him closely.

"Aye, she was."

"Did she ever speak of the First Witch?"

He thought about that for a moment before he said, "No' that I can recall. She was careful about what she said around others."

"I would've been, as well. Did she say anything about spelling the sword you now carry?"

His brows snapped together. "I thought we already spoke about this. I had no idea she'd done it until I fought that witch."

"Then there's a chance she didn't spell it."

"I suppose," he said with a shrug. "What are you getting at, lass?"

Synne bit her lip again as she frowned.

"Lass," he pushed. "Just say whatever it is you're afraid to say."

"Asrail said that a finger bone of the First Witch is inside the hilt of your sword. It's the bone Sybbyl is looking for."

24

Blackglade

Armir couldn't remember ever feeling so anxious before. He paced the confines of his chambers as his mind went over the last conversation he'd had with Malene. As he'd watched her grow into her role as Lady of the Varroki, he couldn't help but be proud. He'd always pushed Malene hard, probably harder than he should have at times, but he'd known she could handle it.

And she'd proven that there was little she was afraid of.

In all his years as Commander, he'd stood beside many Ladies, but not one of them could compare to Malene. She had fought against her destiny like nearly all the girls that he'd brought to Blackglade did. But she was the only one who had fully accepted her role and embraced it. That was the difference between her and all those who had come before her. Malene was the one the Quarter prophesied. The Quarter, the seers of the Varroki, were reclusive yet freely shared such things. They had long foretold the one who would lead the Varroki into a new age. Malene was that one. Armir knew it in his bones.

The fact that she was willing to give her life for the Varroki proved how she had come to accept them—and Blackglade—as her home. The one thing he wouldn't do was simply stand by when he could be preparing her.

Armir stalked to his door and threw it open before he strode outside to the stairs and took them two at a time to the top of the tower that housed Malene's chambers. He knocked, and none other than Helena opened the door.

The witch smiled at him, her green eyes crinkling at the corners. "Hello."

He gave a nod of his head while his gaze searched for Malene. He found her at the table, reading. Ever since she'd learned how to read, she had devoured every book she could get her hands on. She paused and looked up as he entered, her lips curving into a smile.

How easy it would be for him to believe that she cared about him. Armir knew better than to allow himself that bit of fantasy, however. It would only lead him down a road of misery he couldn't come back from. It didn't matter that Malene had changed the rules that allowed his position to marry and father children now. In his mind, his duty was solely to her. Besides, there was no one he wanted.

Well, no one but her.

"I, um, I think I'll go," Helena said and hurried out, closing the door behind her.

Armir frowned as he stared at the door. "What was that about?

"You do have a rather fierce look about you today," Malene said with a chuckle. "I gather that's why you're here."

"It is."

She marked the page she was on and closed the book

before she got to her feet to face him. "All right. I'm listening."

"It's time for training with battle magic."

"You've shown me already."

Armir blew out a breath. "I've barely scratched the surface of what there is. Magic comes easily to you now, but there is a difference in using it to light a fire versus protecting yourself or hurting an enemy."

Malene swallowed as she thought about that for a moment. "Sybbyl could arrive any day. The training you speak of takes years, not hours or days."

"Whatever you can learn now could save your life."

"Hmm," she said as she pursed her lips. "Let me ask you a question. If I didn't have the blue radiance in both hands, would you be talking to me about battle magic? Or would you be considering finding a place to hide me from the Coven?"

Armir clasped his hands behind his back as he walked to the open window and looked out at the churning sea. The clouds had dispersed, but they would be back soon. Winters were always harsh. "The Coven has never come for us before. I'd be teaching battle magic regardless." He turned to face her then. "You're the Lady of the Varroki, the one we follow. Aye, my job is to guide you and protect you when need be— which I freely do. However, we need a leader, and if that means I have to take you out of the battle, I will."

"You will not," she stated in an icy tone.

"I will," he replied. "There's a greater chance I'll stand beside you fighting instead of taking you away if you know how to do battle magic."

She looked away, her lips flattening. Finally, she nodded and returned her gaze to his. "You've made your point. Let's get started."

For the next two hours, he didn't let up as he pushed her

harder and harder. The fact that she soaked up everything he taught her proved how great her magic was. It frightened him how quickly she was growing in power. He wasn't scared because he was jealous of her magic, but because he knew that if she were aware of just how powerful she was, she wouldn't hesitate to go out and try to find Sybbyl herself, taking the battle away from the Varroki so no lives would be lost.

Armir couldn't chance that happening. He hadn't lied. The Varroki needed Malene. His people were strong and courageous but also set in their ways. Malene had begun as just another Lady who balked at what Fate had given her and reluctantly did her duty. But then Malene had changed. She had sought to know everything about her role and the Varroki. Then, she had set out to change things for the better.

Not everyone was thrilled with the changes she'd made, but they were slowly coming to see that Malene did it to ensure that the Varroki prospered instead of their numbers continuing to decline at such a rapid rate.

"You're worried," Malene said after she lowered the cup of water she'd finished.

Armir didn't try to lie to her. "You should be, as well. None of the Coven has ever gotten their hands on a bone of the First Witch before."

"That's true, but then again, we have the Living Heart. Braith, as Warden of the Blood Skull fights with us, as well."

"Maybe. He isn't here, though, is he? He's at his castle."

"It doesn't matter where he is. No one in the Coven, not even Sybbyl, will get their hands on the skull. The Blood Skull is the most powerful piece of the First Witch. Everyone knows that. But I think the Heart is the second strongest."

"Every bone of the First Witch holds triple the amount

of magic that any witch or warlock wields. Sybbyl was already strong. If she finds another bone…"

"It won't do any good," Malene said over him. "She could find every other bone of the First Witch, and it wouldn't matter."

The conviction in her words brought Armir up short. He was reminded of the dream Malene had had of Trea, the First Witch, coming back to life. Had Malene had another vision? Her dreams weren't like other people's. Malene's dreams sometimes were a gateway into someone's life. She'd seen Helena's and Jarin's battle with Sybbyl in just such a dream.

"I'm all right," Malene told him. "I see the worry on your face, but you don't need to be concerned."

"Of course, I do."

She chuckled, shaking her head. "You don't."

"Did you have another dream about Trea?" Malene hesitated, and it was all the answer he needed. "You did."

"Not exactly. I had the same dream. Exactly the same dream."

Armir leaned his shoulder against the wall and thought about that for a moment. "Everything was exactly the same?"

"Everything."

"That isn't normal, is it?"

Malene barked a laugh. "I can't say there is much about my life that *is* normal. I'm here as Lady of the Varroki to keep the shield up so the Coven and outside world can't find Blackglade. That's my sole job."

"Not your only job," he interjected.

She shrugged. "Pretty much. When was the last time a Lady took it upon themselves to change the laws?"

"None lasted long enough or cared deeply enough to try. Until you."

"The prophecy," she said in a low voice. "You wanted to keep that from me."

"You have enough on your shoulders."

She inhaled deeply and softly blew out a breath while looking at the ceiling. Her gaze lowered to Armir. "I'm capable of handling this."

"I know." He knew it all too well, actually. In fact, he was beginning to suspect that she didn't need him at all. That's how capable Malene was.

She said nothing more as she faced him, letting him know that she was ready for more practice. Armir complied, though his mind wasn't completely in it. He was thinking about the upcoming battle as well as his future role.

He was so lost in thought that the next thing he knew, he was on his back with Malene standing over him, the blue radiance in her palms shining brightly as she held her hands over him with one foot on his chest. She was breathing heavily as she stepped back and lowered her hands.

"You either let me beat you, or your mind was elsewhere," Malene said.

He got to his feet and tried to keep his wounded pride from bothering him. "I don't try by letting my students win anything."

"So, your mind was elsewhere." She poured more water and handed him a cup. "Want to tell me what has taken you away from our training? I hope it wasn't me."

Armir drank the water and walked to place the wooden cup on the table. "You excel more every day."

"I thought that would make you happy."

"It does," he hurried to say. "But I've also come to realize that you don't need anyone to guide you."

She grew very still. "Are you saying you want to step aside?"

"Never. I'll stand beside you always. What I'm saying is that you're more than capable of continuing on without anyone else."

Malene turned and walked to the hearth, staring into the flames. "When you first brought me here, I was kept in these chambers away from others."

"So you could learn your position and all it entailed."

"I was still a child, taken from my home and family and thrust into a place I didn't know or want to be."

Armir had heard it many times from other Ladies. He couldn't imagine what they went through, but it wasn't for him to change the way things were done. That wasn't his position. "I'm sorry."

"You said that every day." She glanced his way. "I believed you then, and I believe you now. For many, many months, yours was the only face I saw. You were the only person I spoke with. When I was able to venture out, I didn't want to. At first, I thought this place a prison, but it's my home. I might not like how I was brought here, but I know this is where I belong."

"It has been a long time since any Lady has said those words."

"The magic chooses who is the Lady of the Varroki. I couldn't change that even if I wanted to. But the one thing I don't want to change is you being my second in command. You might think I can do this alone, but I'm telling you I can't. The only reason I'm able to do what I've done is because I know you're here."

Armir fought the need to go to her and touch her. For so long, he had been forbidden to touch a Lady of the Varroki. That might have changed with Malene's decree, but he still didn't freely touch her as he wanted. "And I'm telling you that you don't need anyone, especially me. I'll be here, and I'll remain in this position for as long as you want me. But you're stronger than any Varroki. I've not wanted to tell you because I was worried what you might do. Now, I realize it doesn't matter how much I worry. You'll do whatever you want to do."

"I'll do whatever I *need* to in order for the Varroki—and you—to remain alive."

She had never pointed him out so blatantly before. Armir might hope that she cared for him, but how could she not? As she'd said, he was the only one she saw, the sole person she'd known for months after she had been first brought to Blackglade.

"We're lucky to have you as our Lady," Armir said.

Something moved in Malene's face as if his words hadn't been exactly what she'd wanted to hear. But he couldn't tell her that he couldn't imagine a life without her. That the very thought of something happening to her made him want to destroy everything.

He couldn't tell her that he loved her.

25

After Synne had told Lachlan about the First Witch's bone in his sword, he hadn't said a word. He'd finished his oatcake, then mounted his gelding. Synne realized that she had told him quite a bit, so she didn't push him to say anything, just as he hadn't pushed her earlier. It had taken her hours to digest it all, and even then, she wasn't so sure she knew what to do with the information.

They continued riding, hard and fast. The horses seemed to sense something in the air as well because there were times both she and Lachlan had to hold their mounts back when they wanted to run, even over dangerous terrain.

By the time they stopped for the night, Synne was exhausted both mentally and emotionally. She glanced at Lachlan, but he was as closed off as she had been that morning. Before she could head off to hunt their dinner, he came to her and held out his hand.

"Can I use your bow?" he asked.

She handed the weapon to him. "It's my turn."

"I'll be back," he said and turned away.

Synne blew out a breath after he'd left. Then, she scavenged around to find wood. When she couldn't find that, she went looking for peat. She got lucky and returned to their camp. It wasn't as hidden as their others, but it was the best they could do, given the fact that there were no woods anywhere close. The glen they'd chosen was small, but all it took was one person atop a mountain or a connecting hill to spot them. Thankfully, there weren't feet of snow in this particular area, making it easy to clear a spot for their camp.

She was about to start the fire when she recalled what Asrail had said about the roots of the trees in the ground. Synne removed her gloves and placed her palm flat on the earth. The cold seeped into her skin instantly, but she ignored it as she closed her eyes and listened for the trees. Minutes ticked by with nothing.

"Can you hear me?" she whispered. "My beloved trees, I need your assistance. Do I have enemies approaching?"

When there was no response, she searched deep inside herself to try and hear them. She wasn't sure it would work since she'd always had to touch the trees to sense what they wanted to tell her.

Her eyes snapped open as she realized that wasn't true. She had heard the trees when she was little, and the Gira had been coming for her. She hadn't been touching any tree then. If she could do it once, she could do it again. The difference was, she'd been in the middle of a forest then. Now, there wasn't a tree anywhere near her. But their roots were everywhere, just as Asrail had said.

Synne closed her eyes again. "I'm listening."

The force that went through her palm had her snatching her hand back in surprise. Then, she hastily put it back on the ground as trepidation rushed through her. She reached for her bow, only to remember that Lachlan had it. Whoever was coming wasn't here yet, but they were close. Closer than she'd expected, especially after they had traveled such a distance that day alone.

Was it Sybbyl? No. Surely, the trees would alert her to that. They were the ones, along with Edra's magic, that had kept her from the abbey.

Synne lifted her gaze and found Lachlan standing before her. She slowly rose to her feet. "What's wrong?"

"I'm no' sure. What were you doing?"

"Listening for the trees."

"And?" he prompted when she didn't elaborate.

She licked her lips. "An enemy is close."

"Sybbyl?"

"I can't say for sure, but I definitely felt something. We should keep moving."

Lachlan shook his head. "For once, we know they're coming. We can set a trap."

She opened her mouth to argue, then decided against it. "All right."

"One of us should stay out in the open, and the other should hide."

"I'm usually the one hiding. I can again."

He thought about that for a moment before he walked to her and handed her the bow and arrows. "I'll hide this time. I found a spot no' too far away. It'll give me an advantage since I'll be up on that ridge."

Synne followed his finger and saw where he pointed. It was a good vantage point and still close, but also high enough up that he could see someone approaching as long as they didn't come from behind. "Good spot."

"Are you all right?"

His question surprised her. "Me? I've been worried about you?"

"Why?" he asked, shock lining his face.

Synne's brows rose on her forehead. "Because you've not

said anything since I told you about the bone."

"I've no' even thought about that. I've been thinking about what you told me regarding your parents. You fear the Gira, and now you've learned that you are half-Gira."

"I…" She stopped, unable to find the right words. "I'm not sure how I feel, really. I have no idea whether Asrail told me the truth or not, and I don't know how to find out. Yet there was much of what she told me that…felt…right. I wanted to dismiss everything she said, but I couldn't. It's like I knew it. Here," she said and pointed to her chest.

He nodded slowly. "And being part Gira?"

"I can communicate with trees," she said with a smile. It faded quickly, however. "I've seen for myself how vicious the Gira are. I know if they find out who I am, *what* I am, they'll come for me. What about you?"

Lachlan reached behind his head and grasped his sword to pull it from its sheath. He looked at the pommel. "If there is a bone beneath the leather wrapping, no one told me. I'm fairly certain my grandmother would have said something."

"Maybe not. You were still young when she died. She might have told your father, though."

"I can no' imagine him not passing that information on to me."

"Unless no one knows. It could be that it was done when the sword was first forged. It might have been hidden there by the blacksmith without them telling anyone."

Lachlan thought about that for a moment. "Hmm. That's a definite possibility. The sword is over a hundred years old. It's been strengthened a few times with new metal, but the pommel hasna been altered. At least, that's what I was told. The truth is, I can no' know for certain if there is a bone there or no' unless I look for myself."

"I saw you kill that witch when my arrows couldn't find their mark. That in and of itself tells me there is something special about your sword. My bow and arrows were spelled by witches. I've fought a witch before and defeated her. But what you did, that was something more. It makes me think there is more to your weapon than just it being spelled."

"If Asrail can be believed, then why did the witch Elin no' take it?"

Synne wondered that herself. "That's a good question. I'd have loved to speak with her, but I didn't see her again after I left."

"I tried to follow her, but she disappeared."

"She was with Asrail, I think. And Asrail spoke of working with a witch to help my father change to become human. I knew Giras liked Witch's Groves, but I didn't know they joined forces."

Lachlan walked to her and pulled her against him with his free arm. "I wanted to spend this night with you in my arms."

"I like the sound of that. As soon as we reach Blackglade, we'll make sure that happens."

"Aye," he murmured and lowered his head.

The brush of their lips t sent heat spiraling through her. Synne wrapped her arms around his neck, realizing for the first time how much she'd missed such contact with him. And now that she had it, she didn't want to release him.

"I don't suppose we have time for—"

He chuckled, shaking his head as he said over her, "Nay, lass. I'd never forgive myself if our enemy found us naked while pleasuring each other. As much as I hunger for you, I can wait."

"I'm not sure I can," she replied honestly.

His groan rumbled through his chest. "You do know how to make a man ache."

"Only because I feel the same."

"You've got to stop talking like that," he told her, but there was no heat in his words.

She lifted her head for another kiss. "I can't help it. That's what you do to me."

His mouth settled over hers as his tongue slipped past her lips. She sagged against him, his arm holding her tightly as the kiss deepened, and flames of desire had her firmly in their grip. This was one time she wished she'd worn a gown so she could just lift her skirts and straddle him.

It was Lachlan who ended the kiss. He brushed his knuckles down her cheek and stared into her eyes. "When we reach Blackglade, I need to speak with you. There is much I need to say, and while I want nothing more than to do that right now, we need to keep our minds focused on what's coming."

"You think I can focus now that you've said all of that?"

"Aye," he said with a smile and a wink. "You can, and you will."

"Then just tell me what it is you want to say."

Lachlan was silent for a moment. "Survive this night, lass. You hold my heart in your hands, and we have many years ahead of us."

She was so shocked by his words that she gaped at him. He kissed her forehead and turned to walk away. Synne stared after him, confused, happy, and excited all at once. She hadn't dared to dream that he might want her after this.

"You have mine, as well," she called out to him.

He halted and turned back to her. In the fading light of day, she saw his brilliant smile. He lifted his hand in a wave and continued on.

Synne felt as if she were floating on a cloud, she was so happy. She had to remind herself that there were still many dangers about, and one that was coming their way. She made the fire and took care of the horses before she found the last oatcake in Lachlan's knapsack. She would've split it with him had he been there. Instead, she broke it in half and put the remaining bit back into the bag.

Then, she went to sit by the fire to wait. Synne ate the oatcake and put her hand on the ground. "I'm listening," she told the trees.

A smile pulled at her lips when they answered.

26

Need pounded through him like fire. It scorched him, urging him to return to Synne and give in to the desire. Lachlan wanted it more than anything. Walking away from her after seeing the hunger in her eyes had been the hardest thing he'd ever done.

But he would do it again and again as long as it meant that he'd have her for the rest of his life.

It was a gamble Lachlan took because he was aware that one or both of them may lose their lives in the upcoming fight. He didn't know if his sword was spelled or if it did indeed hold a bone of the First Witch. Frankly, he didn't care as long as it killed anything that came after him or Synne.

Just thinking about her made him smile. Lachlan had never thought he'd find a woman who matched him so completely, but then he'd stumbled upon Synne. Or rather, she had come into his forest. It didn't matter how they'd found each other, only that they had. He couldn't wait to introduce her to his family. His sisters would adore her, and his father couldn't help but be impressed by her skills.

Lachlan gave himself a mental shake. He had to stop

allowing his mind to drift from the present threat that was descending on them. It had never entered his mind to question Synne about what the trees—or roots, this time—had told her. He'd seen the special bond she had with trees. Learning that she might be part Gira explained a lot.

Twilight made it difficult to see into the distance. It was why it was the perfect time to hunt, because it was hard for the animals to see, as well. Lachlan held his sword in one hand and his dagger in the other. Back and forth, his eyes scanned the horizon against the rise and fall of the mountains, looking for anything out of the ordinary.

Just like for the past several days, it was quiet. Too quiet. In some ways, Lachlan could almost imagine that this was a dream. But he felt everything too vividly for it to be anything but reality. He hoped that whatever was coming for them arrived before night had fully fallen, but he'd be prepared either way.

As the night darkened one side of the sky and began moving toward them, he frowned when he thought he saw what looked like mist. He was immediately on guard. Then he blinked, and it was gone. Lachlan's gaze slid to Synne to see that both of her hands were on the ground. He watched her, knowing that she was communicating with the trees. The moment he saw her left hand wrap around her bow, he knew the threat had come.

The drop down from the ledge was significant, but he'd cleared away any loose rock so he wouldn't slip. There was still a chance that he could hit the cold ground wrong or land on a rock buried just beneath the surface, but to go around the way he'd gotten onto the ledge would take too much time.

It seemed as if the darkness suddenly enveloped them fully as the last bit of light dipped behind the mountain. The sky was a beautiful pale blue with just a hint of orange on the horizon. And then, even that was gone.

Lachlan looked around for the mist, but it was now too dark to discern it from anything else. He might have fought against witches and had a witch for a grandmother, but he knew very little about them. What he did know was that he couldn't underestimate them. If he could imagine it, then he had to be prepared for them to be able to do it with their magic.

Seemingly out of the blackness, a woman in a dark cloak appeared across from Synne. The woman moved so delicately that it almost looked as if she glided on air. Lachlan's gaze was riveted. He prepared to throw his dagger since it appeared as if Synne weren't going to defend herself.

Malene spun around from the roof of the tower and started for the stairs. She had to tell Armir that Synne and the warrior were close. It was time to send a Varroki after them. She hadn't taken two steps before she looked up to see Armir coming toward her.

"I know," he told her as he came to a halt.

Malene swallowed. "A witch is coming for them."

"I'll go."

"Nay," she stated. "We'll both go."

Armir's blond brows snapped together in a deep frown. "You shouldn't leave Blackglade. Especially not now."

"You won't reach them in time."

Her second in command merely smiled. "I'll be back."

She wanted to call out to him, to ignore his words and go with him. Then she thought of the Varroki and everyone within the walls of Blackglade who were counting on her. Malene's gaze dropped to Armir's retreating form as he walked down the staircase on the outside of the tower that wound to the ground.

With the spell falling from her lips, she reached the bottom of the stairs and looked up as Armir ran down them. He didn't seem at all fazed to find her there. His long strides ate up the distance as he came to stand before her in the fading light.

"Be careful," she said.

He bowed his head. "I've still some things left to teach you. I'll return."

"You better."

He grinned then, showing even, white teeth. "Is that a command?"

"Aye." The sight of that smile made her heart skip a beat.

"I would never disobey the Lady of the Varroki."

"I-I'm also asking as…a friend."

The smile faded as he moved closer to her. "I am your friend. I've always been your friend. And I will return to you."

He walked past her without another word. She waited until he was at the gates before she used the spell to return to the roof of the tower to watch him.

Lachlan was careful with his movements as he lifted his left arm to throw the dagger. Just before he let it loose, a hand came down on his shoulder. His head snapped to the side to find a man standing, his blond hair pulled back from his face.

The man squatted beside him and whispered, "You've found your destination?"

"How do I know who you are?"

The smile on the man's face was wide. "I like you,

Lachlan MacCullum. We've been waiting for your and Synne's arrival for some time."

"I'll ask again. And you are?"

"A friend."

Lachlan wasn't going to just take anyone at their word. "If you're who I think you are, then do something to help Synne."

"She doesn't need my help."

"The hell she doesna," Lachlan stated.

The stranger put a finger to his lips and pointed toward Synne. Lachlan found his gaze drawn to the woman he loved.

<hr>

She was here. Synne didn't have to look up to know the witch had found her, because the roots far below the ground had told her. Synne knew the location of the Gira all across Scotland and England. And she also knew where Sybbyl was. However, as soon as she got a lock on the witch, the connection vanished.

Synne let that go for the moment since another witch was standing before her. Synne slowly opened her eyes and met the brown gaze of the witch across the fire. There was something about her that seemed familiar.

"From everything I've heard about the Hunters, I expected more from you," the witch stated.

Synne smiled, more at ease than she had ever been in her life. "Everyone has to deal with disappointment."

The witch peeled back her lips in a fake half-laugh. "Very funny. I've been tracking you for days. If I'd known how easy it would be to kill you, I would've taken my time to reach you."

"If I'm so easy to kill, what are you waiting for?"

"You can't be the one who has killed three of us."

Synne shrugged and glanced skyward. "That's me."

The witch's gaze narrowed as she stared. "Then why aren't you preparing to fight me?"

"Who says I'm not?"

"Stop toying with me."

Synne couldn't stop the smile on her face. She didn't want to look Lachlan's way, but she couldn't help but wonder what he was doing. Could he hear their conversation? Did he realize that she had things under control? He must. Otherwise, he would've already made himself known. "Aren't witches the ones usually toying with their prey? It doesn't feel good, does it?"

"Just for that, I'm going to make your death painful."

"What are you waiting for?"

The witch pulled up her hands as deep orange magic flared between her palms. Synne was on her feet in the next instant with an arrow nocked and pointed at the witch.

"Impressive," the witch said with a smile. "It's almost too bad that you have to die."

Synne twisted her lips. "I don't feel the same about you. You deserve what's coming. You chose the wrong side."

The witch laughed as the magic grew, expanding as she pulled her hands apart. "We can't be stopped. You should accept what's coming."

"I fight for the freedom of all," Synne stated. "And I stand against those who would kill without thought or mercy."

"You would've been a great witch," the woman said and flung the magic at her.

27

The way Synne moved was mesmerizing. Lachlan was awed at the ease in which she flipped her body to miss the magic thrown at her. Then land and fire off an arrow before nocking another. He'd known that she was agile by the way she climbed the trees and that she had hinted at different training, but Lachlan had never seen anything like this before.

"The Hunters are very skilled," the man said.

Lachlan's gaze followed Synne as she ducked, rolled, flipped, and spun around the witch, who turned in circles, trying to hit Synne with magic. Unfortunately, none of Synne's arrows had found their mark yet.

"Synne said that she never misses her mark. This is the second witch she's faced that she can't strike," Lachlan said.

The man made a sound in the back of his throat. "This witch is using magic to move the arrows out of the way. I bet the other did, as well."

"Then Synne needs help."

"Does it look like she needs anything?"

Lachlan looked back at his woman. In fact, it appeared as

if Synne had things well in hand. He realized as she moved around the witch that Synne was getting closer and closer to her. Lachlan couldn't wait to see her finish off the woman.

"Come," the man said.

Lachlan frowned. "I thought you said that Synne didna need help."

"She doesn't. I do. More witches are coming."

With one last look at Synne, Lachlan followed him. As he fell in step behind the warlock, Lachlan realized that the man had never given his name, said anything about the Varroki or Blackglade, nor had he done anything to help Synne.

Lachlan halted suddenly. "Where are the other warriors?"

The man didn't turn around. "You and I can take care of the witches that are coming."

"Who are you?"

"I told you. A friend."

"I want your name."

This time, the man stopped. He slowly turned to face Lachlan so the light from the rising moon fell upon his face. "I could say any name. How would you know I spoke the truth?"

"I doona think anything you've said is the truth."

The man chuckled. "You're smarter than you look, though it took you long enough to catch on."

Lachlan stared in bewilderment as the man before him shifted into a woman. Three others came out of the darkness then. He widened his stance and looked at all four of them. "If you think to frighten me, it'll take more than that."

"Did you really think I was some Varroki come to save you and that Hunter?" the witch who had pretended to be a man asked. "How pathetic."

The shortest of the group eyed him. "Maybe, but he is handsome. I'd like to have him in my bed for the night."

"As if you'd get first pick, Gelda," the oldest of the group snapped.

The first one rolled her eyes and said, "Gelda. Hester. Enough. At least Ruth is smart enough to keep her mouth shut."

Lachlan shook his head. "The only thing the four of you are getting this night is death."

"Oh, I do like your spirit," the leader said. "Too bad you have to die."

They came at him together. Lachlan threw his dagger, but one of the witches easily moved it aside. He lifted his sword, shielding himself as their bodies and magic reached him. Lachlan braced himself in a lunge, but even still, he slid back in the snow and dirt. The witches bounced from his sword and lay sprawled around him.

Lachlan didn't hesitate to plunge his blade into the one nearest him. Her scream stopped mid-cry as she turned to ash. The other three stared in shock. The leader was the first to gather herself and come at him again, this time with only magic.

He blocked it, only to move his blade in time to stop two more shots of power sent by the other witches. Lachlan used Synne's technique and maneuvered himself closer and closer to the witches until he was able to spin and lunge, piercing Hester's heart.

The witch burst into ash just as a man came out of nowhere, landing beside Lachlan and battling the remaining two witches. The man struck Gelda down in short order, and then joined Lachlan to take out the leader. Lachlan didn't stay to find out who the man was. He turned and ran back to check on Synne, except she was no longer near the fire.

Lachlan scanned the area and caught sight of movement in the dark, seconds before Synne rushed to him and flung herself into his arms. He held her tightly, thankful that both of them had survived another attack.

"You were amazing," he said as he drew back to kiss her.

She smiled up at him, but before she could reply, her gaze moved to the side. "Armir," she said in greeting.

The man bowed his head of blond hair. Lachlan saw that it was shaved on either side with various tattoos showing. The rest of his hair was gathered in a queue at the top of his head and bound with leather strips every few inches.

"Lachlan, this is Armir, the second in command of the Varroki, and a formidable warlock," Synne said. "Armir, this is Lachlan MacCullum, the best warrior of his clan."

"I saw his skills," Armir said as his gaze moved to Lachlan. "You're very good."

"I appreciate the assist."

"I'm not sure you needed it," Armir said with a grin, then he held out his hand.

They clasped forearms as Synne looked on with a smile.

"Come," Armir said. "Let's get the two of you to Blackglade."

In short order, Lachlan and Synne had their horses and were getting ready to leave when Armir paused and turned his head to Synne. The silent way the warlock watched her put Lachlan on guard.

"What is it?" Lachlan demanded.

Synne glanced at them as she settled the reins over the mare's head. She quirked a brow at Armir. "Why are you looking at me that way?"

"What happened to the witch you were fighting?" the warlock asked instead.

Lachlan immediately became defensive. His lips parted as he readied to give Armir a piece of his mind, but at the last moment, he held off. His gaze swung to Synne.

"What?" she asked as she looked between them. "Both of you are staring at me as if you don't know me."

Armir lifted one shoulder in a shrug. "I know you very little, actually."

Synne then turned her attention to Lachlan. "And you? What's your excuse?"

Lachlan thought about the days he'd spent with Synne. From the first moment he'd met her, she'd been fiery and determined. She gave all of herself in everything she did, including lovemaking. She had been winning against the witch before Lachlan's attention was diverted.

"You can't be serious," Synne said, a hint of anger and confusion in her voice. "Lachlan, you know me."

He blew out a breath as the fire he'd been about to put out crackled between them. "I was tricked by a witch moments ago. She made me believe that she was a man, a Varroki. I saw her transform right before my eyes into a woman as three more witches came at me."

"I can see how they would trick you since you didn't know Armir or any of the Varroki, but you can't say that about me."

No, he couldn't. And yet…he found himself unable to decide. He looked around for any ash from the witch and found nothing.

Armir said nothing as his gaze remained locked on Synne.

"Tell me about the battle," Lachlan urged Synne. "Tell me how you defeated the witch because I doona see any ash."

"Because I didn't get a chance to kill her. She got away."

It was possible that Synne spoke the truth. Lachlan wanted to believe her, but he wasn't sure he could.

Synne walked from the mare and came to stand beside him. She took his hands in hers and gazed into his eyes. The red-orange glow of the flames danced around them, casting dark shadows across her face. "You felt my kiss. Did I taste different?"

"Nay," he replied with a shake of his head.

"The Varroki have kept themselves hidden from the Coven. How would I know Armir unless I'd met him?"

Lachlan looked at the warlock, but Armir wouldn't look away from Synne. Lachlan's eyes slid back to the woman he loved. "I doona think I'm the only one you need to convince."

"You're the only one I care about. You told me I had your heart," she said in a soft voice.

He couldn't believe he had doubted Synne, all because Armir—a man he didn't know—looked at her oddly. For all Lachlan knew, Armir was the one who wasn't who he said he was. Lachlan smiled at Synne and pulled her into his arms. "I'm sorry, lass. I doona know what I was thinking."

In the next breath, Lachlan was thrown to the side. He gave a shake of his head to clear it and searched for the culprit to find Armir standing over Synne with his hand outstretched above her. Words Lachlan didn't recognize fell from the warlock's lips. Shocked to his core, Lachlan half-crawled, half-ran toward Synne.

Armir's shout of, "Nay," stopped Lachlan in his tracks. The warlock's pale green eyes landed on Lachlan as he jerked his chin to the left. Lachlan followed it and saw his sword lying near Synne's outstretched hand.

Lachlan reached behind him, but even before his hand came up empty, he knew that was his sword on the ground. He hadn't felt Synne reach for it, hadn't felt the blade being drawn from its scabbard.

"This isn't Synne," Armir stated.

Synne—or whoever it was—began to laugh, the sound evil and cold enough to chill Lachlan to his bones.

Armir's lips peeled back as he glared at the woman. "Who are you?"

"Wouldn't you like to know?"

Lachlan got to his feet as rage pounded through him. "What did you do with Synne?"

The face Lachlan had come to love turned to him, and while this woman looked like Synne—and even sounded like her—it wasn't her.

"I'll never tell," the witch replied with a smirk.

Lachlan strode to his sword and grasped it before he turned to the witch. "Oh, you'll tell," he threatened, the blade at her throat.

The witch threw back her head and laughed.

The sound was suddenly cut off. Lachlan frowned, not understanding why he could see the witch laughing but no longer hear her.

"I didn't want to listen to her anymore," Armir said. "I used a spell that will keep her imprisoned and unable to hear us."

Lachlan could barely fathom what was happening. He looked to the warlock as Armir pivoted and walked away, keeping his back to the witch. After a moment, Lachlan joined him.

"When you speak, keep your back to her," Armir cautioned. "She might not be able to hear us, but she could read our lips."

"Bloody hell," Lachlan mumbled and ran a hand down his face.

Armir blew out a breath. "I can't take you to Blackglade now."

"I would do the same in your shoes."

"We know it's only a matter of time before the Coven finds us, but I'm more concerned with why the witch wanted your sword."

Lachlan glanced at the weapon in his hand. "Synne told me a bone of the First Witch was in the hilt."

Armir's eyes widened. "Did you know this?"

"Nay."

"And how did Synne come to learn this?"

Lachlan fought not to look back at the witch in the hopes that it was Synne there. "From a Gira named Asrail who claims to be her grandmother."

"Interesting," Armir said to himself as he looked away. He caught Lachlan's gaze and said, "If you do hold something of the First Witch, you need to get to Blackglade immediately before Sybbyl finds out. She's close."

"I'm no' going anywhere without Synne."

A woman with flaxen hair and gray eyes suddenly appeared before them. "Actually, you are."

28

"Easy," a voice said as Synne tried to open her eyes.

She recognized the woman's voice but couldn't put a face to it. Her body felt weighed down as if something were making sure she couldn't rise.

"The spell will wear off, but you've got to give it time, Synne."

She licked her lips and tried to talk but couldn't find a voice for her words. Synne attempted to open her eyes again and managed to see a glimpse of bright light before her lids fell shut once more.

"You're safe now," the voice told her. "Be easy. I've got you. I won't let anything happen to you."

It didn't matter what the woman said, Synne wasn't going to believe anything until she saw it for herself. But no matter how hard she tried, she couldn't force her eyes to open or move her body. Even as the blackness pulled her under, she fought until she couldn't fight anymore.

When Synne next came awake, she lay still. Her body still felt heavy, but not as bad as before. Fire crackled. The smell of fresh bread and herbs filled the air. Someone hummed lightly while a spoon scraped the sides of a bowl. Footsteps moved about short distances, coming from the same direction as the humming.

There was a fog around Synne's mind that she wanted gone so she could remember.

Aye! You need to remember!

The thought that went through her mind made her blood freeze in her veins. Something had happened, but…what? She needed to be somewhere, there was some*one* she needed to be with.

A gentle hand was placed on her shoulder. "Easy."

The same woman as before. It did little to soothe Synne's nerves. If anything, the woman made things worse by not telling Synne what she wanted to know.

"You took a heavy dose of magic meant to kill you. It's only because of who you are that you're still alive."

This time when Synne tried to open her eyes, her lids obeyed. She looked up at the ceiling of a small cottage with dried herbs hanging everywhere. Synne turned her head and found herself staring into brown eyes that she felt she was supposed to know.

The woman smiled. "It'll take you a little longer before your memory returns. I'm Elin."

Synne remembered the name. "Asrail told me."

"Aye, Asrail," Elin said, her smile brighter.

When Synne tried to rise, Elin was there to help her sit up. Synne had never been so weak before, and she didn't like it. It took Elin helping her hold the cup for her to drink the water. Even that little bit of effort tired her out. Elin used some pillows so Synne could prop herself up.

"You had me worried," Elin told her as she got to her feet. She walked to the kitchen area of the tiny cottage and asked, "Hungry? I've made some soup."

Until that moment, Synne hadn't realized that she was famished. "Please."

Elin began dishing out some of the liquid into a bowl.

"Tell me what happened," Synne asked.

The witch said nothing as she returned to the bed and sat on the stool beside it. She pursed her lips. "You need to give yourself some time."

"I don't think I have it."

"That blast of magic you took was meant to kill you."

Synne leaned her head back against the pillows and blew out a breath. "But I'm alive."

"Barely. Have you heard nothing I've said?"

She turned her head to look at Elin. "Every word. Now, tell me what I'm missing."

Elin set the bowl on her lap and lowered her eyes to the floor. A moment later, she met Synne's gaze. "Do you remember meeting me?"

"I do."

"And Asrail?"

With every question, the fog thinned. Synne nodded. "She claims to be my grandmother."

"She is your grandmother."

Synne remained silent, waiting for Elin to continue.

The witch filled a spoon with broth and brought it to Synne's lips. Only after Synne had taken it did Elin speak again. "After you departed, Asrail wanted to follow you to make sure you remained safe. I convinced her to remain where she was and said that I would trail you. I caught up with you when you stopped for the night."

"Wait," Synne said with a frown. Something was missing, something she was supposed to know. She closed her eyes and thought back to meeting Asrail, and how she couldn't wait to get back to… The name escaped her, and no matter how hard she tried to see the face, she couldn't.

Synne relaxed her body. Then she went through her memories again. This time, she didn't see a face. Instead, she saw the back of a man. Long, black hair. Memories of a beard over a hard jaw. A laugh that made her grin. A Scottish brogue she couldn't get enough of.

"Lachlan." The name came to her out of nowhere. Synne opened her eyes and looked at Elin. "I was with Lachlan."

Elin smiled, but it didn't quite reach her eyes. "That's right."

Fear gripped Synne. "Tell me he's all right. Tell me he isn't dead."

"I don't think so."

"What do you mean, you don't *think* so?" Synne's entire body shook from anger and panic.

Elin's gaze was steady, her voice smooth. "I got there to find you already in battle with the witch. I heard another fighting not too far away and gathered that was Lachlan. When you took the hit of magic, I stepped in and took you."

"So, Lachlan might think I'm dead? You need to find him and let him know that I'm okay."

"We'll look for him."

Synne shook her head furiously. "Now. We need to go now."

"We can't. You aren't ready."

"Put me on a horse. I'll be fine."

"You won't."

Synne whipped back the covers, intending to throw her legs over the side of the bed, but she could hardly move them an inch.

Elin's voice was soft when she said, "I told you it would take time."

"What exactly happened to me?"

The witch set aside the bowl and covered Synne with the blanket once more. "The spell was meant to kill you."

"You've told me that twice already. What are you leaving out?"

Elin straightened and reluctantly met Synne's gaze. "The witch got into your mind."

"Meaning?"

"She knows everything you know."

Cold hands of terror squeezed Synne's heart. "Lachlan's sword. The witch will know about it."

"Aye."

"Don't you see? I've got to get to him."

"There's a chance the sword is already in Sybbyl's grasp."

"I don't care if it is. I have to find Lachlan. I have to know he's all right."

Elin's face sagged with regret. "But you're in no position to do anything right now."

Synne fought not to give in to the scream of frustration that welled up within her. "How long have I been here?"

"Two days."

Two days! That was two full days that Lachlan would've been on his own. He was good, and with the sword, he might just be able to ward off attacks. But an assault by Sybbyl? Synne wasn't so sure. She wished her body was healed. It looked fine, but inside, she felt something altogether different.

"It's your mind, not your body," Elin said.

Synne cut her eyes to the witch. "Did you read my mind?"

"I didn't have to. I could see it on your face. I've only seen the spell that was used once before. The witch gets into the mind of the person she uses the magic on. It allows her to know everything that person does."

Synne asked, "Does she have to kill the person to use the spell?"

"Nay, but she prefers to because it allows her to carry out the second part of the hex."

The fact that Elin knew so much about the witch and the spell led Synne to believe that Elin knew the witch personally. "And what's the second part?"

"The witch makes herself look like the one she's now killed."

"So, Lachlan may very well believe I'm alive and with him, when in fact, it's the witch."

Elin glanced away. "Aye."

"Who is she?" There was something in Elin's face that made Synne aware that the witch knew the other woman.

It took a long time before she answered. "My sister, Avis."

The hits just kept coming. Synne squeezed her eyes closed as she tried to hold back the tide of anger. "If you knew what she was doing, then you should've stopped it."

"I was worried about saving you!" Elin exploded. "Perhaps I should've let you die and saved Lachlan instead."

"That's exactly what you should've done. Saved Lachlan and killed your sister."

Elin's nostrils flared. "Regardless of what she's done or who she is, she's my sibling."

"And she chose a side. Just as you did."

"It's easy for you to sit there and tell me what to do. You wouldn't be so demanding if your sister were still alive."

Synne gasped as if kicked in the stomach by a horse. She had no time to react because Elin spun around and walked out of the cottage, slamming the door behind her.

For long minutes, Synne sat there with Elin's words going around and around in her head. She'd had a sister? Why couldn't she remember that? Why had Asrail not said anything? Synne wanted to discount everything Elin had said, but she wasn't sure she could. Elin had no reason to lie. She had spoken out in anger, which meant it was likely something Elin hadn't meant to share—and wouldn't have shared if she hadn't been so furious.

Synne leaned forward and managed to get a hand on the bowl. She couldn't pick it up, however. Instead, she lay back down and turned on her stomach as she pulled the stool closer. It took her several tries and more soup on the floor than in her mouth, but Synne finally managed to eat. With each spoonful, she could feel her body getting stronger.

"Elin said it was in my mind, not my body."

That meant that Synne simply had to use her mind to get past the weakness. Edra used to tell her all the time that a person could do whatever they wanted if they only set their mind to it. And Synne wanted to get to Lachlan. Nothing would stop her.

Not a spell, not weakness, and certainly not Sybbyl.

29

"I doona like this," Lachlan grumbled for the fifth time that morning as he paced the tower in Blackglade.

Malene turned the page of the book she was reading and casually said, "None of us do."

"I should be out there with Armir and Jarin." He'd met the Varroki warrior after Malene had brought him and Armir back to Blackglade. The fact that the two were out searching for any sign of Synne without him made things worse.

Helena came into the room, her green eyes moving from Malene to Lachlan. The witch was comely with delicate features. While Synne had mentioned that the witch carried Jarin's child, Lachlan could see no evidence of that as yet.

"We've been over why you need to remain here," Malene told him.

Lachlan halted and scrubbed a hand down his face. "Aye, I know. The bloody sword. But I could leave it here."

"That wouldn't be wise at all," Helena told him as she walked toward where Malene sat at the table.

"Because I'm nothing without the sword," he snapped.

Malene softly closed the book and looked at him. "You

need to remain here because you're the owner of the sword. Anyone might be able to wield it, but it's been part of your family. It was given to you, and you chose to come here with Synne. That means you're in charge of it. If you go out there with the others and encounter witches without the sword, you might not return. Armir will come back with Synne. I don't want to be the one to tell her that you died simply because your pride couldn't stand being left behind with the women."

Lachlan stalked to her as anger simmered inside him. He didn't hide it from his face or his voice when he said, "I want to be out there looking for Synne, the woman I love. It has nothing to do with anything else. If you knew me, you'd understand that."

"You're upset," Helena said as she put a hand on his arm. "And rightly so. No one is questioning that, Lachlan."

He dropped his chin to his chest and shook his head. "I can no' lose her. She's…"

"Everything," Malene finished for him.

Lachlan lifted his gaze to her and realized for the first time that she understood exactly how he felt. How had he missed it before? Then again, he hadn't been looking. He probably wouldn't have seen it now had she not said the words. Or perhaps she was allowing him to see what she usually kept hidden.

Who was it that she loved? Lachlan had seen very few since he'd been brought to Blackglade. They hadn't walked through the gates but arrived by a spell that had left him emptying his stomach for far longer than he cared to remember.

"Aye," he said with a nod. "Synne is everything to me."

Helena's hand dropped from his arm. "Does she return your feelings?"

"I think so." He looked at the witch.

"Then she'll find her way back to you."

"If she isna dead." Lachlan turned away. His mind had been spinning with those thoughts.

Malene stood and walked past him as she said, "Come with me."

Lachlan watched her before he looked to Helena, who raised a brow and said, "I suggest you do as the Lady of the Varroki commands."

He followed Malene as she walked out of her chambers and took the stairs to the roof of the tower. Lachlan had known that he was high up in the structure, but he hadn't realized they had been at the top. Nor had he realized there was a way to reach the roof of the building. His steps slowed when he saw the stone pillars that were curved inward.

"There is much about the Varroki you don't know," Malene said from the middle of the roof. Her soft gray eyes held his in the morning sunlight. "There was much I didn't know either. I've only recently come into this power."

As she said the words, she lifted her hands out, and blue light shot from her palms. The blue radiance that Synne had told him about. Lachlan took the last few steps to the roof but didn't go farther. He wasn't sure if he should.

"I'm meant to keep this city from view of the Coven and the outside world. For a long time, I resigned myself to that simple act. Until I realized there was so much more I could do, so much more I wanted to do. So much more I *needed* to do. I never asked for any of this," she continued. "But it's mine to bear, and I do it with as much grace as I can. But if for one moment you think I enjoy being here instead of out there looking for Synne or hunting the Coven, you're wrong."

Lachlan released a breath. "You stay because people are counting on you."

"Each time I leave, I do so at the peril of those who look

to me for protection. They put their Fates in my hands. It's not a burden I assumed easily at first."

"I understand."

She gave him a hard look. "Nay, you don't. Synne told you about the Coven, but you don't truly know what they're capable of."

"I heard stories."

"Hearing isn't the same as seeing. If I'd have known you had one of the First Witch's bones, I would've come to get you and Synne days ago. Every day the two of you were out there, Sybbyl had a chance to realize what you had and come for you. I can't allow that to happen."

Lachlan pulled his sword from his scabbard and held it out to her. "It may be in my possession, but I'm giving it to you."

"Why would you do that?"

"Because I know it'll be safe here."

Malene shook her head of flaxen hair. "As I told you inside, the sword is yours. You were given it, and because of that, you must wield it."

"Anyone can use it," he argued.

"Tell me something. Since you've had it, have you ever been defeated?"

"Nay."

She quirked a pale brow. "What about before?"

"Only a few times."

"Not in battle, though."

Lachlan shook his head slowly. "Nay, no' in battle. All that shows is that I know how to handle myself."

"What that proves to me is that the bone chose you."

"My father gave me the sword. No one else decided that."

Malene smiled and flashed him a pointed look. "How old were you, Lachlan?"

That's when he realized how young he'd been when his

father had first handed him the sword. Even then, Lachlan—as well as others in the clan—had been surprised by the move. A laird held onto his sword for a long time before passing it on.

"Exactly," Malene said into the silence. "No matter what you may think, the sword chose you. With it, you've protected your clan."

"And yet, I left them."

"For something bigger. You did the right thing."

"Would you feel that way if you left Blackglade for something bigger?" he asked.

Her gray eyes briefly looked away. "That decision may yet lie before me." She drew in a sharp breath and motioned him toward her. "Come. Look out over the Varroki."

Lachlan walked to her side before he turned to view the city. He'd seen some of it from the windows of the tower, but it was nothing compared to what he saw now. The city was much bigger than he'd first imagined. There were shops with various-sized buildings and streets lined with cobblestones. In the distance, he could see farmland and pastures.

"What do you see?" Malene asked.

Lachlan turned his head toward the sea and the churning waters. He kept turning until he looked out past the huge gates that closed Blackglade off from the rest of the world. He wondered why there were gates if the city was hidden by the Lady of the Varroki, but he had to admit, he would've erected such a wall around the city, as well.

"I see a place that has withstood time," Lachlan said as he looked down at Malene. "I see a place and its people who are separate from the rest of the world. Somewhere that is beautiful and strange and needs to remain hidden."

She cocked her head to the side as the wind lifted the ends of her hair. "Why would you say that?"

"Because there will always be magic, and the Varroki need to be here to keep witches in line."

"You assume the Varroki won't stray to do evil."

"You haven't before."

Malene's lips split into a wide smile. "You think of me as a Varroki?"

"You call it your home. So, aye."

"Thank you," she replied with a bow of her head. "As for your earlier statement, every being must choose good or evil. Sometimes, the battle happens when we're young, and we don't even know it. Other times, it happens much later in life, and the choices a person makes lead them to that point. What I'm trying to say is that we're not perfect. We make mistakes just like everyone else. Some of the Varroki chose to leave this place and forget the teachings. Some don't make that choice on their own."

Lachlan frowned as he listened. "You would allow someone to know of this place and its location and leave? That isna verra smart."

"I never said they retained the memories of Blackglade or anything about the Varroki. Magic is used to erase it from their minds."

"What would happen of a Coven member stumbled across such a person?"

"Let's hope that never happens."

"Because the Coven could undo the magic put into place to make that person forget about Blackglade and the Varroki," Lachlan stated.

Malene nodded. "That's right."

Lachlan pinched the bridge of his nose with his thumb and forefinger. "Why are you telling me all of this?"

"Because you're a part of this world now. If you leave without the sword, you put the Varroki and everyone fighting the Coven at risk, because the Coven will find you and force the information from you."

"And if I leave with the sword?"

Malene held his gaze. "Then you're giving Sybbyl the chance to take it from you and possess another bone of the First Witch."

"Aye. So, I remain."

"So we both remain," she said and looked out over the gates of the city.

Lachlan watched her for a moment. It was then that he realized what he'd glimpsed below. "You care about him."

Malene tucked a strand of her hair behind her ear and said, "Does it show?"

He was surprised that she didn't try to deny it because it was obvious she didn't want others to know. "Nay."

"Obviously, it does, or you wouldn't have said anything." She turned her head to him, locking their gazes.

"It was the way you knew how I felt about Synne when we spoke in your chambers. I guessed then that there was someone who had your affections."

"Sometimes, I think it might be easier if he could discern them for himself."

"Why no' just tell him?" Lachlan asked.

She smiled sadly and turned away. "Things are never that easy."

"If you love him, then it should be that easy."

"Maybe it should."

Lachlan stared off into the distance. "What happens if Armir and Jarin can no' find Synne? We're no' even sure she isna dead."

"I have no answers for you."

"Can you no' search for Synne?"

Malene's shoulders lifted as she drew in a deep breath. "I've tried many times and found nothing."

"Does that mean she's…gone?"

"Magic could be shielding her. I don't know."

Lachlan nodded, his mind turning to another issue. "And the witch we have who looks like Synne? Why is she no' dead?"

"It isn't her time yet."

"It should be," he said and stormed off.

Malene watched Lachlan walk to the stairs and descend them. She didn't know where he was going, but she knew he wouldn't leave Blackglade. He finally understood why he needed to remain, even though every fiber of his being wanted to search for his beloved.

A gust of wind whipped her skirts around her legs, pushing against her body so she had to lean into it so as not to topple over. There was much she hadn't disclosed to Lachlan. While she'd admitted to using her magic to look for Synne, she hadn't told him that she had found something that could be Synne. It was faint, so indistinct, Malene wasn't sure it was even the Hunter. It could be a trick by Sybbyl and the Coven.

As for the witch who now wore Synne's face, Malene had a feeling she would be useful soon. Until then, she would remain locked in the magical prison Armir had put her in.

Yet, for all the turmoil awaiting Sybbyl and the Coven, Malene felt more confident now that another bone of the First Witch had been found and was in their hands.

Malene closed her eyes and tried once more to search for Synne. Within moments of the magic swirling around her, she knew she wasn't alone. Trea, the First Witch, was with her.

"*She's alive.*"

She was almost there. Synne was half-crawling, half-pulling her way to the door. After eating the bowl of soup, she'd tried to stand up. That had been a mistake, but once she was on the floor, she could only think of leaving and finding her way back to Lachlan.

Her hands hurt, and she'd torn several nails down to the quick as she used her fingers to dig into the floor and help her arms drag herself along. She was exhausted, but Synne wasn't going to give up. She kept moving, inch by agonizing inch. Sweat beaded her brow and dripped into her eyes. Her hair stuck to her face, making it itch. More frustrating than all of that was the fact that her legs refused to obey her.

The door suddenly swung open, and skirts brushed across Synne's face an instant before Elin demanded, "What are you doing?"

"What does it look like?" Synne snapped as she rested her forehead atop her hands.

There was a beat of silence, then Elin stepped over her and closed the door. "You should've called for me if you'd fallen."

"I need to get to a tree." The statement came out of nowhere. Synne hadn't even realized that's what she wanted until the words fell from her lips. She lifted her head and turned onto her side to look up at Elin. "Please."

Elin stared at her for a long moment before she sighed and went down to her knees beside Synne. "All right."

Whatever elation Synne felt quickly dissipated when it took them what felt like hours just to get Synne off the floor and into a chair. Both were out of breath when they finally managed it.

"Well," Elin said as she wiped her brow. "That was difficult."

Synne pointed to her boots. "Can you hand those to me?"

"You're going to need help."

"I can do it."

Elin's look of doubt was hard to miss as she handed the footwear to Synne.

"Why didn't you use magic?" Synne asked as she lifted her leg and put her foot into the boot.

"My mother taught us that it's easy to use magic, and while it's sometimes necessary, when it isn't, we shouldn't get lazy and use it. Sometimes, it requires more intelligence and strength of character to *not* use magic."

Synne smiled up at her. "That's sound advice."

"If only my sister would've heeded it."

"What happened to her?"

Elin turned away and began picking up what little there was in the cottage. "We lived quietly far from the village. Mum worked as a healer and midwife, but she didn't advertise her services. She only helped those she knew. One day, we had to go into the village for the market, and a woman went into labor. It was a difficult one, and the other midwife was tending to another birth. Mum didn't want to help, but she also knew that if she didn't, the woman and baby would likely die. She bade Avis and me to return to the cottage."

Synne paused after getting one boot on. "Where was your father?"

"Never had one," Elin replied with a shrug. "Birthings can take days, so I didn't get worried until the third day when Mum still hadn't returned home. That's when Avis and I went back to the village. It wasn't even dawn yet, so few people were about. I'm still not sure what they would've done to us had anyone spotted us. I'll never forget hearing the creak of the rope in the silence of the morning. They'd strung Mum up in the nearest tree and left her there for the crows."

"I'm so sorry, Elin."

The witch squatted down before her and lifted Synne's other leg to put her foot in the boot. "I found out the woman who died was a lord's wife. They had been traveling through the village, and it was just luck that we'd been there when she went into labor. Mum managed to save the baby, but the mother was too weak and didn't make it. The lord claimed that my mother must have done something to her. It wasn't long before word got to him that she kept to herself and had a way with herbs."

Synne had heard this many times before from others. "Naturally, he assumed she was a witch."

"Aye. So many times, they get it wrong, but this time, they were right. Mum was a witch. However, she never used magic when assisting with births since there is always a price to pay when magic is used. She'd seen that price come in the form of the life of the newborn."

Synne leaned forward and put her hand on Elin's shoulder. "I can't imagine what you and Avis must have gone through."

"Avis kept asking why Mum hadn't used magic to get free. I asked myself that same question." Elin stood when she finished buckling Synne's boot. "Mum was proud to be a witch, but she also knew how important it was to keep her magic from others. She didn't free herself because she was thinking of us."

"So many of us lost parents because of magic. It isn't right."

"Few things in life are." Elin held out her hand to Synne. "Ready?"

Synne took the witch's hand and set her jaw. "As I'll ever be."

This time, Synne was able to keep on her feet while Elin's arm wrapped around her. They smiled at each other. Standing was much different than walking, and the first step nearly had both of them on the floor.

"I've got you," Elin said as she managed to keep them both standing.

Synne swiped at her hair that kept getting in her face. "I keep telling myself that my body is fine. That it's only my mind that's off."

"You've made significant progress since you woke. More than I could've hoped, actually. I've stayed longer in one place than I normally do, but I couldn't leave you."

One difficult step at a time, they walked. Synne kept her gaze on the ground in front of her as they made it out of the cottage. The cold hit her instantly, but it was a welcome reprieve from the sweat of exertion.

Synne swallowed but needed something to occupy her mind as she tried to walk. "When did you and Avis part ways?"

"We stayed on our own for several years. Mum had taught us how to provide for ourselves. I sold herbs to help. I thought we'd continue on like that forever, but I could see that Avis wasn't happy. Within a few years, she began lashing out at anyone we came into contact with in the village. She didn't understand how I could speak to them. I tried to tell her that we needed to survive. I hadn't forgotten what had happened to Mum, but Avis didn't see it that way. Then, she began using magic for everything."

Synne grimaced. "That put you both in danger."

"It did. By that time, anything I said automatically caused us to argue. One morning, I woke up, and she was gone."

Synne didn't remember her parents, but Elin was different. She had seen her mother there, had known her sister when she left. "Did you remain there long?"

"A few months. That's when I began noticing people looking at me strangely. It wasn't until one little boy asked me if I could do magic like my sister and my mum that I knew Avis had done something. I generally didn't speak with too many or listen to gossip, so I had no idea that Avis had found out which of the men hung our mum and killed them. The last I heard, she'd found out the name of the lord to track him down."

"Did she kill him?"

Elin made a sound at the back of her throat. "I don't know. I didn't try and find out."

"You've been on the move ever since."

"I find a place and stay for a handful of days, then I'm gone again. At first, it was to keep away from anyone who thought I might be a witch. Then it was to stay out of the Coven's way."

Synne's legs were starting to wobble. She wasn't sure she could make it. This had been a mistake, but she didn't want to say that, not after everything Elin had done. To take her mind off the pain, Synne kept the conversation going. "How did you meet Asrail?"

"By accident. Some members of the Coven were tracking

me. I'm not sure how they knew about me, but they were relentless."

"As they are," Synne said.

Elin chuckled. "Very true. Anyway, Asrail hid me from them. I'd known of the Gira, but I'd never spoken to one. We spent a few days together in those woods, talking. She told me about the bones of the First Witch being discovered, and of the Coven's upheaval. Both of us had been alone for so long, we liked having someone else to talk to. Without even knowing it, we formed a friendship." She looked up. "Don't stop, Synne. We're almost there. Look."

Synne lifted her gaze and saw the trees just a few feet away. Hope sprang up even as her body fought against her mind. Tears fell from her eyes as she gritted her teeth and kept moving. Elin was patient while taking the brunt of Synne's weight as they closed the distance. As soon as Synne was close enough, she reached out her free hand for the tree and fell against it.

Her cheek slid against the bark, the roughness cutting her skin, but she didn't care. She sighed in contentment, feeling instantly better.

"You really are part Gira," Elin whispered.

Synne turned over so that her back was to the tree. She realized after shifting that she hadn't had to fight her body to move, it had done it on its own. "Why do you say that?"

"The Gira look like trees because they need them in order to survive. They can go a little while without them, like we can hold our breath underwater. The trees allow the Gira to live. And it's a tree that's healing you right before my eyes."

Synne couldn't stop smiling. "The numbness and pain are leaving. I can't explain how good it feels."

"You don't have to. I can see it on your face." Elin sat beside her, uncaring about the snow. "You've not asked about what I said earlier regarding your sister."

"Nay."

Elin licked her lips and turned her head to her. "I shouldn't have said it."

"Is it true?" Synne asked as she looked at Elin. "Did I have a sister?"

"Aye."

"Why didn't Asrail tell me?"

"You'd just learned your parents were killed by Gira, and you're half-Gira. It was a lot to take in. You didn't speak of a sister, so Asrail thought it might be easier if you didn't know."

Synne moved her toes in her boots and looked back to the cottage and the thin smoke that rose from the chimney. "Was she older or younger than me?"

"Younger. The two of you were playing in the forest. She had walked away, but you didn't. Asrail tried to call her back and keep an eye on you. Everything happened so fast. Your parents came running, with the Gira chasing them. And Asrail—"

"Had a decision to make," Synne finished. "She told me she chose to save me instead of my parents."

Elin blew out a breath, and it puffed out around her. "She said you were turned away, so you never saw the Gira take your sister before your parents. Asrail refused to allow all of you to die, and you were closer. She did what she had to do."

"I know. None of it is her fault."

"She doesn't feel that way. None of it would've happened had she not helped her son turn human."

Synne shrugged. "Love finds a way. My parents would've come together regardless. Asrail shouldn't blame herself for any of it. Without her, I wouldn't be here."

"You should tell her that."

"I should. And I will. But first, I need to find Lachlan."

31

The longer Armir was away from Blackglade, the more his anxiety grew. And it was then that he realized it wasn't the city he wanted.

It was Malene.

"I'm beginning to think that Synne is dead," Jarin said from beside him.

Armir halted and looked around the forest. If Synne got away, he figured she'd find a way to get to the trees for shelter and to know if enemies were coming. "Until we find a body or Malene tells us Synne is dead, we'll keep looking."

"When the Coven is looking for us? I'm not sure how wise that is."

Armir turned his head to the warrior. "Do you want to be the one to tell Lachlan why we stopped looking? Or how about Malene? Then there's Helena."

"I get your point," Jarin replied testily.

"I would rather be at home, as well, but Synne knows… things about—" Armir specifically left off saying, "*the bone in Lachlan's weapon*" as he saw something out of the corner of his eye for the second time since entering the forest.

"The Coven could already have that information. Though they can do nothing about it."

Armir quirked a brow. "And just what lengths would you go to if they had Helena?"

Jarin looked away, his gaze focused off to the side. "I'd do anything."

"Lachlan loves Synne, and he'll do anything for her."

"Including giving up the one thing he shouldn't," Jarin said with a nod. He looked back at Armir. "Anyone could have her."

Out of the corner of his eye, Armir saw something move again. Jarin had seen it as well, though neither man said anything. They didn't need to. By his count, four Gira surrounded them. Why the nymphs hadn't called to them, Armir didn't know.

Jarin moved his head just enough to nod at Armir. Before they could attack the Gira, another nymph flew through the air and impaled the Gira nearest him with a stick that shot from her hand. Armir didn't have time to ask what the Gira was doing as the others attacked him and Jarin. He took out one with Jarin, and the Gira helped them kill the remaining two.

The Gira met his gaze and said, "My name is Asrail. I'm Synne's grandmother. You need to find her and get her to Blackglade immediately. The other Gira have already told Sybbyl who Synne is."

"She's really half-Gira?" Jarin asked.

The nymph glanced at Jarin and said, "I would never lie about that. She's in danger. She must be found."

"You don't know where she's at?" Armir asked.

"I've been looking for her, but I can't find her or Elin."

Armir frowned. "Elin? Is that the witch who helped you talk to Synne?"

"She's not part of the Coven, but they've been after her for some time."

Jarin leaned on his staff, his lips twisting. "You're in danger as well now that you've killed a Gira."

Asrail snorted and moved to a tree to touch it. "That isn't my first time killing one of my kind, and I doubt it'll be the last. I've been hunted by the Gira for years, simply because I allowed my son to follow his heart. That won't ever change. Right now, I don't care. Let them come for me, as long as Synne is safe."

"I wish we could help, but we haven't found any clues to her whereabouts," Armir told the nymph.

Asrail's lips parted, then her head jerked to the tree. Suddenly, she smiled. "The trees have told me where Synne is, but if I know, the other Gira do, as well. You must go now."

"Come with us," Armir urged her. "It may take all of us to get Synne to safety."

The nymph hesitated but a moment before she nodded. "We're going to need to travel by magic."

She held out her arm and waited for the men to take it. Armir had never trusted a Gira before, but he was putting his life in the hands of one now. Literally. He took her palm and waited for Jarin to do the same on her other side.

"Don't worry," Asrail said before he could. "I'm not going to betray you. You've no reason to trust me, but I'm asking you to."

Jarin blew out a breath. "I hope we're doing the right thing."

"You are," Asrail said right before everything went dark.

A moment later, Armir found himself out of the forest and staring across a vast expanse of rolling hillsides and mountains. He blinked, thankful that his stomach didn't rebel at the magic. His gaze shifted to Asrail to find the Gira leaning against a tree with her eyes closed. Armir's eyes then slid to Jarin, and he found the warrior wearing a frown as he looked at something behind Armir.

"Asrail," a woman said frantically from behind him.

Armir spun around and found a woman with brunette hair rushing to the Gira. Movement near the ground caught his attention, and he looked down to find Synne twisting from her position at the base of a tree to see what was going on.

Her gaze locked with his. "Please tell me Lachlan is all right."

"He's with Malene."

Relief caused Synne to breathe in quickly as she looked away. When she had herself under control, she turned back to him. "What about Avis?"

"Who is that?" Jarin asked.

Armir watched as Elin didn't hesitate to help Asrail, but she had barely looked at them. He'd never heard of witches helping the Gira. By the look of things, there was a friendship between Asrail and Elin, one that had saved Synne's life.

It was Asrail who answered after she opened her eyes. "Avis is a witch who lost her way. She forgot who she was."

"That doesn't really answer my question," Jarin stated.

Elin's brown eyes moved to Armir. "She's my sister."

"Elin saved me," Synne said. "I wouldn't be here without her."

Jarin eyed the witch. "Are you with the Coven?"

"Nay," the three women answered in unison.

Jarin turned his head to Armir, while he kept his gaze on Elin. The witch lifted her chin as if daring him to call her a liar.

Finally, Armir asked, "If you aren't part of the Coven, then will you stand with us against them?"

Asrail turned her head to Elin and put a hand atop the witch's. "It's time."

"We need all the help we can get," Synne said as she moved onto her hands and knees.

Armir reached a hand down and helped Synne to her feet. She gave him a nod of thanks then turned her attention back to Elin.

"What are you afraid of?" Jarin asked her.

Elin's eyes snapped to him as she gave him a hard look. "How easy it is for you to ask that question. As a man, you can move about as you wish, do what you want without fear of someone trying to rape you."

"You have magic to keep them away," Armir replied.

Elin turned her head away. "And I've used it when I had no other choice."

"The Coven has been after her for years," Asrail interjected. "I helped to hide her, and she helped to hide me when it was necessary."

Jarin moved his staff to his other hand. "I can well understand all of that, but we're in a position now where we need all those who oppose the Coven to take a stand."

"You need to decide now," Asrail informed Elin.

The witch's brows snapped together. "Why the hurry?"

"Sybbyl," Armir guessed.

At the sound of the Coven leader's name, everyone grew wary. Synne looked over her shoulder to the cottage. She stood on her own, but she didn't appear steady.

"We need to get moving," Jarin stated.

Asrail nodded. "All of you."

"You mean all of us," Synne said.

Asrail smiled at her, holding out her hand. Synne hesitated only a heartbeat before taking it. "Child, someone has to stay behind to give all of you time to escape."

"Not you," Elin whispered.

The Gira shrugged. "Who else? The Varroki need to return to Blackglade. I spent my life ensuring that Synne wouldn't be harmed, not to mention, Lachlan awaits her return." Asrail paused, her lips curving into a soft smile. "Then there's you. I always warned you that one day you'd have to take a stand against the Coven and your sister. That day has arrived."

"I agree with Elin," Synne said. "I don't want to lose you."

Jarin's lips flattened. "We could be making headway if we'd stop talking and get moving."

Armir looked into the distance where Asrail's gaze kept moving. She felt Sybbyl's approach. That could come in handy, but Sybbyl used magic to cross great distances. She would catch up with them on foot, even if Asrail remained behind. Armir went through several scenarios as the other four began to bicker.

"Enough," he said and looked at Asrail. "I appreciate your willingness to sacrifice yourself for your granddaughter and the rest of us, but it wouldn't do much good. Once Sybbyl finished with you, she'd find us before we could return home."

Asrail studied him. "I could hold her off for a significant period of time."

"You know how far we are from Blackglade. You know it won't be enough. It would be better if you came with us."

Asrail bowed her head. "So be it."

"Can you use magic to take us back to where we were?" Jarin asked.

Elin shot him a harsh look. "You have eyes. You can see how bringing you here has affected her. It takes a lot to move herself. But to add others? She's going to need time to recover."

"Time we don't have," Asrail said.

Synne straightened her shoulders. "We can talk about all of this while we walk, but we need to get moving." She then looked at Elin. "Did you bring my bow and arrows?"

"Avis already had them at that point," the witch said.

Synne's lips pressed together. "Looks like I'll be getting them back from her."

32

This was the fourth time Sybbyl had found herself changing directions while looking for the bone. Either someone was moving it, or the staff was intentionally misleading her.

There was laughter in her head, and it wasn't her voice.

Sybbyl tightened her grip on the staff and said, "Enough! Tell me what I want to know."

There was no response, which only infuriated Sybbyl more. She was trekking all over Scotland, looking for the bone to grow her power. She had the staff, and it was supposed to obey her. Sybbyl turned in a circle and looked at the mountains surrounding her. Snow flurries swirled, the gray sky threatening a snowstorm at any moment.

This might be her first time in Scotland, but Sybbyl had a difficult time believing that there were no people about. It was like she had been intentionally led away from any villages. Her gaze slid to the staff in her hand. There was no laughter in her head, or even the voice. But she knew it was listening.

"As long as I hold you, I control you," she stated.

"You control nothing."

"I have the Staff of the Eternal, which means, I control it. You can try and thwart me all you want, but in the end, I will win." Sybbyl took a deep breath, then in a voice laced with anger, she commanded, "Now tell me where the bone is!"

The silence that followed only enraged Sybbyl. She threw back her head and released a scream of fury to the heavens. This wasn't how any of this was supposed to go. She had the staff. That meant she was in control. Why wasn't it listening to her? Why wouldn't it obey her?

She looked at her hand that was wrapped around the wood of the staff's handle. The moment she had touched it, the First Witch had gotten into her head. Her bones were supposed to hold great magic, but no one had told Sybbyl what else the bones could do.

The voice in her head chuckled in response.

Sybbyl narrowed her gaze on the staff. She didn't like the fact that the First Witch was somehow in her mind, but it was a small price to pay to get what she wanted. No matter how much she hated it, Sybbyl would deal with the laughter and comments from the bone. After all, she was the one wielding the Staff of the Eternal. If the First Witch was so powerful, she would bring herself back. Or, she would've at least made sure that no one could get to her bones. But she wasn't that strong. She was weak. And now, others controlled parts of her.

There was a smile on Sybbyl's lips when the voice remained quiet. She hadn't figured that the First Witch would appreciate such words. It was time the voice understood who was in control.

"*I'm very aware of who is in control.*"

"Remember that," Sybbyl ordered. "Now, tell me where the bone I search for is located."

"*Far from where you can reach it.*"

"Tell me!"

"*In the hands of a Highlander, who is even now with the Varroki.*"

Sybbyl had never felt such rage, such uncontrollable savagery before. She had wasted valuable time trying to find a bone that could've been hers had she not been led on a merry chase. Now, it was with the Varroki. But that didn't matter. She had the staff, and the Varroki didn't have any other bones. They would be easy to take down. Without them, the Hunters and anyone who might have a bone of the First Witch wouldn't stand a chance against her.

She lifted the staff and slammed it into the ground. "In which direction are the Varroki?"

The voice was silent, which simply wouldn't do.

Sybbyl slammed the staff into the ground a second time, harder than the first. A vibration ran through the wood before sinking into her palm and moving through her body. "Which direction are the Varroki?"

"*North.*"

She shifted north and was about to take a step when the voice stopped her cold.

"*South. East. West. The Varroki are everywhere. They are all around you, in people you don't even realize. They've been watching the Coven from the moment it was created. And they've made it their mission to stop you.*"

Sybbyl took a deep breath before she slammed the staff a third time. It was such a violent move that her hand slipped down the smooth wood. "Tell me!"

Silence filled her mind. Then, in a voice laced with fury, the bone spoke. "*Northwest.*"

With a destination in mind, Sybbyl began walking. But she wasn't finished with the bone. "Where exactly is this Highlander?"

"You'll never find him."

Sybbyl laughed. "Oh, I know I will. The fact that you won't give me the answer tells me that he is out here somewhere. The Varroki may be with him, but they aren't in their hidden city yet. That means I can still get the next bone."

Her laughter grew and echoed around her when the voice had no pithy reply. It had tried to outwit her, but that wouldn't happen. It was a remnant of a powerful witch, sure, but one that had been dead for ages. Whatever magic lingered was hers to command. The voice was a hindrance meant for those with weak minds. That wasn't her.

And she'd just proven that.

"Tell me where he is," Sybbyl said in a voice laced with danger.

"Headed to the Varroki city."

Sybbyl ignored the pull of pain in her neck from her wound. It had grown, festering, but the pain was manageable. She would deal with it once she had rid herself of the Varroki and had the next bone in hand. Her neck and wrist might pain her, but they didn't dampen her power or her ability to do magic. And that's all that mattered at the moment.

She started to say the spell that would allow her to travel over vast distances, but she stopped mid-sentence. She had wasted time and magic moving around all of Scotland, looking for the bone. The staff could be misdirecting her yet again. However, she needed to get to the Highlander quickly. It seemed she needed more than just the staff right now.

"Avis," she said, sending out a summoning spell with the name.

When she didn't get an immediate answer from the witch, Sybbyl remained where she was, waiting for her magic to bring Avis to her. But as the seconds passed, she realized that something or someone was keeping Avis from her. The witch wasn't strong enough to stay away herself. Besides, Avis was loyal. She would come when called. That could only mean one of two things. Either a Hunter had somehow managed to best Avis—which Sybbyl didn't think likely. Or…the Varroki had gotten to Avis.

That seemed the more likely scenario, but it did little to appease Sybbyl. She thought back to when she had last been in a forest. The Gira could aid her since they had sided with her. But once more, she paused. The Gira had chosen her because they believed her strong enough. If they saw any weaknesses, they would turn on her. That meant she couldn't go to them for help.

Sybbyl didn't trust any other witches, especially those in the Coven. The only one she slightly cared about was Avis, and only because the witch had shown great potential and all but worshipped Sybbyl. It looked as if she were on her own. It was how it was meant to be anyway. Sybbyl had always been on her own, and she always would be. The only person she could trust and rely on was herself.

She began walking in the direction the staff had directed her. Even when the snow began to fall heavier, she kept walking. When night fell, she continued on. She didn't stop, didn't rest, didn't eat. That would come later when she had the next bone.

Every few hours, she demanded that the staff tell her which location the Highlander was in. Every time, the staff told her northwest.

After hours of walking, Sybbyl heard the Gira calling to her from a nearby forest. The moment she entered the woods, she was assaulted by their hurried words. Sybbyl was stunned to hear that there was a half-human, half-Gira walking around—and that same person just happened to be a Hunter.

Fury coursed through Sybbyl. "Where is she?"

The Gira gave her the location. Without another word, Sybbyl used the travel spell.

33

They weren't going to make it. Synne knew it in her bones. Their small group was traveling quickly, but it wasn't going to be enough. She didn't need to ask if they were a significant way from the gates of Blackglade, she could see it on Jarin's and Armir's faces.

She glanced at Asrail. The Gira looked better than she had after first arriving, but she still wasn't strong enough to use magic to take all of them to the Varroki.

Armir held up a hand, and they paused beside a stream to drink and take a brief rest. Synne might have trained diligently but wasn't used to running for long distances. She drew in gulps of air to try and slow her breathing as she looked around the landscape while Elin, Asrail, and Jarin knelt next to the water and drank.

"Are you all right?" Armir asked.

It was the first time any of them had asked her that, which surprised her, considering that she had needed help getting to her feet a short time ago. Her limbs were still weak at times, but she refused to give in to the feeling. Even the instances where she stumbled, she managed to remain standing.

"I've been better, but you don't need to worry about me," she told him.

Armir grinned as he held her gaze. "It's not just your skill with the bow that Edra and Radnar saw in you. They sensed your determination, your loyalty."

"If I was as good as I should be, Avis wouldn't have been able to use that spell on me."

"You can't blame yourself," Elin said to Synne as she wiped her mouth with the back of her hand and got to her feet to face them. "Avis is a master at making others believe she's vulnerable. As soon as they do, she strikes. She's as good at it as you are with a bow."

Asrail shifted to sit on the cold ground. "Elin's right. Avis is more devious than people first think."

Synne shifted, uncomfortable that four pairs of eyes were on her. "I'm only here because of Elin. Had she not arrived in time, I'd be dead."

"Avis won't be bothering anyone again," Armir stated.

Synne jerked her head to him. "Did you kill her?" She winced then and shot a look of regret in Elin's direction. "I'm sorry. That was callous. She's your sister."

"She might be of my blood, but she stopped being my sister when she sent the villagers after me," Elin replied.

Jarin got to his feet and joined them. "I met an Avis when Sybbyl captured me. What does she look like?"

"Blond hair, brown eyes," Elin said with a shrug.

Jarin's brows drew together. "Demure. Mousy, even?"

Elin's face went white. "Always. That's why I was so shocked when she turned on me."

"What is it?" Armir asked Jarin.

The warrior gave a shake of his head, his face a mask of disbelief. "She appears to be Sybbyl's favorite."

Ice slid through Synne's veins. "And Sybbyl sent Avis after Lachlan and me. Sybbyl must know that Lachlan has the bone."

"Sybbyl wouldn't send a witch after a bone," Asrail said. "That's what the elders did with her, and look who ended up with the Staff of the Eternal and in control."

Armir crossed his arms over his chest. "I agree with Asrail. If Sybbyl knew that Lachlan had a bone, she would've come for it herself. I think she just wanted to stop you from getting to us."

"Maybe." That made Synne feel a little better, but not much. "Now what?"

Jarin jumped on a nearby boulder and looked the way they'd traveled. "We keep moving."

"Agreed." Armir motioned Synne to join him in getting some water.

The moment she put her hand in the icy water, she began to shiver. As out of breath and sweaty as she was, the water cooled her instantly. She drank as much as she could, then got to her feet. Synne dried her hand then fisted it in an effort to keep as much warmth as she could.

Then, they were off again. It reminded Synne of her travels with Lachlan to Blackglade just a few days ago. It was like she couldn't reach her destination. At least, Lachlan was there. He was safe with his sword that held the bone of the First Witch. Synne couldn't believe the luck she'd had in meeting him. Had she been looking for him or the bone, she never would've encountered him. Yet, their paths had crossed. When she thought about everything that'd had to line up for that to occur, it boggled her mind.

Despite their fast pace and few stops, Synne still didn't think their chances of reaching Blackglade in time were all that great. Asrail could leave and save herself. She was fairly certain that Jarin and Armir could also use magic to disappear. Even Elin could find some spell to hide herself as she had for years. The only one without magic, the only one incapable of saving herself, was Synne.

She came to a stop, the others passing her. It took a few moments for them to realize she had fallen behind. Asrail was the first to halt and look her way.

"What is it?" Jarin asked, his chest rising and falling quickly from exertion.

Synne looked at each of them. "Why are you here? Right now, with me?"

"You know why," Armir answered. "We came to find you."

Synne shrugged. "You did. Then you discovered that Sybbyl wasn't far away and would be coming for us. Or worse, lying in wait as we rush back to Blackglade."

"We're wasting time," Jarin told Armir.

Synne nodded, her brows raised. "You are. All of you. Each of you could use magic to get as far from here as possible. That would put you away from Sybbyl. Why aren't you doing it?"

"Because we're in this together," Asrail said in a soft voice.

Armir glanced at the sky, and the snow that began to fall in earnest. "You think because you don't have magic that you're inferior."

"It's the truth," she answered.

Armir's pale green eyes locked with hers. "But you do have magic. You might not conjure spells, but you are far from magicless."

"I can shoot a bow accurately. I can communicate with trees. Aye, I can do both of those things. But I don't have my bow now."

Asrail walked to Synne and took her hands. "Do you remember what I told you? You don't need to have a tree next to you for you to hear them. Their roots run beneath us, carrying their message."

"That's how I know we won't make it to Blackglade," Synne said. She looked from her grandmother to the rest. "You all need to go. Now. Scatter in different directions. Asrail spoke of staying behind to give us time. Now, I'm saying it."

Jarin stalked to Synne until he stood inches from her. "If you'd seen Lachlan's face when he thought he'd lost you, you wouldn't be standing here talking like this. Your arse would be finding a way to get back to him."

"I want nothing more," Synne said, her throat closing at the mere thought of never seeing Lachlan again. "But this is about more than just me. This is about the survival of the rest of the world."

Armir dropped his arms and walked a few steps closer to Synne. "Why do you think Malene made Lachlan remain behind with her and Helena? The bone is safe. For now. Do you think it'll remain that way if Sybbyl gets her hands on you?"

Jarin gave a shake of his head. "What do you think your man will do if Sybbyl tells him she'll let you live if he turns over the bone? What would you do?"

Synne looked away, unable to answer.

"She has a point," Elin said into the silence that followed.

All eyes jerked to the witch.

Elin twisted her lips and shrugged. "We all have magic. Asrail got the two of you to me and Synne, but she won't be able to do that again for several more hours, at the very least. Individually, we could probably manage to find a way to get to Blackglade with magic. We're making good time, but Synne's right. We won't make it."

"What do you suggest?" Armir asked.

Elin glanced at Synne and grinned. "We pool our magic together."

"Could that work?" Jarin asked with a frown.

Asrail chuckled and looked at Elin with bright eyes. "It just might."

"All five of us?" Synne knew it took an obscene amount of magic to move one person any amount of distance. To add four more to the mix meant it would take *a lot* of magic.

Armir put his hands on his hips and stood there silently for several minutes, staring at the ground. Finally, he looked up and let his gaze meet each of them, landing lastly on Synne. "It might."

"What will happen if it doesn't?" she had to ask.

It was Asrail who said, "It could kill one or more of us."

"But we'd be away from Sybbyl," Elin added.

Jarin shrugged. "That's a reason to chance it right there."

Synne couldn't deny that she wanted to get back to Lachlan more than anything. She didn't care that he had a bone of the First Witch. He was what she wanted. It was Lachlan that she loved. If they didn't take this chance, she'd never make it back to him. But…if they tried to pool their magic to get to Blackglade, she could be in his arms in a matter of minutes.

"We need to make a decision now," Asrail said suddenly.

Synne didn't need to ask to know that her grandmother sensed that Sybbyl was closer than ever before. "All right. I'm game. Not that I have much to contribute."

"Not true," Asrail said as she came to stand beside Synne. "You're part Gira. You have more magic than you realize. I know how to call it forth."

Asrail put her hand out. One by one, they put their hands atop the others. Then Asrail began the spell. Synne was shocked into a stupor when she actually felt the magic running from the others into her hand and then into Asrail's.

When the rest began saying the spell along with her grand-mother, Synne joined in, too.

The force of the magic was so strong that she put her other hand atop Armir's in an effort to hold on. The more she tried to cling to them, the more it seemed as if someone or something was pulling her away.

"Don't let go," Asrail called out to her.

Synne looked into her grandmother's eyes and realized then that someone was trying to pull her out of the group. Synne dug in her heels and clenched her teeth. No one was going to take her away from her friends…her family.

Armir put his free arm around her, drawing her against him as even more magic poured through their hands. The snow falling around them began to swirl in a giant circle, moving faster and faster as the power grew, and the spell continued. Synne started to smile. They were going to get away. And soon, she was going to be in Lachlan's arms. This was actually going to work.

She had to close her eyes because the wind was blowing so fast around them, it flung her hair into her eyes. The wind howled in her ears like a scream. And then, there was silence. An instant later, they fell to the ground. Synne blinked up at the sky above her. There was no snow here. That thought immediately vanished as her stomach rebelled. She rolled onto her side and emptied what little was in her belly.

"Lass."

Arms she recognized came around her, holding her gently as she finished being sick. Then she turned and pressed her face against Lachlan's chest.

"I thought I'd never see you again," he whispered.

She clung to him, happier than she'd ever been before, ecstatic to be back in his arms. No longer would she deny what was in her heart. "I love you."

"And I love you. More than anything."

Synne looked up at him when he pulled back. They shared a smile. She saw the love in his eyes and knew that nothing could stand between them. Against all odds, they had made it to Blackglade. There was so much she wanted to say to Lachlan, but it was put on hold as others came up, talking to the group.

Lachlan helped her to her feet, and she looked to find that they were in the middle of the city. Malene was with Armir, Helena with Jarin, and some unknown Varrorki warrior was tending to Elin. But there was no sign of her grandmother.

"Asrail?" Synne called.

That got Elin's attention, and she also looked around for the Gira.

"I'm sorry," Jarin said as he came to stand before her.

Synne swallowed. "What for?"

"I tried to hold onto her."

A tear slipped down Synne's face, and she hastily dashed it away. "What happened to her?"

"She was held behind," Armir answered.

Elin stumbled as she tried to get to her feet. Finally, she managed it, her entire body shaking from either sickness or anger, it was hard to tell which. "What do you mean, she was held back."

Armir's gaze moved to Synne. She then looked at the witch. "Something tried to hold me there. I could feel it."

"It was Sybbyl," Malene said. "I'm sorry."

Elin's face went white. "Sybbyl will kill her."

"We can't let that happen," Synne said.

Jarin had his arm around Helena as he said, "Sybbyl could've taken any of us."

"But she didn't," Synne stated. "She took my grandmother."

"Who let herself be taken."

Synne jerked her head to Armir. "What did you say?"

"She let go," Armir replied.

Synne shook her head. "She wouldn't do that."

"Aye, she would," Elin said and wiped her eyes. "She would've done anything to protect you."

That's when Synne remembered Asrail telling her to hold on. Her grandmother had known what Sybbyl was doing. Tears choked her. Synne turned her face into Lachlan's chest once more as both of his arms came around her. He held her, letting her cry.

"Sybbyl is too crafty to kill Asrail outright," Malene said.

Synne sniffed as the words penetrated her brain. She lifted her face and looked at the Lady of the Varroki. "What do you mean?"

"She means that Sybbyl will use Asrail against us," Elin said through silent tears.

Jarin nodded gravely. "Just as she would've used you against Lachlan."

"What do we do, then?" Lachlan asked.

Malene drew in a deep breath. "We prepare."

"To save her?" Synne asked.

Armir glanced at Malene before he said, "To kill Sybbyl."

34

"What are you doing?" Lachlan asked as he hurried to catch up with Synne.

There had been a lot of planning and ideas for how to take out Sybbyl, but through it all, Synne had remained silent. Lachlan knew it was because she was worried about her grandmother. A Gira.

It was odd since she had been so terrified of them before. But discovering that the only remaining member of your family was one of the magical nymphs could change things. He knew it would with him. Why should Synne be any different?

"Lass," he said in a whispered hiss.

She halted and turned to look at him. "I don't know what I'm doing. I feel helpless and unable to contribute."

"From what the others told me, you did just as much as they did."

"It's not the same."

"Because you doona have magic?"

She looked away with a sigh. "A witch used a spell on me. I was trained better than that. I should've known it was coming, but I didn't. I let myself believe that I was better than Avis. That I could defeat her. Instead, she nearly killed me. Because of that, Sybbyl now has my grandmother."

"Doona blame yourself for something that could've happened to anyone."

"I'm a Hunter, Lachlan. It shouldn't have happened to me."

He reached for her, and thankfully, she let him pull her against him. "Lass, I understand the pain you're feeling. It's the same thing I dealt with while Armir and Jarin were out searching for you, and I was here."

"I don't want to lose Asrail," she said, her voice muffled against his chest as her arms came around him.

Lachlan kissed the top of her head. "Asrail was the queen of the Gira. That means she's smart and capable. She'll find a way to get free."

Even as he said the words, Lachlan knew they were a lie to make his woman feel better. He had Synne back in his arms. It shouldn't be all that mattered, but it was.

Synne leaned her head back to look at him. "Do you know where they're keeping Avis?"

"Doona do this, lass," he said with a shake of his head.

Synne gave him an innocent look. "What? I'm just asking."

"Because you've got some plan concocted in that brain of yours. Something the others would shoot down immediately."

"The others. But not you," she said with a smile.

Lachlan blew out a ragged breath. "Tell me what you're thinking."

"I'm going to get my bow back."

"You're in a city full of witches and warlocks. Any of them could make you another bow and spell it and the arrows, just as Edra did."

Synne stared at him. "I want my weapon."

"That isna wise. Malene put Avis somewhere no one could see. She did it for a reason."

"Maybe Malene just wanted to keep her away from you."

Lachlan crossed his arms over his chest and quirked a brow. "I can refrain from attacking someone who is imprisoned."

"I wouldn't be able to," Synne stated.

He wanted to disregard her words, but he couldn't. Because they were true. He had wanted to find Avis and exact his revenge. It didn't matter that Lachlan had warned Synne to let go of vengeance. She was his. The woman he loved. And Avis had harmed her. When the witch had been captured, Lachlan hadn't known if Synne was alive or dead. But he knew he wanted to take it out on the one person responsible—Avis.

"Bloody hell," he murmured as he dropped his arms and turned away.

"You don't have to help me. Just don't stand in my way."

His head swung back to Synne. "I love you. That means that no matter what you do, I'm going to stand beside you."

A smile broke out across her face. "Really?"

"Really," he said and pulled her against him for a kiss. "I may no' agree with this, but I willna let you do it alone."

Synne wore a frown as she looked up at him. "I wasn't entirely truthful with you about Avis."

"I hadna guessed," he replied, his words heavily laced with sarcasm.

She chuckled and ran her hands over his chest. "I'm ready for all of this to be over so we can have some time together."

"We can have that time now."

Synne bit her lip as her frown grew. "You mean instead of trying to find Avis."

"Aye, lass," he murmured and put a finger under her chin to tilt her head back so he could look into her amber eyes. "I thought you were dead. I couldna eat or sleep as I waited to learn of your Fate. Now that you're here, all I want to do is throw you over my shoulder and find a quiet place to strip you so I can have my way with you."

He wanted her to know how much she meant to him. He hadn't expected his words to affect her, but the moment he saw her gaze darken with desire, he continued.

"We've had one night, but I've relived it every time I close my eyes. I think of the ways I want to bring you pleasure. I think of how you clung to me when I filled you with my cock. I think of holding you against me, feeling your breath on my skin once more. I think of how good it feels when our bodies are joined."

She put a finger to his lips, the pulse in her neck quickening. "I'm a fool. From the first moment I realized you weren't with me, I've been trying to return to you. And once I was back in your arms, all I could think about was battle." Her hand lowered to his chest as she gave a single shake of her head. "You're right. We need this time because we don't know what tomorrow brings."

"Shall I throw you over my shoulder?" Lachlan asked with a grin.

She chuckled and took his hand as she turned them. "Armir mentioned something about a place."

They were smiling as they hurried back to the tower. Once there, Armir stood at the base of the stairs and said, "Second door. The chamber is all yours."

"Thank you," Synne said as Lachlan pulled her up the stairs after him.

The door shut behind her, and Lachlan pushed her up against it, his mouth covering hers as need clawed at him. He'd discovered how quickly Synne could be snatched from him, and it had left him reeling. He needed to feel her against him, to sink into her wet heat and feel her flesh against his.

They tore at each other's clothes, removing one item at a time as their kisses grew frantic and fiery. Just as the last piece of clothing hit the floor, someone knocked on the door. Synne's head swung toward the sound.

"Ignore them," Lachlan told her and kissed her once more.

But the knock sounded again.

"We should answer it," she said.

Lachlan bit back an angry response when a third knock sounded. Synne reached for the blanket on the bed and wrapped it around herself. Lachlan stalked to the door, not bothering to cover his nakedness. He halted at the entrance, his hand on the lock. "Who is it?"

"We've got hot water for your baths," came a soft voice from the other side of the door.

Lachlan was about to tell them to come back when Synne said, "Oh, a bath sounds amazing."

With a sigh, Lachlan opened the door and stepped back so the women couldn't see him. Six of them came in, carrying buckets of steaming water that they dumped into a large tub he hadn't seen. Though, he hadn't really looked at anything in the room since he'd been otherwise occupied with Synne.

The women filed back out. Lachlan began to close the door behind the last one when it was stopped. He looked around the edge to find Armir holding the door open with his arm while wearing a smirk.

"You need to leave," Lachlan said.

Armir glanced at Synne, who had walked to the tub with the blanket still wrapped around her. "I'm sorry to interrupt."

"Then leave," Lachlan said in a low voice.

The smile left Armir as he met Lachlan's gaze. "I know what you were doing before. You won't find Avis."

"I doona want my woman anywhere near that witch."

Armir stared at him for a little while longer before he bowed his head and stepped back. But Lachlan still wasn't able to close the door as the six women returned with more buckets. It took another two trips before the tub was filled. Lachlan had never been so happy to close a door in his life. When he turned back, Synne stood in the middle of the room, naked.

She held out her hands and smiled. "Look at this place."

"Aye," he said.

She flattened her lips. "You didn't look."

He shrugged and let his gaze move around to see the bed, the hearth with a nice fire built, the table and chairs, two windows with the shutters closed, and the tub. "It's nice."

"It's amazing," Synne said with wide eyes. "I can't believe I'm in Blackglade. I honestly thought I'd never find my way here."

Lachlan ate up the distance between them until he stood before her. He reached up and smoothed her blond hair from her face. "There's only one thing I find amazing in this place. And I'm staring at her."

Synne rose up on her tiptoes and kissed him. "I love you."

He bent and lifted her in his arms before he lowered her into the tub. She grabbed his hand and pulled him in with her. It was large enough to fit them both comfortably, which Lachlan really enjoyed.

"This is nice," Synne said when he pulled her back to his chest and held her. Her head leaned back against him.

He watched the long strands of her golden hair float in the water before his eyes moved to her breasts and her hardened nipples. "Hmm."

Synne chuckled and turned to face him. Her gaze met his as her hand wrapped around his cock. "We might want to hurry before we get interrupted again."

"I'll be taking my time, lass," he informed her. With a smile, he grasped her hips and brought her against him tighter.

There was no more need for words as the flames of desire took them.

35

It felt so good to be back in Lachlan's arms. Synne hadn't realized how much she needed his touch until it was gone. She had come to depend on him in short order. More than that, she had come to love him with all her heart.

And she had nearly lost what they had because she'd been overconfident.

The steam from the bath caused her hair to stick to her face as she ran her hands up and down Lachlan's arousal. His lids lowered as he leaned forward and placed his lips against hers. It was gentle and soft, completely different than when they had first come into the chamber. But if she'd thought he would take things slowly, she was wrong.

He spun her around so she had to grab hold of the side of the tub. Then he came up behind her. Synne moaned when the blunt head of his cock found her entrance. The moment he filled her, her body throbbed, waiting for the pleasure she knew was coming. And she didn't have long to wait.

Lachlan reached around and slowly twirled his finger around her swollen, aching clit while thrusting his hips.

Every pump sent her higher, made her body crave more. He kept the tempo slow, and each time she tried to increase it, he'd stop moving.

"Please," she begged.

His mouth was close to her ear, his breath fanning her cheek as he asked, "What do you want?"

Didn't he know? Couldn't he tell? "You."

Warm lips wrapped around her earlobe as his tongue licked it while he continued thrusting with agonizing leisure. "How do you want me?"

She turned her head to the side so her lips were near his. "Everywhere. Anyway. Always. Forever."

A heartbeat passed where Lachlan didn't move. When he did, it was in a frenzy of need and desire that made her stomach clutch with excitement. He held her hip with one hand while his other moved to her breast to roll a nipple between his fingers. He kissed her while driving into her hard and fast.

Water sloshed over the sides of the tub to splatter on the floor. Synne closed her eyes in ecstasy as Lachlan's mouth traveled down her neck. His hips moved faster and faster, driving harder, deeper.

"Synne," he whispered in a strangled voice.

She understood because she too was close to release. The sound of her name on his lips tipped her over. Then she was falling, the pleasure enveloping her. Lachlan gave a shout and joined her. This time, he remained inside her, filling her with his seed.

It was a long while before either of them moved. Synne opened her eyes to look at the fire and smiled. She had never been so happy before, and she never wanted it to end. Lachlan pulled out of her and reached for the soap. He lathered his hands and turned her toward him. He was gentle and seductive as he washed every inch of her body, then turned to her hair.

When she was clean, Synne took the soap from him and washed him. She had never touched a man like this before, and she liked it. By the contented look on his face, so did Lachlan. After his hair and body had been cleaned and rinsed, they rose together from the tub and dried off.

Synne sat before the fire and combed her hair. She looked away from the flames to find Lachlan watching her as he reclined on his elbow. "What?" she asked.

"I'm enjoying watching you," he said. "What are you thinking about?"

She smiled. "You."

"Oh?" he asked, his brows raised on his forehead.

"When I woke with Elin, I knew who I was, but I had no memory of recent events. Worse, I couldn't move."

Lachlan's smile vanished, replaced by a frown. "You didna say."

She shrugged. "There wasn't time to tell the story. My memories returned soon enough, especially the ones about you. As I lay there, trying to get my body to move, I kept thinking about all the events that had to happen for us to meet."

"Aye. So many things had to go just so. Otherwise, I wouldna have been there that day."

"Some would call it destiny."

"I think it is."

Synne nodded slowly as she smiled. "Me, too. That means you and I were supposed to meet."

"Aye, lass. Just as we were supposed to fall in love."

"And be together for the rest of our lives."

He sat up and moved to her. "Exactly. I doona want to live without you."

"And I don't want to live without you."

"Then it's settled."

She stopped combing her hair. "Is it? I'm a Hunter. I can't just stop doing this."

"And I'm to be laird of my clan. I can no' just stop doing that. Can you no' be a Hunter in Scotland?"

"I'm not sure I could survive the cold."

"I"d be there to warm you," he said with a wink.

Synne licked her lips. "You would let me Hunt?"

He chuckled and gave her a quick kiss. "If there's one thing I've learned about you, it's that no one tells you what to do. You're your own woman, Synne."

"I don't want either of us telling the other what to do. I want us to have a partnership."

"I like that idea. I'd also like the women in my clan to have the option of learning a weapon if they so desire."

That shocked Synne. "You mean you'd allow them to train with me?"

"Actually, I thought my clan could be one of many places that others could come to be trained to be a Hunter. If we win this war, that doesna mean the Coven will disband. There will always be witches out there who wish to do others harm. Who better to train the next group than one of the original Hunters?"

"I…I don't know what to say."

Lachlan smiled as he stood and pulled her up with him. "How about we think about this later. There's something I'd rather be doing now."

"What's that?"

"How about I show you," he said as he brought her to the bed.

Before she knew it, she was on her back with Lachlan between her legs. Synne forgot about Hunters and training and Scotland as his tongue licked her sex.

Synne rolled over, seeking Lachlan's warmth. They'd spent the day making love, talking, and eating. It had been glorious. When only cool sheets met her hands, Synne opened her eyes to find an empty bed.

"Lachlan?" she called.

When he didn't answer, she sat up and rubbed her eyes while yawning. With half-opened lids, she scanned the room. The moment she saw Lachlan lying on the floor before the hearth with an arrow in his chest, she came instantly awake. Synne threw back the covers and started toward Lachlan.

"Stay where you are."

The sound of her own voice drew her up short. Synne looked over to find…herself…walking from the shadows. "Avis."

The witch drew out another bolt from the quiver slung across her body. She casually strolled toward Lachlan while nocking the arrow. "I can see why you like this weapon."

"What do you want?" Synne demanded as she glanced at Lachlan.

He was alive, his gaze on her as blood slid down his chest to pool in the rug. Pain contorted his features as he struggled to breathe.

Avis laughed and swung the bow to Synne. "Your death. Had my sister not interfered, everything would've gone as planned."

"If you think Lachlan wouldn't have guessed the truth, you're wrong."

The witch shrugged. "I would've gotten into this city regardless. I was only supposed to kill you, but then I thought…why not find the Varroki city and destroy those within?"

"You're taking credit for something that hasn't happened yet."

"How would you know? The two of you barely even knew I was here, you were so wrapped up in each other."

Synne wanted to go to Lachlan, but she knew if she tried, Avis would either shoot her or Lachlan. Then it hit her. "You came here first. You've not tried to take out any Varroki."

"I wouldn't necessarily say that," Avis replied with a smile. "I had to get free somehow."

Synne refused to believe that any of the Varroki would betray one of their own. The only outsiders besides Avis were Synne, Lachlan, and Elin.

"Oh, you're trying to figure out who released me," Avis said with a laugh. She lowered the bow and smirked. "The Varroki are so worried about the magic they used to keep others out that they never thought to use magic within their gates."

Synne didn't believe that for a moment. Malene was too smart for that. Besides, Armir would've thought of that, as well. "You might kill us. You might even take out a few Varroki, but you'll never get to them all. You'll be dead yourself before Sybbyl gets here."

"You got one thing right. I'm going to kill you and Lachlan. Everyone still believes I'm imprisoned. I'll hide your body and take over as you just as I intended. I'll tell the others that Lachlan turned on me, and I had no choice but to kill him. I'll claim he gave me his sword to watch over with his dying breath."

Synne tried to see if the weapon was on the other side of the bed where Lachlan had put it, but she couldn't see it. "And when someone goes to check on you in your prison?"

"I've seen no one since I was put in that prison," she stated angrily.

Lachlan coughed, blood spilling from the corner of his mouth.

Synne slowly climbed out of bed. Avis had the bow raised before Synne's foot hit the floor. She didn't like the fact that her own weapon had been used to hurt Lachlan—or that it was now pointed in her direction.

"You think to battle with me again?" Avis asked with another laugh.

Synne couldn't believe how calm she felt. Maybe it was the fact that the odds were stacked so high against her that she had nothing to lose. Perhaps it was because she knew there was only one option open to her—win. Or, maybe it was because Lachlan lay dying at her feet, and both their lives depended on her. Whatever the reason, she had never been more focused, had never felt so sure of her abilities.

She quirked a brow at the witch. It was weird staring into her own face. "Afraid of fighting me again?"

"Afraid?" Avis snorted loudly. "I've not been afraid in a very long time."

"But that isn't true, is it? You're afraid of Sybbyl."

Avis's eyes narrowed at her. "I'm not afraid of Sybbyl. I respect her power."

"Let's be honest. You're terrified of her. You recognize the power the Staff of the Eternal gives her, and you know you'll never be able to best her to rule the Coven." Synne had no idea where the words had come from, but once said, they made perfect sense.

"Sybbyl can't live forever. She'll name an heir."

Synne took a step toward the witch. "There's so much you don't know about the bones. But more than that, Sybbyl won't share any kind of power. The moment she thinks someone is gaining too much of it, she'll kill them."

Avis's cocky smile slipped. "You know nothing of us witches."

"I've spent my life learning how to protect the innocent and kill witches like you and Sybbyl. The power struggle within the Coven isn't any different than anything else in life. Just because you have magic doesn't make you better."

"I disagree. You need a weapon to protect yourself. I use magic," Avis replied with a lift of her chin.

Synne took another step toward her. "That's still a weapon. Call it what you want, but it is what it is."

"If you think your talk is going to stop me from killing Lachlan, you're wrong."

"I'm just stating facts."

Avis gave her a hard look. "Then what's your answer to this?"

Synne knew the instant Avis released the arrow that it was for Lachlan. Synne wanted to go to Lachlan, but to save them both, she had to take out Avis. When the arrow was fired, Synne used every bit of speed she had to race toward the witch. She knocked her bow out of Avis's hand as she flipped over the witch's head and landed behind her.

As Synne spun around, she dropped to her knee and swung out her other leg, knocking Avis to her back. Synne tucked her head and rolled away just as a blast of magic came at her. Avis released a scream of rage as she got to her feet. Synne's gaze locked on the arrows that had fallen from the quiver.

Synne had to get to them. She rolled again, coming up to stand behind Avis once more, slamming her foot into the back of the witch's knee, knocking her to the floor again. Synne used that time to gather two of the arrows, but she wasn't quick enough. Magic grazed her left arm, causing pain to shoot through her body.

She then started running toward Lachlan. At the last minute, she turned and threw the arrows at Avis. Just before they were about to find their mark, the witch vanished.

Synne landed heavily. She took a moment to make sure that Avis wouldn't return, then she went to Lachlan. The second arrow had landed in his right thigh. She leaned over him, tears coursing down her face when she found his eyes closed.

"Lachlan?" she whispered.

She heard sounds outside her door. In an instant, Synne was on her feet with her bow in hand, and three arrows nocked. When the door was thrown open, she found herself staring into Malene's face with Armir and Jarin behind her.

36

Fear had never held her so firmly in its grip before. Synne could only watch in shock as her friends rallied around Lachlan to save his life. She stood there, numb and gutted to see the man that she loved fighting for his life.

"Synne."

She heard someone calling for her, but she couldn't tear her gaze away from Lachlan, lying so still upon the floor. He was a warrior full of life. A man who stood up to anyone who dared threaten his family or clan. It wasn't right that he was so…still.

"Synne."

This time, someone shook her. Synne looked to find Helena standing before her with concern in her eyes.

Helena refused to let her look away. "Malene is doing everything she can. I need you to get dressed."

Dressed? Synne glanced down to find that she was still naked. She hadn't even thought about that as the others rushed into the chamber. Synne took the clothes Helena held out for her and began to put them on. But her gaze returned to Lachlan. She struggled to hear the words Malene and Armir exchanged, but she couldn't make them out.

"Tell me what happened?" Helena urged.

Synne shrugged. "I woke to find the bed empty. Then I saw Avis. Well, she still looked like me, but she was standing in the room."

"That can't be possible," Jarin said from his position guarding the door. "She was imprisoned."

Synne shook her head helplessly. "She said something about someone freeing her."

Armir's head jerked to Jarin. No words were exchanged in that heartbeat. Jarin bowed his head, and with a glance at Helena, the warrior quietly left the chamber. Synne was torn. She wanted to go with Jarin so she could do something instead of standing there powerless to do anything but watch. But the idea of leaving Lachlan made her physically ill.

"Go on," Helena said.

Synne wanted to refuse, to tell the witch to leave her alone, but Synne also knew that everyone needed information, down to the tiniest detail that could unravel this current mystery. She swallowed and drew in a deep breath while she closed her eyes. The last thing she wanted to do was relive everything that had happened, but she didn't have a choice.

"Lachlan and I spent the day alone. We fell asleep in each other's arms, but something woke me. I reached for him because I was cold. When I couldn't feel him, I opened my eyes to find the bed empty. I sat up to look for him and saw him lying there." Her eyes opened, remembering how he had looked at her with steady eyes filled with pain—but conviction, as well. "I saw the arrow sticking out of his chest and started to go to him. That's when Avis stepped out of the shadows and told me to remain where I was."

Helena took Synne's hands in hers. "You're doing good. I know this is hard."

With as much detail as possible, Synne recounted the rest of the story, right up until the door had opened to reveal the others.

"None of this makes sense," Helena said, more to herself than anyone else. "How could Avis just disappear? From Blackglade?"

Synne pulled her hands from Helena's and walked toward Lachlan. Malene sat on her haunches with her hands over Lachlan with the blue radiance glowing from both hands. Still, Lachlan didn't move.

Synne wrapped her arms around herself, suddenly cold to her very bones. "Why isn't he opening his eyes?"

"We're working," Armir said.

Malene blew out a breath and lowered her hands to her thighs, then looked at Synne. "Avis used arrows to strike Lachlan, which made me believe it was a simple matter of removing them and healing the wounds."

"Avis used magic, as well," Synne guessed.

Malene nodded once. "She took Edra's magic that was meant to kill witches and altered it before adding her own."

"Altered it how?"

"To kill someone without magic. Specifically, Lachlan," Armir answered.

Synne's knees buckled as she crumpled to the floor next to her love. This couldn't be happening. He was the wielder of a sword that held a bone of the First Witch. He was in Blackglade, protected from anyone from the Coven. They were safe.

Her throat clogged with emotion, and it took her three tries before she was able to get any words out. "Can you save him?" she asked Malene.

"Nothing I'm doing is making a dent. The magic within him is acting like a poison, infecting his blood, bones, and organs."

In other words, he was slowly dying, and there wasn't a damn thing Synne could do about it.

Or was there?

Synne jumped to her feet and went to the other side of the bed where Lachlan had set his sword. When she didn't find it, she began tearing apart the room.

"What are you doing?" Armir asked.

She ripped the linens from the bed and lifted the mattress. "Looking for Lachlan's sword."

In less than a second, Armir joined her as Helena went to Malene and helped her. It didn't take long for Synne and Armir to realize that, somehow, Avis had gotten the sword, as well.

Fury replaced Synne's fear. Someone within Blackglade's walls had not only freed Avis but had also allowed the witch to get Lachlan's sword. And Synne was going to find out who it was.

She turned to Armir, but before she could even get any words out, the Commander said, "I know. You don't need to say it. I'm going to find out who freed Avis."

"You should find Elin. She might know what kind of magic her sister used. It could stop whatever's happening to Lachlan," Helena said.

Malene pinned Armir with a steely look. "Bring Elin to me. I'd like to question her."

"What?" Synne asked in confusion. "Elin helped us. She wouldn't turn on us now that she's finally protected from the Coven."

The Lady of the Varroki remained calm as she said, "People lie all the time. This could've been a ploy by the Coven to get inside our gates and swing the tide in their favor."

Synne didn't want to believe it. She opened her mouth to defend Elin, but then hesitated. What did she know about the witch? Nothing other than the fact that she had helped Asrail. And while Synne hadn't wanted to believe the Gira about everything, she had. Why? Was she so desperate for a family that she would grab hold of any story someone—even a tree nymph—gave her?

If she hadn't believed Asrail, none of this would've happened. Synne wouldn't have believed that Elin was a friend and convinced her to join them on their journey to Blackglade. How stupid she had been. Synne had wanted more people to stand with them against the Coven, when she should've been doing everything she could to determine whether the stories she'd been told were true or not.

Synne looked at Lachlan. She couldn't do anything to heal him because she didn't have magic. But she was a Hunter. And she had spent some time with Elin.

Her head swung to Armir. "Let's go find the witch."

The two of them walked from the chamber and down the stairs to the rooms below theirs. Synne hadn't realized that Elin had been in the tower, as well, but it made sense. Malene would want to keep strangers close instead of letting them find quarters inside the city.

Armir knocked on the door. "Elin? We need to talk."

Seconds passed with no response. It was very early in the morning, so the witch could still be asleep. Armir tried a second time. When there was still no answer, he used magic to unlock the door and enter. Synne followed behind him to find that the bed had been slept in but was now empty.

Armir said nothing as he pivoted and walked out. No sooner had he descended the stairs than he was barking orders to guards Synne hadn't seen before. She stood on the stoop outside of Elin's chambers and looked at the city. The Varroki's numbers had declined, but there were still a significant number of them.

"Synne."

Her head moved toward the nearby trees. The call had come from the forest, but the trees had never spoken in words to her before. It intrigued her that she now heard actual words. She longed to go to them. They might be able to help her with the pain in her heart. Tears filled her eyes and fell down her cheeks before she could stop them. She wanted to find Elin, but her mind was filled with Lachlan. Synne turned and headed back up the steps. When she entered the chamber, there was no change with Lachlan, despite Malene and Helena both using magic.

No one needed to tell her that Lachlan was dying, and there was nothing anyone could do about it. The only way Synne could help him was to find who had betrayed them. She would uncover everyone involved, those who had torn her world apart and taken the man she loved from her.

Synne retraced her steps and went to locate Armir. It wasn't difficult to find the Varroki as he stood near the tower, looking out over the city with a critical eye. She came to stand beside him.

"I have a hard time believing a Varroki would betray us," he said.

Synne fisted her hands, wishing she had her bow. "You think it's Elin?"

"She's not in her chambers. That doesn't look good. However, I'll wait until the city has been searched to state my final opinion on the matter." He looked at her. "I'm about to go look where Avis had been held. Want to join me?"

"I'd like that very much."

She walked with Armir away from the city to the trees. Synne frowned the closer they got. Was it a coincidence that the trees had called to her, and Avis had been held here? She didn't think so. But why hadn't the trees spoken sooner? Why hadn't they alerted Synne that something was going on?

The moment they entered the forest, Synne put her hand

on a tree. The chaos within her dimmed enough that she didn't feel as if she were being crushed under the weight of everything anymore. Several moments went by as she felt the tree enveloping her with comfort. Some might call it solace, and perhaps it was.

She didn't ask it anything at first. Not because she didn't want to know the answers, but because she hadn't realized how much she needed the trees until that moment. She soaked up all the positivity radiating from the tree she was touching as well as the others. Bit by bit, she felt herself standing taller, feeling more confident. Finally, she opened her eyes to find Armir watching her.

"It's amazing to see your connection to them," he said.

She looked at the tree and smiled at it before letting her hand smooth down its bark. "So many believe that plants don't have feelings. They would be wrong. The cry of a tree that is being felled is more painful than I could ever put into words."

"What did this one tell you?"

"Nothing. It passed energy from itself into me because it felt my pain and wanted to help. All of the trees around me shared their energy."

Armir glanced around them. "I could see it. I didn't know what was happening, but your appearance changed. It looked as if you were getting stronger."

"I need the trees, just as the Gira do. There is no denying that."

"You believe Asrail is your grandmother?"

Synne shrugged. "I believe I'm part Gira."

"Why not ask the trees?" Armir asked.

She narrowed her gaze on him. "Aren't we going to Avis's prison?"

"Aye. I put her in the forest because of your connection

to the trees. I knew they would stand as guardians around her."

Synne's heart pounded in her chest. She looked at the tree and placed her other hand on it. She was hesitant to ask any questions because she feared the answers, but if she was to catch Avis and find who'd double-crossed them, she had to do it.

"Am I half-Gira?" she asked.

The trees had never shared words with her before today. She wasn't sure if they had actually said her name earlier or if she had imagined it. She prepared herself for a flood of feelings like usual, but she heard her name instead.

Synne jumped back in shock.

"What is it?" Armir asked with a frown.

Instead of answering him, she put her hands back on the tree.

"*You are Gira,*" replied a multitude of voices.

Synne put her forehead against the tree. This time, using only her mind, she asked, "Is Asrail my grandmother?"

"*You are blood of Asrail, once queen of the Gira.*"

Tears fell from her eyes once more. "Is Asrail dead?"

"*Not yet, though she is in the hands of the Coven.*"

Synne looked at Armir and told him, "Asrail is my grandmother."

"You have answers. That is good. Though you have more questions."

He meant he had more questions, but in truth, they were the same ones she had. Synne lifted her eyes to look at the trees around her in the dark. She heard them creaking overhead as they swayed with the wind. Some found the sound scary. She found it comforting. She used to imagine that the limbs were reaching out for her in reassurance.

"*You are one of us,*" the trees replied.

She smiled. Then, keeping the questions in her mind

only, she asked, "Was the witch Avis imprisoned in this forest?"

"Aye."

"She wore my face."

"Confused us. We tried to talk to you."

Synne jerked as it dawned on her what had happened. "You thought I was imprisoned by the Varroki, so when someone came to free the witch, you didn't call out?"

"Nay."

The pain and anguish that came from the tree was enough to cause Synne to smooth her hands over the bark in comfort. "Thank you for trying to help me." Synne dropped her hands and faced Armir. "Take me to where Avis was kept."

He turned and waved her to follow him. As they fell into step together, he asked, "What did the trees say?"

"They believed Avis was me."

Armir halted suddenly, surprise on his face. "And they thought you were being held against your will. Did they free you?"

"Nay, but that's why I didn't hear any kind of warning."

"Did they say who released Avis?"

"I didn't ask," Synne said and kept walking. "Yet."

They said nothing until she saw the first felled tree. Armir said something she didn't make out, and then light flooded the area. That's when they saw the multitude of trees that had been felled and blown up, fanning out from a central location. She didn't need to ask to know that's where Avis had been held.

Synne touched one of the felled trees and felt nothing. Its bark was black as if burned, and it was cold.

"Bloody hell," Armir murmured.

Synne walked to the center where Avis had been held and turned in a slow circle. The violence that had occurred took out more trees than she had first guessed. How had she not heard their screams?

"No one should've been able to get through my magic," Armir told her.

She met his gaze. "Someone did. And we're going to find out who."

37

The destruction of the trees was like a punch to Synne's gut. But it was nothing compared to knowing that someone's magic was strong enough to break through Armir's spell.

Synne went to one of the evergreens that still stood. The limbs nearest the center of the blast radius were charred and now bare. She put her hands on it and gasped at the suffering she felt. Its soft cry reminded her of a whimpering dog that had been tortured.

She turned her head to Armir and asked, "Can you heal the trees that are still alive?"

He blinked, taken aback by her question. "You want me to—"

"Heal the trees," she finished for him. "Aye. Can you do it? They're suffering tremendously."

He ran a hand down his face and shrugged. "I've never tried. I can't promise anything, but I'll try."

"That's good enough." She then spoke to the tree in her mind. "I'm so sorry. I know you are hurt, but the Varroki here is going to try and help you."

Instead of asking that evergreen because of its pain,

Synne walked farther until she found a deciduous that wasn't hurting. She put her hands on it. "We're trying to sort out what happened."

"*We know.*"

Synne licked her lips, forgetting that the trees spoke to each other, as well. "Did you see who freed the witch?"

"*We did.*"

"Who was it?"

"*Another witch. Elin.*"

"Thank you," she told the tree.

Synne faced Armir, gutted at what she'd learned. She didn't interrupt as he crafted a spell. It was impressive to watch him work. She had seen witches, but she wasn't used to seeing warlocks. Not that there was any difference in their magic. Yet Armir was different in that he put everything he had into a spell. He used his hands, his body, and words to shape the enchantment.

And when it moved from his hands to shoot out in all directions to the trees, Synne watched the pale blue light move like tiny fireflies. She wondered if he was aware that his magic was the same color as Malene's radiance. Surely, he knew. But did she?

When he finished, and they both stood watching the spell begin to heal the trees, she found a reason to smile. That ended when Armir turned to her and said her name.

"You know who did this, don't you?"

She nodded and slowly turned to him. "Elin."

"We asked her to join us," he said angrily and paced away.

She understood his reaction because she felt the same. "I know. It must have been part of her plan."

Armir whirled back to her. "And Asrail? Her story is true? How does Elin tie into that?"

"We might never know. Asrail is my grandmother. I don't

know if the story she told me is true, but I can believe we're blood. As for her friendship with Elin, there was genuine affection between them."

"You can't know that," Armir stated. "After all, we both believed Elin was against the Coven. We need to get back to Malene and tell her."

Synne put out a hand to touch his arm and halt him. "Your spell will continue with the trees?"

"Aye. Each of them hurt by the blast will be healed."

"Thank you."

He put a hand atop hers. "I may not feel their pain, but seeing the damage done here still causes me distress. Now that I know they hurt, we will do whatever we can to help any we come across."

Synne hadn't expected such a statement, and it must have shown on her face because Armir chuckled and pulled her along with him as he began the trek back to the tower. After a few steps, their hands fell by their sides.

"You've heard the tales of the Celts and the Norse?" Armir said.

Synne nodded. "Of course."

"So, you know about the Tree of Life."

She glanced at him. "I do."

"The Varroki revere all life, whether it's animals, plants, or people. I'm ashamed to admit that I never imagined the trees could communicate with us."

Synne smiled at him. "Now you know. More than that, you recognize the importance of all life."

They reached the tower in record time and returned to Synne's chamber. She hoped when she walked in that a miracle had happened, and Lachlan would be sitting up, but that wasn't the case. Disappointment weighed heavily on her.

Malene lifted her gaze when they walked in. "I've done all I can."

Synne didn't reply as she rushed to Lachlan and knelt beside him. She touched his face as the tears blurred her vision.

"It was Elin," Armir announced. "She released Avis. The result was a blast in the forest that took down dozens of trees."

Malene got to her feet and blew out a breath. "That means Sybbyl will have a second bone."

"You assume Avis and Elin are bringing it to Sybbyl," Helena said.

Synne no longer cared. Her heart was too broken to think about the Coven or the upcoming battle. She rested her cheek on Lachlan's chest and let the tears fall.

"It could be a power play between the two sisters," Armir said.

Malene snorted. "Do you honestly think either of them would share the power? Only one of them will wield the sword."

"But do they stand a chance against Sybbyl?" Helena asked.

Synne had had enough. "Shut up!" she shouted as she turned to look at the trio. "Lachlan is dying, and all you can think about is a stupid bone. Who cares who has it now? A good man, one who was willing to sacrifice his life for us, is dying. If you aren't going to respect that, then get out!"

"Forgive us," Malene said and briefly put a hand on Synne's shoulder before walking to the door.

Helena lowered herself to the floor next to Synne and took her free hand in hers. "That was thoughtless of us. I'm sorry."

Synne no longer had any words. The tears were coming faster now. She looked at Lachlan. He appeared to be at peace, but she knew it was an illusion. The poison that was killing him was no doubt painful. Perhaps it was a blessing that she couldn't see the agony he was in. If only someone could help.

Of all the people to attempt to heal Lachlan, Synne had expected Malene's magic to do it. After all, she was the strongest of the Varroki. But it had done nothing. She squeezed her eyes shut and thought back to the brief time she'd had with Lachlan.

Somehow, a memory of her first encounter with Asrail filled her mind. Synne's tears dried instantly as she sat up. "I need to get Lachlan to the forest."

"Wait," Helena said as Synne got to her feet and attempted to lift Lachlan. "You're going to need help."

Synne ignored her. She had one of Lachlan's arms around her shoulders and was struggling to get him to sit up. She hadn't realized how heavy dead weight was. At this rate, it would take her years to get him to the forest.

Suddenly, she was able to get Lachlan upright. When she looked to the side, she saw that Jarin was there. He gave her a nod, and Synne stepped away to allow him the room he needed to get Lachlan over one shoulder.

Synne rushed to the door as Jarin followed her. She ran into the forest and waited for Jarin, who was followed by Helena. When Jarin finally reached her, Synne helped him lower Lachlan to the ground and then covered him.

"The Gira can heal themselves," Synne said. "But only with the help of the trees. Asrail said I would never be without the trees because their roots run beneath the ground."

Jarin moved back a few paces. "I hate to state the obvious, but Lachlan isn't a Gira."

"I know."

Synne didn't want to think about what might happen if this last-ditch effort didn't work. She had no one else to turn to, and nothing left to lose. She sat at Lachlan's head and put one hand on him and the other on the ground.

"Hear me, my friends," she said aloud. "You have protected me, sheltered me, and given me peace. I didn't realize our connection until recently, but it never mattered. You were part of me. You were always there, wherever I went. Now, I come to you with a request that I realize you might not be able to help with. The man I fell in love with, Lachlan, has been hurt by a witch, using my own arrows. That same witch killed many of your kin earlier as she broke free of her prison. Nothing the Varroki have done has been able to help Lachlan. He's a good man. He's…everything to me. I have no magic, but I'm begging you to help heal him."

Seconds turned to minutes, and nothing happened. Synne squeezed her eyes closed again as a torrent of tears came. She wasn't angry at the trees. It wasn't their fault that she didn't have magic. She was only half-Gira, and while that half allowed her to communicate with the trees, it didn't give her anything else that could save Lachlan.

"I'm sorry," she told him.

When she heard his last ragged breath leave his body, Synne knew her heart would never be the same. She was sobbing freely as she moved to lay beside him in the same position they had fallen asleep in the day before. The sun was just cresting the horizon, the light chasing away the darkness.

The gray world around Lachlan went dark. Then, he was blinded by a light. In the next instant, he felt a body beside him. He knew without looking that it was Synne. He frowned as he realized that he was lying naked on the cold ground. Then, he heard crying.

He wasn't going to stand aside and let someone hurt his woman. He wrapped an arm around her. "Lass? What is it?"

"Lachlan?" she asked, her head lifting from his chest.

The shock in her voice worried him most of all. He opened his eyes, blinking several times until he could focus on her tear-stained face. "Your nose is red."

"Because I've been crying," she said with a smile.

He raised his brows. "Then why are you smiling now?"

"Because I thought you were dead."

"Dead?" As he searched his memories, he recalled being pulled from the bed and thrown to the ground before an arrow landed in his chest.

He'd tried to call out to Synne, but the witch had taken his voice. It had been disconcerting to see Synne's face on the one who fired the arrow, but he had known it was Avis. The real Synne, the one who had stolen his heart, still lay in the bed they shared together.

"Avis poisoned you," Synne said as she cupped his face and rained kisses upon him.

Lachlan wrapped both arms around her and held her against his body. "I think you need to catch me up on everything. First, I'd really like to get off the cold ground."

"It's that ground and the trees that saved you," she told him with a bright smile.

"And you said you didna have magic."

She jumped up and pulled him to his feet. "I don't."

"You do, or the trees wouldna have heard you."

Synne shrugged. "I don't care. Come. Let's get you some clothes."

Lachlan grabbed the blanket that had fallen to the ground and covered himself as they headed to the tower. Jarin and Helena were at the base speaking to Armir and Malene. The moment Jarin saw them, his mouth fell open.

He shrugged at the group as they reached them. "I'm as shocked as you all."

Everyone waited until he was dressed before they knocked. Synne let them in and proceeded to tell them the story, all while holding Lachlan's hand.

"Did you feel any pain?" Malene asked.

Lachlan shook his head. "I felt nothing once it all went dark. I was in pain after Avis shot me with the first arrow, but she must have done something because I couldna call out to Synne. The darkness began to close in around me after the second arrow."

"You're damned lucky," Armir said. He then looked at Synne. "Good job, going to the forest."

She shrugged, still grinning. "Asrail told me how the Gira could heal themselves with the help of the trees. I had nothing to lose, asking them for help."

"So, what now?" Lachlan asked.

Jarin blew out a breath. "One of the sisters got your sword."

Lachlan couldn't remember if he had seen Avis with his weapon or not. He could only recall her holding Synne's bow and arrows. "So, everything has been in vain? Sybbyl will have the second bone?"

"I don't think so," Malene said. "Only one person can wield the bone, and I don't think the sisters are bringing it to Sybbyl. If we're lucky, the two will kill each other while trying to determine which one will wield the weapon."

Helena twisted her lips. "If Sybbyl doesn't attack them first."

"Elin has more magic than anyone guessed," Armir said, crossing his arms over his chest.

Synne grunted. "I went head-to-head with Avis, and I can attest to how powerful she is."

"The sword is gone," Lachlan said. "That's what we should be discussing. No' which of the sisters is more powerful."

Malene clasped her hands before her. "But that is an important factor. If we can determine which of the sisters has the greatest magic, then we might be able to guess who will go up against Sybbyl."

"It doesna matter." Lachlan looked around the group. "Whichever sister takes control of my sword, will have a lot of magic. I also believe they willna bring it to Sybbyl, but from what I've learned about the Coven leader, she willna stand for that. She'll go after them. And that, my friends, buys us some time."

Jarin frowned. "For?"

"Locating another bone," he said with a smile.

The room was silent after his announcement. Everyone was looking at each other, thinking over what he'd just said.

Synne was the first to speak. "Lachlan is right. Helena, as the Living Heart of the First Witch, you should be able to locate another bone. And if you can't, surely Braith can as Warden of the Blood Skull."

"I'll be damned," Armir said with a grin. "This could work."

Malene's lips curved into a smile. "We just might be able to pull this off, but a lot will hinge on whether the sisters bring Sybbyl the sword or not."

"They won't," Helena said.

Lachlan looked at the witch. "How do you know?"

"Because when you hold that kind of power as a witch, you don't freely give it up," Malena answered.

The six of them exchanged looks, smiles forming.

Hours later, Lachlan and Synne were finally alone again. As soon as they were, he pulled her into his arms. "You saved me."

"I didn't want to live without you."

"And I doona want to live without you. Our bond is greater than any I've ever imagined. You are my life, Synne, the breath in my body. You're the blood that makes my heart beat, and my soul sing. I love you more than anything else on this Earth."

She put her hands on either side of his face and smiled up at him. "You are everything to me. I can't face a day without you."

"Then will you be my wife? It'll mean being the wife of a laird," he cautioned.

Her arms wound around his neck as she shrugged. "The wife of a laird who teaches others to be Hunters."

"Ah, lass. I'll give you anything you want. Just say you'll be mine."

"I've been yours from the moment we met."

He crushed his mouth to hers and lifted her in his arms to carry her to the bed, his heart bursting with joy. They might have stumbled in their war against the Coven, but he was leaving with the prize—Synne.

EPILOGUE

Lachlan wished there was a way for him to speak to his father and tell him about Synne. He also wanted to return to his clan for a quick visit, but there wasn't time. War was approaching. The fact that Elin had betrayed them cut deeper than anyone had expected—most of all, Synne.

He still couldn't believe that she was his.

His gaze moved to her as their small group stood in Malene's chamber and began to plan for Sybbyl's attack. They also had to take into account Avis and the fact that she had his weapon. Lachlan couldn't believe that he'd lost it, but he would go through everything he had endured again, as long as he got Synne.

"I want to find Elin," Synne said.

Lachlan shook his head as he crossed his arms over his chest. "Lass, remember what I said about revenge?"

Her amber eyes slid to him. "Aye. Yet I've spent time alone with Elin. Maybe I'm a fool, but I can't see her betraying Asrail and me as she did."

"She has a point," Armir said. "The way Asrail and Elin

interacted, it was obvious they were close. Like a mother and daughter."

Jarin shrugged, unswayed. "Daughters betray their mothers all the time. Elin and Asrail weren't even blood relatives."

"That doesn't mean the bond wasn't there. And, sometimes, that kind of tie is even stronger," Synne pointed out.

Helena's lips twisted. "I can see both sides of this."

"Perhaps Elin set all of us up," Malene said. "Including Asrail. Yet I find that difficult to believe. From what I know of the Gira, they aren't easily manipulated. Asrail kept her secret of Synne's true origins to herself, and while some Gira knew of it, the fact that Asrail hadn't been near Synne in years might have made them forget."

Lachlan wrinkled his nose. "I doona think Asrail would share her knowledge of Synne with just anyone. Elin would've had to gain her trust over a long period of time."

"And Elin couldn't know what Asrail might share to use against her," Helena added.

Jarin sighed loudly. "I admit, that is a good point."

"But why release Avis?" Armir asked.

Synne looked to Lachlan. "Maybe she didn't have a choice."

"Meaning?" Jarin urged.

Synne licked her lips and turned her gaze to the warlock. "She said Avis might be her blood, but she didn't care about her. However, Elin's response to learning that Asrail was gone was true. She was gutted, just as I was. Possibly more so."

Malene looked at each of them. "We're going to find Elin because the witch needs to answer for her actions."

Avis ran to the Witch's Grove with a smile on her face. She had gotten the sword, and the Highlander was dead. She couldn't stop laughing as she recalled Synne's face when she realized that her lover couldn't be saved.

Avis looked at the sword. Had she not learned that the weapon held the bone of the First Witch, she wouldn't have thought twice about it. Now, she had a bone. And she could stand with Sybbyl as they battled the Varroki.

A part of her knew that Sybbyl would try and take it from her, but Avis wasn't stupid. She had gotten the bone on her own. And no one would take it from her.

No one.

With her arms pumping and her legs moving as fast as she could, Elin ran. Her breath was loud in her ears, and her heart pounded in her chest. Strands of hair tangled in her lashes, blocking her eyes, but she didn't notice or care. All that mattered was getting away.

Though she knew it was pointless. They would find her. And they would kill her.

Thank you for reading **EVERNIGHT** I hope you loved Lachlan and Synne's story as much as I loved writing it. Last up in The Kindred series is EVERSPELL.

Nothing stays secret forever.

Buy EVERSPELL now at
https://donnagrant.com/books/everspell/

To find out when new books release
SIGN UP FOR MY NEWSLETTER today at
http://www.tinyurl.com/DonnaGrantNews.

Join my Facebook group, Donna Grant Groupies, for exclusive giveaways and sneak peeks of future books.

Keep reading for a excerpt from EVERSPELL and a special sneak peek at the rest of THE KINDRED series…

Buy EVERSPELL today at
https://donnagrant.com/books/everspell/

New York Times **bestselling author Donna Grant "skillfully melds history and legend" (RT Book Reviews) in a thrilling series – The Kindred.**

Nothing stays secret forever.

Runa's world is full of mysteries. Skilled at dwelling in the shadows, she is prepared for everything.

Except the truth.

To save the family she never knew she had, she has to make a plan. A plan that doesn't involve the sexy, mysterious stranger that keeps finding her again and again… and taking her breath away every time.

Faced with the impossible, Brom must make a choice. Finding the Varroki and taking his birthright was inevitable… until he finds Runa.

She is captivating. She is beautiful. She is dangerous. He

can never have her as a Varroki warrior because they swear to live only for the cause, never taking a lover.

Falling for her means revealing all his secrets. But with life and death – and the battle between good and evil – on the line, he might have to break his own heart.

Chapter One

Western Scotland

Her quarry wasn't far now—though Runa enjoyed the hunt. Long ago, she'd been taught to become a master of patience. Only when her target was close did her heart begin to pump excitedly. There was nothing more satisfying than taking out evil.

Stars blinked above her in the inky sky. Large, gray clouds slowly made their way across the heavens, their silhouettes highlighted by the crescent moon. The night was her favorite time. She could pretend the world was hers alone during those dark recesses of the night when most slumbered.

The one thing Runa *didn't* like was people. They were liars, thieves, and deceivers. Their hypocrisy knew no bounds, and no matter how many times she gave them the benefit of the doubt, they continued proving why she was better on her own. Morea had told her that she belonged with the humans, but Runa knew better.

Her short time with them had only reinforced her decision.

She blew out a breath as she thought about the woman who had raised her. Morea had passed away several years ago, but Runa still missed her with the same ache. The woman had been Runa's family—the only family she had. Or…the only one that mattered.

Runa pushed aside the tinge of melancholy that always came when she thought of Morea being gone. She couldn't let her thoughts get in the way of her hunt. Especially not this one. It was too important.

There, in the distance, she picked up the sounds of her quarry. She heard the rapid, harsh breaths, proving that they had been running for some time. Runa smiled when her prey came over the small rise, making themselves visible. When she was younger, she had rushed out to meet her targets in her eagerness to finish the job. Now, she waited for them to come to her.

It was almost too easy, really. She had a knack for knowing the path they would take. Then, all she had to do was lay in wait for them. Morea had told Runa that something passed down from her birth parents had given her that ability. She didn't care how or where she got it. The fact that she had it was enough for her.

But once she realized that she had such an ability, hunting lost some of its appeal. She had enjoyed the chase. Liked tracking her quarry and then finally catching them. There was no getting around trailing them. That was now her favorite part of the job.

Her target was getting closer. Runa cautioned herself to wait, to remember the patience Morea had taught her. Only when her prey was nearly upon her did Runa step into their path. Her eyes locked with black ones that widened in surprise—that brief instant when her target wondered if they could get away.

"You can't," she stated.

A small frown creased the Gira's bark-like skin. Even the tree nymph's hair looked like limbs, reaching toward the sky.

The young Gira stared at Runa, fear and apprehension filling her visage.

Runa blew out a breath as she pulled her short swords from their scabbards that crisscrossed her back. She then placed the flat side of the blades against her shoulders. The nymphs tended to stay in groups, and because the Gira blended in so well with the trees, few forests didn't have their fair share of them.

"You know who I am?" Runa asked.

The nymph nodded slowly, never taking her gaze from Runa.

"The Gira have put a price on your head for dishonoring your clan."

At this, the nymph snorted. "I'm not the one who dishonored anything."

"I'm not here to pass judgment. I'm here to carry out the sentence. Besides, you wouldn't be running if you hadn't done…something."

The nymph rolled her eyes. "You think you're so high and mighty. You, Runa, know nothing. So much has been kept from you. You were sent to kill me for dishonoring my clan. What do you think your precious Morea did? If it hadn't been for the old queen, Asrail, Morea would've been killed."

"I know the story you speak of. Morea and Asrail were close friends for years. When Morea found me and decided to raise me, Asrail didn't stand in her way."

The Gira's smile was slow before she began laughing. She tilted her head to the side and regarded Runa. "Asrail is your grandmother. You've been kept alive because she and Morea made sure that neither you nor your sister could be found by the rest of us. But that's all about to change. Asrail has been caught, and your sister has been found."

Runa felt as if she had been kicked. *Sister?* Surely, everything this Gira said couldn't possibly be true. Could it? But she remembered being very young and asking Morea why they weren't with other Gira. Morea had told her it was because she preferred to live apart from the others.

Runa never had a reason to question that. Not even when she began to see for herself that the Gira rarely went out on their own. They nearly always remained in packs. Their strength was in their numbers and the many whispers that drew unsuspecting humans straight to them.

"You're lying," Runa told the nymph.

The Gira shook her head, the smile now gone. "I'm not. I'm running from my clan because they want to kill Asrail. After they use her to draw out your sister, that is."

Runa didn't want to believe any of it, but something within her said there was truth in the Gira's words. She didn't want to think about why Morea hadn't told her about Asrail or her sister. There had to be a good reason.

It would be easy for Runa to finish her mission and forget anything the nymph had told her. But she wasn't going to. Now that the words had been spoken, Runa would always remember them. And if she wanted to discover the truth, she needed to seek out her sister and Asrail to get it.

"Where are they holding Asrail?"

The Gira stared at Runa for a moment before she replied, "North."

Not once had Runa ever let someone she hunted go. She wasn't sure what would happen if she didn't finish the job now. But none of that mattered at the moment. Her mind was too full of the fact that her grandmother was alive, and the knowledge that she had a sister. Neither of which she had known.

"What are you going to do with me?" the nymph asked.

Runa pulled herself from her thoughts. "I was paid to do a job."

"I'm not the only one who doesn't agree with what

Sybbyl is doing, but I'm the only one who spoke up," the Gira said.

"Who is Sybbyl?"

The nymph jerked back as if struck. "How do you not know of the Coven leader?"

"The Coven is led by three elders," Runa corrected.

"Not any longer. Sybbyl took the Staff of the Eternal and killed them."

Runa began to wonder if she was dreaming. She felt as if the world were turning a different way than she was. "What is the Staff of the Eternal?"

"You really don't know anything, do you?" the Gira asked in disbelief.

Runa gave her a flat look and lowered her arms so the blades of her short swords pointed downward.

"All right," the nymph said while lifting her hands, palms up. "The staff contains a bone of the First Witch. The Coven elders have been trying to locate and possess them ever since the Coven was formed. The Blood Skull was only found recently, but not by the witches. A Witch Hunter and a lord located it. The Blood Skull chose the lord to be its Warden and protect it."

Runa digested that bit of information. She knew of the Hunters. She had even spotted one a few times, but she never saw them go up against a witch. "The Coven lost out on the skull, which I assume belonged to the First Witch?"

"Exactly. It was a race between the Hunters and the Coven to get the next bone. One of the Hunters got close, but an elder actually got hold of it first. Her mistake was letting Sybbyl get her hands on it. Then, Sybbyl killed the others and took over."

"I gather this bone she managed to get her hands on made her powerful?"

The Gira chuckled. "You could say that. There was no

other way she could've killed the elders. The more bones she has, the more powerful she becomes."

"What does Sybbyl want?"

The Gira shifted uneasily. "She wants to rule."

"The witches?"

"Everyone. She wants to make sure witches are in power while those without magic live in fear."

Runa glanced away. After all the years of people killing those they thought were witches, she could see Sybbyl's side of things. Maybe it was time for witches to live out in the open. But the thought of the Coven in charge sent a chill of foreboding down Runa's spine.

"How many bones are there?"

The nymph shrugged. "I don't know, but Sybbyl has twice been denied a bone. Well, one wasn't a bone exactly. It was a witch named Helena, who is the Heart of the First Witch."

"A descendant? You're telling me a witch of the Coven wouldn't give herself to Sybbyl?"

"That's the thing. Helena wasn't part of the Coven. She stood and fought them, along with a Varroki warrior."

Now that got Runa's attention. Morea had told her stories of the Varroki, but she'd thought they were just made-up stories since she'd never encountered one herself. "The Varroki are real?"

"Very," the Gira said with a shudder. "And extremely powerful. Sybbyl was on her way to take out the Varroki after she wiped out the Hunters."

Runa frowned. "The Hunters are gone?"

"I was with the Gira and Sybbyl when we attacked the abbey and wiped out any and all who lived there. Sybbyl didn't care if they were witches or not. She said that anyone who stood against the Coven deserved death."

The more Runa heard about this Sybbyl, the more she

didn't like her. Though, Runa had never really made any kind of stand in the human world. But how much longer could that continue if everything the nymph said was true?

"Go on," Runa urged.

The Gira swallowed and glanced around. "On the way to find the Varroki, Sybbyl ordered one of her followers, Avis, to track down your sister."

"How do you know this woman is my sister?"

"Because she has Gira blood. Something Synne—your sister—didn't realize until Asrail told her."

Jealousy that Synne had spoken with Asrail rose up within Runa. She cautioned herself against such emotions. She wasn't sure if anything this Gira told her was true. While she wanted to believe it, she knew she had to tread carefully.

"You seem to know a lot about my family," Runa said.

The nymph briefly lowered her gaze to the snow-covered ground. "Your grandmother told everyone what she had done after Sybbyl captured her."

Runa quirked a brow in question. "Tell me."

"Asrail saved Synne when your parents were attacked by the Gira. Asrail then brought Synne close to the abbey where the Hunters lived so that she could grow up without the fear of being discovered by the Gira. The leader of the Hunters, Edra, took Synne in and raised her. Your sister had no recollection of Asrail or you until recently."

Runa tightened her fingers around the hilts of her swords. "I'm supposed to believe you?"

"I'm telling you what I know. I was there to witness most of it. Some of it I heard from others."

"If Synne was raised as a Hunter, how did she escape the slaughter?"

The Gira shrugged. "I don't know. What I do know is that after Asrail saved Synne and you disappeared, she was removed as queen of the Gira."

"What of my sister?"

"She met a Highlander named Lachlan, who had a finger bone of the First Witch in the pommel of his sword. Together, the two of them went north to find the Varroki."

Runa frowned when the Gira paused. "Is that all?"

"With the help of a young witch named Elin that Asrail befriended, Synne met Asrail on her trek north. That's when Sybbyl trapped Asrail."

Runa wasn't sure what to make of Asrail. She had been queen, but had given that up to save her grandchildren. Then she'd lived alone for years before befriending a witch? That wasn't something a nymph did. Or maybe Runa was the one who didn't know what the Gira did or didn't do. "And the rest? Did Synne make it to the Varroki?"

"She did. As did the Highlander and Elin. Unfortunately, so did Avis, who happens to be Elin's sister."

Runa really didn't like what she was hearing. "Was my sister harmed?"

"Synne and the Highlander fell in love, which was unfortunate because Avis made her watch as she killed Lachlan and took his sword. What Avis doesn't know is that the Highlander survived."

Runa didn't care. The need to avenge her sister was strong. It felt strange to have such intense feelings about someone she didn't even know. But they were there, nonetheless. "Was Elin part of all of this?"

"No one has seen Elin since, so I can't answer that."

"What do the Gira have planned now?"

"They have pledged themselves to Sybbyl because she has the staff. The plan is to use Asrail to draw Synne out, find Avis, and get the sword. Then kill the Varroki."

"What about the other bones?"

"If there are other bones, Sybbyl will go after them."

"It isn't easy for a Gira to live alone."

"Asrail did it. So did Morea. Others have, too."

Runa shrugged a shoulder. "You don't really have an option. You either live alone, or you die with them."

"Are you…?" The Gira blinked, hope filling her eyes. "Are you going to let me go?"

Runa knew it was the wrong decision, yet she found herself saying, "I am."

"So, you believe me?"

"I don't know what to believe, but something is telling me that I need to find out the truth." Runa slid her blades back into their sheaths. "I'm going to check out your story. If you've told me lies, I'll come for you. There won't be anywhere you can hide."

"They aren't lies."

"Good luck, then. I hope I don't see you again."

The Gira bowed her head. "Half-human or not, you still have royal blood."

"A lot of good that has done Asrail."

"It might do you and Synne some good."

Runa grunted and stepped around the Gira.

She had more hunting to do.

Buy EVERSPELL today at
https://donnagrant.com/books/everspell/

ABOUT THE AUTHOR

New York Times and *USA Today* bestselling author Donna Grant® has been praised for her "totally addictive" and "unique and sensual" stories. She's written more than one hundred novels spanning multiple genres of romance including the best-selling Dark King series that features a thrilling combination of Dragon Kings®, Druids, Fae, and immortal Highlanders who are dark, dangerous, and irresistible. She lives in Texas with her dog and a cat.

www.DonnaGrant.com
www.MotherofDragonsBooks.com

facebook.com/AuthorDonnaGrant

instagram.com/dgauthor

bookbub.com/authors/donna-grant

amazon.com/Donna-Grant/e/B00279DJGE

pinterest.com/donnagrant1

9 781942 017585